P9-CFY-148

Fingerprints
and
Facelifts

Books by Rick Copp

THE ACTOR'S GUIDE TO MURDER

THE ACTOR'S GUIDE TO ADULTERY

THE ACTOR'S GUIDE TO GREED

FINGERPRINTS AND FACELIFTS

Published by Kensington Publishing Corporation

Fingerprints and Facelifts

Rick Copp

KENSINGTON BOOKS
http://www.kensingtonbooks.com

KENSINGTON BOOKS are published by

Kensington Publishing Corp.
850 Third Avenue
New York, NY 10022

All Kensington titles, imprints, and distributed lines are available at special quantity discounts for bulk purchases for sales promotion, premiums, fund-raising, educational, or institutional use.

Special book excerpts or customized printings can also be created to fit specific needs. For details, write or phone the office of the Kensington Special Sales Manager: Attn. Special Sales Department. Kensington Publishing Corp., 850 Third Avenue, New York, NY 10022. Phone: 1-800-221-2647.

Kensington and the K logo Reg. U.S. Pat. & TM Off.

Library of Congress Card Catalogue Number: 2007925429

ISBN-13: 978-0-7582-0962-7
ISBN-10: 0-7582-0962-2

First Printing: July 2007
10 9 8 7 6 5 4 3 2 1

Printed in the United States of America

For Mike
My world is so much richer with you in it.

Acknowledgments

I would not even be writing books if it was not for my incredibly talented editor John Scognamiglio. I also consider myself lucky to be counted as one of his friends.

Many thanks to Linda Steiner, Vincent Barra, Brian Levant, Rob Simmons, Joe Dietl & Ben Zook, Charles Marcus, Laurice and Chris Molinari, Joel Fields & Jessica Sultan, Yvette Abatte, Milan Rakic, Robert Waldron, Marilyn Webber, Mark Greenhalgh, Lori Alley, Woody and Tuesdi Woodworth, Betty Paquet and Sheila Storey, Craig Thornton, Alan Burnett, Sharon Killoran, Laura Simandl, Susan Lally & Priscilla Botsford, Sarah Kiefer, Diane Gordon, Chris Fahland, Kevin Brown, and Dara Boland.

To Joanne Moore, thank you for challenging me as a writer.

My love and thanks to my family: my parents Fred and Joan Clement, my sister and best friend Holly, my fantastic nieces and nephew, Jessica, Megan and Justin Simason, and my sisters in Chicago, Nancy Schroeder and Sue Bergeron.

I'd also like to thank my Writers' Group including Dana Baratta, Melissa Rosenberg, Liz Friedman, Matt McGuiness, Rebecca Hughes, Rob Wright, Allison Gibson, and Greg Stancl for all their notes and suggestions on both the outline and manuscript of this book.

Also to my team of William Morris agents, Andy McNichol, Carey Nelson Burch, Cori Wellins, Lanny Noveck, Ken Freimann, Jim Engelhardt, and James Wynne, I am always grateful for your patience and support.

CHAPTER 1

*T*opanga Canyon, 25 years ago . . .

The sun blazed on a beautiful April afternoon as Benito Coronel, a wildly successful furniture designer and manufacturer, welcomed fifty guests, mostly well-heeled customers, to his sprawling backyard that stretched to the edges of a hilltop overlooking the Pacific Ocean in the distance. The dress was casual, as Mr. Coronel held court and regaled his guests with his intoxicating personality.

Tess Monahan, wearing a bright yellow sundress and no bra, her wavy auburn hair flowing to her bare shoulders, walked into this lovely setting on the arm of her date Ronaldo, a strapping hulk of a man, who beamed from ear to ear, proud to be escorting such a staggeringly beautiful young woman. Ronaldo was one of only a handful of employees who were invited to Mr. Coronel's home and Tess fit the bill of the kind of woman he should bring—stunning, well-mannered, and of course braless. Tess played the role of the wide-eyed small town girl to the hilt, prattling on about how she had never been anywhere like this, how Ronaldo was such a sweetheart to invite her, how she would never find a way to thank him.

Ronaldo broke into a wolfish smile. "Oh, I'm sure we can think of a way."

Tess knew it would take at least three cocktails to dull Ronaldo's senses. She had expertly studied his habits for the whole week they had been dating. Within twenty-five minutes he was on his third, and his eyes were droopy, and he had a fixed lascivious smile on his face as he insisted on groping Tess's ass. She played along, rubbing his belly and giggling and slapping his hand away, but inside she was recoiling.

How many more times was she going to have to play the role of the clueless bimbo in order to get what she wanted? This was just the latest in a long line of Neanderthals she had allowed to kiss and feel her up all in the name of getting the job done. She was sick of it. And she told her partners she was sick of it. But they didn't take her seriously. They actually thought she enjoyed this part of the job. Playing the slut. Maybe because when she wasn't on a case, she went through boyfriends like Bluebeard went through wives. But that was because she had a knack for falling in love with the wrong guy. Once she realized her mistake, she'd dump him and move on to someone else. At least she didn't stay like a lot of women. Didn't she at least get points for that?

There were a few nice ones. The French race car driver she had just spent a month with was a sweetheart. Not to mention sexy, especially with that accent and his lust for speed. But he lived halfway across the world so it never would have worked out. And then there was Dan. Dear sweet puppy dog Dan. That was dangerous because she broke the cardinal rule of never dating a client.

He actually proposed. She almost said yes. But if she had, it would have been disastrous because there was someone else who loved him, someone close to her. So of course she was painted as the harlot who tried stealing him away. Nobody seemed to consider the fact that she actually might love him. And she did. God, she was so tired of her reputation. But it was okay because after this case, she was going to announce her retirement and never have to be the slut ever again.

"Look at all the guards patrolling this place. Sure is a lot of security for a furniture salesman," Tess said, snapping out of her reverie and getting back to the matter at hand.

2

"*Mr. Coronel is much more than just a furniture salesman,*" *Ronaldo growled, feeling his own position called into question.*

An international drug smuggler too, Tess thought.

Tess squeezed Ronaldo's arm. "*Oh, I know that, honey, don't get grumpy now. But what I want to know is, if all these guards are up here with us, then who's watching the hillside? I mean anyone could just sneak on up here and rob the place.*"

"*He's got cameras everywhere.*"

"*Really? Are they watching us right now?*" *Tess said, fixing her hair and checking her lipstick in a silver compact she pulled out of her bag.*

Ronaldo smiled and nodded.

"*Then let's give them a show,*" *Tess said. She grabbed his face with her hands and kissed him softly, running her full luscious lips over his.*

Ronaldo gently pushed her away and glanced over to make sure Coronel wasn't watching them. "*Baby, we can't do this here.*"

"*Well, where can we go where there are no cameras watching?*"

He had an idea. One that she had planted without him even knowing. He took her hand in his giant paw and led her quickly away.

They reached the guard shack in less than a minute. Ronaldo entered first and Tess followed. Inside was a wall of television monitors, each showing a separate portion of the retreat both inside the house and outside. A cute fourteen-year-old Mexican boy sat in a chair in front of the monitors. His eyes were closed and he was snoring softly. Ronaldo's face darkened and he kicked the chair. The boy grunted and jumped.

"*Marco, you think Mr. Coronel will hire you as a guard if he catches you sleeping on the job?*"

"*I'm sorry,*" *the still-startled boy said as he quickly wiped his eyes and stared intently at the monitors.*

"*Go get something to eat,*" *Ronaldo barked.* "*I'll keep an eye on things while you're gone.*"

The boy fixed his gaze on Tess. He was fascinated by her bright auburn hair and alabaster white skin. And the fact she wasn't wearing a bra

*probably had something to do with his interest as well. Tess loved the ef-
fect she could have on men, and boys for that matter.*

Ronaldo stepped in front of her to block the boy's view.

*"Now go on, Marco. Get out of here!" Ronaldo barked. "And don't
come back for at least twenty minutes."*

The boy skittered out of the shack. Ronaldo shook his head.

"I'm training him. He wants to work for Mr. Coronel."

*Tess smiled, checked her watch again, and then purred, "So is any-
one watching us now?"*

*Ronaldo took Tess by the shoulders and backed her up against the
wall. He devoured her mouth with his and forced his tongue inside. He
tasted of cigar and she almost shuddered, but moaned to cover her re-
vulsion. Tess made a silent promise to herself before she went undercover for this assignment that this would absolutely be the last time she
would do this. Never again would she demean herself by seducing a guy
who repulsed her. After this case, she was done.*

*Tess positioned herself to face the monitors as Ronaldo ripped at her
sundress. God, she detested every moment of this. Why was she always
the one chosen to do this kind of dirty work?*

*On one of the monitors trained at the hillside on the back end of the
property, a shapely figure draped in black stealthily moved through the
brush towards the main house. It was Dani. Even on the grainy security monitor Tess could make out Dani's flawless caramel complexion
and short jet-black hair.*

*Tess had to keep Ronaldo hot and bothered for at least another fif-
teen minutes until Dani got inside the house and found the evidence
they needed.*

*Tess continued to moan at Ronaldo's touch and it stirred him into a
complete frenzy. He pinned her to the wall by gripping her wrists,
stared lustily into her eyes, and then soaked her neck with big wet
sloppy kisses.*

*How long was this going to take? She stole a quick glance at the
monitors and saw Dani on another one, this one aimed at Coronel's office. Good. It wouldn't be much longer. Ronaldo was now fumbling with*

his zipper. He was a handsome brute, no question, but it was his per-sonality and his violent streak that made him so revolting to her. She just wanted to go through the motions as quickly as possible.

But then, suddenly, the door to the shack opened, surprising both of them. The boy had returned.

"I told you to stay away for at least twenty minutes!" Ronaldo roared.

The boy stuffed an empanada in his mouth. "I don't know what time it is. I don't have a watch."

Ronaldo angrily released Tess from his grip and marched over to the boy. Tess kept her eyes on the monitor. Dani was in plain view. All Ronaldo or the boy had to do was move just a hair and they would see what was happening on the screen. They would be finished.

Ronaldo ripped off his watch and handed it to the boy. "Now you do. Twenty minutes, you hear me?"

"Okay," the boy said, pocketing the watch. He turned to go. His back was now to the monitors as was Ronaldo's. Tess breathed a quiet sigh of relief. Dani was rifling through desk drawers and photographing some papers with a mini camera.

Ronaldo returned his attention to Tess, an apologetic smile on his face. He approached her again, working to unclasp his belt buckle. Just a few more minutes and Tess could feign a headache and get the hell out of there.

But before closing the door to the shack, the boy turned back around. "You want me to take the gun?"

Tess hadn't noticed the machine gun, like the kind you would find in an old Jimmy Cagney movie, perched on top of a desk next to the row of TV monitors.

Ronaldo was about to explode. "No! Just get out of here!"

The boy's eyes fell on the monitors. He saw Dani and then his mouth dropped open. "Look!"

Ronaldo spun around and let out a gasp. He raced for the telephone. He still didn't suspect Tess, but she had to do something. She had to alert Dani that she was exposed. The gun. Tess dove across the room, grabbing the machine gun, surprising both Ronaldo and Marco. They just looked at her. What was she doing? And then, Ronaldo's shock turned to fury. He had been set up. Tess knew what she had to do. She fired the machine gun. The TV monitors exploded. An alarm blared throughout the property. On one monitor Benito Coronel and his guests looked around, confused.

"Step away from the door," she ordered Ronaldo and Marco, who both raised their arms in the air and moved aside. She ran out past them. She saw guards racing for the shack, and she fired the machine gun into the air. The guards ran for cover.

Guests screamed and dropped to the ground, covering their heads with their hands. She knew it was only a matter of seconds before the guards got their bearings and started firing at her. She caught a glimpse of Dani racing out of the house, her own gun drawn. All three of them hated guns and rarely used them. But it would have been irresponsible of them not to carry them in case of a situation like this.

In the distance, several guards quickly ushered Benito Coronel away from the gunfire as the majority of the men began firing at Tess. She hit the ground and rolled behind an upended table tipped over during the confusion of the guests scattering. She fired back.

Suddenly out of the corner of her eye off to the side she saw one of Coronel's bodyguards take aim at her with his pistol and start to pull back on the trigger. From out of nowhere, a silver serving tray flew at him like a Frisbee. It cracked him in the side of the head and he dropped his gun. That's when Tess saw Claire, dressed as one of the waiters in a white blouse, black pants and red vest, her blond hair pulled back in a bun, charge at the surprised guard. Tess's other partner had been keeping watch from the vantage point of one of the catering staff, serving the guests champagne.

As the dazed bodyguard reached out for the gun, Claire hurried up to him, swung her leg up and clocked him across the face with the heel of her boot. Tess once again owed her life to Claire, which was strange in a way since the two were barely speaking.

The door to the shack flew open and Ronaldo came barreling out, Marco on his tail.

Tess was trapped, surrounded on one side by a handful of Coronel's guards and on the other side by Ronaldo and Marco. There was no escape. Ronaldo had seized another gun from the guard shack. He raised it, his eyes blazing with fury, and pointed it right at her. Marco watched, horrified as Ronaldo was about to execute her.

But then a hail of bullets rained down on all of them. Was it Dani and Claire? Tess was crouched down behind the table using it as a cover so she couldn't see what was happening. More likely it was Coronel's men trying to take her out once and for all. Tess ducked farther down, desperately trying to avoid getting hit. Behind her she saw a bullet suddenly rip into Marco's chest. It had to be from one of the guards. Or maybe it was Dani or Claire. Oh God, she prayed it wasn't one of them. He's just a boy. Marco sunk to his knees, blood seeping through his orange T-shirt, and then he flopped forward on his stomach.

Tess could hear sirens in the distance. Police cars were approaching from the service road leading to the retreat. Someone must have called them when the alarms went off. Thank God, Tess thought. Thank God.

When the police swarmed the property, they found Benito Coronel in his office desperately trying to find any papers tying him to his drug smuggling operation so he could destroy them. But they weren't there. Dani had already confiscated them and would eventually hand them over to the police and the DEA. Coronel was arrested and charged with a litany of crimes connected to his drug operation. But the girls weren't satisfied. They wanted Coronel for murder.

The whole reason they'd gone after him in the first place was to prove he'd murdered one of his employees, a young mentally challenged man whose concerned sister had hired them when the boy went missing a month earlier. Soon after the showdown at the party, the girls ultimately found the murder weapon Coronel used to beat the boy to death, *a table leg from one of his antique furniture pieces. It was enough for the DA to try and convict him for murder.*

All three of them, Tess, Dani and Claire, testified at the trial. Coronel got twenty years for drug smuggling. But for murder, he got life without the chance for parole.

On the day Coronel was sentenced, the three of them were there. They were a team. It was only right they all show up. It was a bitter-sweet moment when the judge read the sentence. They had gotten justice for their client, but they also knew this was going to be the last day they would spend together. For seven years, they had been known as the LA Dolls, one of the only private investigation firms owned and operated by women. But internal strife had torn them apart, and it was time to move on. As Tess said good-bye to her longtime partners Dani and Claire on the steps outside the courthouse, she knew it was the end of an era. Never in her wildest dreams would she ever imagine what would bring them back together almost twenty-five years later.

CHAPTER 2

Sherman Oaks, California . . . Present Day

She was quite possibly the hottest woman he had ever seen aside from his fiancée of course, who he was marrying to-morrow. But this woman was unbelievable. Smoking hot. And as she peeled off the Ray Ban sunglasses, black bowtie and white tuxedo shirt to the sounds of the Royal Gigolos' dance remake of "California Dreamin'" it was hard to stay focused on his wed-ding happening in a matter of hours.

Monica was her name. Or at least that's what she told him when she first arrived with her boom box. He knew strippers rarely gave their real names. Damn his buddies for tempting him like this on his last night of freedom. His college roommate, Ted, and childhood best friend, Anson, were behind this. And he'd make them pay just as soon as he sobered up.

Monica had arrived in drag, dressed as a best man. What had his real best man, Ted, been thinking? This was way too Freudian. But now was not the time to analyze. As the black silk dress pants fell away and Monica let her platinum blond hair fall freely from its restricting bun, the groom-to-be was finally able to behold her perfect figure as she swayed seductively to the thumping techno track. Her only costume at this point was a candy-red satin brassiere, matching panties, and high heels.

Anson raised his cell phone to snap a picture of Monica as she jiggled her giant breasts in front of Zak. Ted blocked the shot with his hand. He was smart enough to know they should avoid any evidence that their buddy's new bride might stumble upon later.

Monica reached behind and unsnapped the brassiere. She ripped it off and stroked her lips with her tongue. Man, she was sexy. The bulge in his pants got bigger. Zak was surprised he was even capable after six tequila shots.

She straddled the chair he was sitting in, tossed her hair back and leaned in to whisper in his ear.

"What's your name, honey?"

"Zak . . ." he said, embarrassed that it came out more as a squeak.

"Are you staying here at the hotel, Zak?"

Zak nodded. "One floor up."

He and his buddies had gotten a couple of rooms at the Marriot Courtyard on Ventura Boulevard because his mother had insisted upon it. She knew how much drinking went on at bachelor parties.

"I never do this, but I find you so sexy, Zak. I want to give you a private lap dance in your room," Monica said, stroking a finger down his cheek.

"I probably shouldn't . . ." Zak said as thoughts of his fiancée swirled about in his head.

"I'll be gentle, honey. I promise," Monica said.

Ted poured Zak another shot and slapped him on the back. "Last chance, buddy. After tonight, you won't be getting another opportunity like this ever again."

Who was Ted kidding? He had only been married two years,

and was already whoring around on business trips all over the country for his job for US Tobacco. But Zak loved Celeste. He wasn't about to cheat on her, despite his wild past. No, he was going to stay faithful. But the vows weren't until tomorrow. After the vows, then he'd be faithful. And could this even be classified as cheating? Hell, it was only a lap dance. It wasn't like he was going to have sex with her.

He downed the shot of tequila. He was feeling virile and horny. His inhibitions were history. Never a good sign. The next thing he knew he was grabbing Monica's hand and dragging her out the door to the loud cheers of Ted and Anson.

His head was spinning as he and Monica got on the elevator. He had to focus in order to press the eighth-floor button. He stumbled a bit.

"I'm getting married tomorrow," he said, the words slurring.

When the elevator reached the floor and the doors opened, Zak fell out, grabbing the wall to keep his balance. Monica giggled. He tried focusing on her. She was still in her panties but she was topless.

Just then, a room service waiter balancing a silver tray with empty plates and glasses sailed by, and without even a cursory glance, said, "Good evening."

Zak smiled and tried his best to block Monica from his view. "Good evening."

Monica held him up as he led her to a room at the end of the hall. Zak pulled out his key card and tried inserting it into the slot, but suddenly he stopped.

Zak was having severe second thoughts. Every instinct he had was telling him not to go into that room. Celeste would never forgive him if she found out. Even in his alcohol-induced haze, he knew what he was doing was wrong.

"Listen, Monica . . . I really shouldn't . . ."

"Come on, baby. Trust me, you're going to love it," Monica

said as she snatched the key card out of his hand and opened the door. Before he could protest any further, she snatched a fistful of his shirt collar and shoved him into the room ahead of her.

Zak lurched forward and fell to his knees. It was dark. He couldn't see anything.

"Monica?"

The lights snapped on. Zak turned around to see Monica step aside to allow two husky men to enter the room. Both were well north of six feet tall and looked as if a shot of steroids was part of their daily diet.

"Who are you?" Zak managed to croak out before one of the men stepped forward and kicked him with the heel of his shoe right in the face. His nose cracked and blood spurted everywhere. Zak raised his hands to his face but not before he saw the other man step forward and slam a boot into his ribs. Zak doubled over in pain, and looked up to see Monica sitting on the edge of the bed, reapplying red polish to her fingernails, completely uninterested in the vicious beating happening only a few feet away. After that, everything went black.

CHAPTER 3

Ciudad de Mexico

Bowie Lassiter didn't want to blow this one. It was his first international case as a private investigator. Sure, he had successfully retrieved a few lost dogs and some stolen property in his hometown of Miami, but this was a big-time client. An heiress to a chain of coffee houses was convinced her much younger, layabout husband was cheating on her. If she could gather the right amount of evidence, it would help in her divorce case since she had been too blinded by love to listen to her lawyers' pleas and lock up a prenup.

She had come to Bowie by way of his mother, who was the Assistant Chief of Police in San Francisco, and very plugged into the political scene there. The heiress kept homes in both San Francisco and Miami, and was introduced to his mother at a party.

Bowie didn't mind his mother tossing a case his way. Nepotism wasn't an issue with him. Paying the rent on his houseboat docked in the harbor front along Ocean Avenue was.

He had met his new client over coffee at her palatial estate on

Star Island, a private enclave for the rich and famous just off Miami Beach. The heiress's husband was off working on a new business deal, but that's about as specific as he ever got with his wife, so she just assumed he was with the suspected girlfriend, a gorgeous young Cuban hottie who Bowie found out worked as a cashier at one of the local Walgreens.

The husband had told Bowie's client he was going to Mexico City to research a real estate investment, but she was convinced it was a weekend getaway with *her*. Bowie pretty much confirmed it on the spot by calling Walgreens and finding out from the manager that the hot cashier was taking a few days off and wouldn't be working her shift again until Tuesday.

The heiress wanted proof for her divorce lawyer so she booked Bowie a first-class seat on an Aeromexico flight to Mexico City. Armed with his trusty Fuji digital camera, Bowie was prepared to e-mail photos of whatever he found to his client. He felt bad for her. She was one of the richest women in the country, and yet she looked so sad. It was hard not getting personally involved with his clients. He was more like his mother than he cared to admit.

After checking into the Fiesta Americana Hotel in the artsy, colorful Zona Rosa district of the city, Bowie hired a private driver named Arturo to chauffeur him around and be on call in front of the hotel if he needed him. Arturo spoke no English, but Bowie's mother was Latina and taught him Spanish when he was very young, so he spoke it fluently.

Arturo lit up when he learned Bowie was a private investigator working a case. Arturo was a closet James Bond fan, and was anxious to help in any way he could. So Bowie gave him the photo of the suspected cheat who was staying at the same hotel, and told Arturo to call him in his room if he spotted him leaving the hotel.

Bowie had just showered and put on a fresh shirt and a pair of jeans when the phone rang. He picked it up.

"*Buenos tardes,*" Bowie said.

He heard the excited voice of his driver Arturo speaking a mile a minute. The eagle had landed. He grabbed his room card, and hurried out the door.

Arturo had his buddy Jose, the hotel bellhop, take his sweet time flagging down a taxi for the husband and his girlfriend to give Bowie enough time to take the elevator down to the lobby, rush out and hop in the back of Arturo's small, dusty chocolate-brown sedan.

As Jose slowly opened the back door of the taxi for the husband, Arturo gripped the wheel with his hands, ready for action, a giant grin on his sweet-natured, chubby face.

They followed the taxi twenty-eight kilometers south of the city to Xochimilco, a district of meandering canals and tiny islands, and one of the most picturesque tourist spots in all of Mexico. It was built on a lake by the Aztecs five centuries ago. Its name means, "The place where the flowers grow." In other words, very romantic.

The husband paid the taxi driver and he and his mistress strolled down the dock, boarding one of the many multicolored punts that lined the edge. An enthusiastic local sipping a beer happily took their cash and, using a long yellow pole, pushed the boat out to make the trip down the canal alongside floating groups of musicians and older local women hocking succulent snacks. Bowie jumped out of the sedan and raced down to hire his own boat. Arturo followed closely on his heels.

Bowie tossed some pesos at a corpulent husband and wife team who rocked their punt every time they made a gesture. Bowie told them to follow the boat with the happy young couple. Arturo, still wearing that big grin, climbed in behind Bowie.

They pushed off and drifted along the innumerable canals in the shade of the towering cypress trees. A woman in a small canoe floated past, offering them hash made of corn.

Bowie politely shook his head. "No, *gracias.*"

The couple steering his boat were so close to the punt in front of them, he thought they were going to bang into it. He needed a plan. And then it hit him. Why be discreet? He was half Spanish, and fit right in with the locals. The captain of his boat was wearing a straw hat. He offered to buy it for fifty pesos. And then, he bought a rainbow colored shawl from a passing canoe and slipped it over his muscled, six-foot frame before taking out his digital camera. He told the driver to ride up alongside the boat in front of them.

Bowie raised his camera and started shooting. Luck was on his side. The husband and his mistress were curled up in a chaise lounge in the middle of the boat, kissing and fondling one another, completely oblivious to the beauty of their surroundings.

Bowie snapped and snapped until he felt he had enough proof for his client. The husband sleepily opened his eyes between kisses and noticed him with the camera. He sat up and glared at Bowie.

Bowie spoke in broken English and a thick Mexican accent. "You like picture for keepsake?"

"No," the husband growled. "Now get lost."

"*Si, Señor,*" Bowie said. As the captain of the other boat pushed the pole harder to put some distance between the two punts, Bowie checked the photos, pleased he had gotten some good shots.

Suddenly, the serene, almost dreamlike setting was shattered by a loud, sharp crack. Bowie jumped, nearly dropping his camera in the canal. The husband and wife ducked. Several Mexicans partying in a neighboring boat screamed and nearly tipped over their vessel. Bowie spun his head around to see a boatful of musicians just sitting there frozen, not sure what had just happened.

There was another crack, and Bowie felt something whiz past his right ear. He dove to the bottom of the boat. He hadn't even tried bringing his gun because he never would have gotten security clearance, and this was such an easy, supposedly nonviolent case.

He lifted his head up slowly. Another bullet shot past him. Bowie hunkered down and waited. If they tried to board the boat and finish the job, he'd have to defend himself with no weapon. They could easily take him out. Man, this was not how he pictured his first big case ending.

After a few minutes, there was stillness again. And Bowie raised his head to see a punt carrying two Mexicans and one Caucasian glide down the canal at a high speed and disappear around the corner. He never saw their faces.

He turned and his heart nearly stopped. His driver Arturo was slumped down in the back of the boat, his glassy, still eyes staring lifelessly, while blood seeped through his white cotton shirt.

CHAPTER 4

Rio de Janeiro, Brazil

Bianca Cardoza only agreed to meet her two best pals Isabel and Fabiana because they were hanging out at Bofetada Café and Bar. Bofetada catered primarily to a gay clientele, which made it much easier for the stunning eighteen-year-old Rio native to relax and catch up with her friends without the hassle of some drunken, pot-bellied tourist trying desperately to pick her up.

She had recently broken up with her boyfriend who owned his own paragliding business. He spent his days strapping wide-eyed tourists to his back and running off a cliff to give them a bird's-eye view of the dazzling beaches and grand mountains of her home city. But predictably, like most of her suitors, he was only after her money. Sure, she was beautiful, and had even done some local modeling, so that was usually what got them interested in the first place.

However, when they discovered that her late father was a billionaire with real estate holdings and shipping companies all over the world, that's when everything would inevitably change.

She never had to wait too long before they would bring up the subject of some kind of investment or loan. Why should she care? What they needed was chump change compared to what she had in her trust fund.

But she did care. She would love to meet a guy who wanted to get to know her, not just her bank statement. She hated the fact that she was the same as every other poor little rich girl, like the Onassis kid, and so many others, but she was not going to let that bother her tonight. She was determined to have fun.

Bofetada was packed with a post-beach crowd that was getting louder by the minute thanks to the free-flowing caipirinhas, a tangy lime drink made with potent Brazilian liquor, muddled with sugar. Fabiana and Isabel had already downed three of them before she'd even arrived. They were giddy and giggling and acting more like adolescent girls with each round.

"You need to forget about Ricardo, and get back out there," Isabel said to Bianca as her head swayed back and forth. She then licked the sugar off the edge of her glass.

Bianca smiled, "I don't think so. I'm done with men for a while."

"Like him for instance," Fabiana said, pointing toward the back of the bar. "No, don't look yet."

It was too late. Both Bianca and Isabel swiveled their heads around to see a striking man with blond hair sitting alone at a corner table. His shirt was open, revealing a smooth bronzed chest. He raised his glass at the three gaping girls and flashed a gorgeous smile.

They all laughed and whipped their heads back around.

"We are so busted," Isabel said.

"So what? It's not like he's interested in any of us," Bianca said. "He's gay."

"All the attractive ones usually are," Fabiana added.

"I'm not picking up a gay vibe," Isabel said.

"You didn't pick up a gay vibe with your ex Miguel, and he was sleeping with your brother," Bianca said.

Isabel tossed a napkin at Bianca who dodged it by moving her head to the side. A strong, tanned, masculine hand caught it.

"How are you ladies doing tonight?" It was the blond man from the corner table.

Isabel leaned forward coquettishly. "Love your accent. Are you from England?"

"Australia. Melbourne."

"What's your name?" Isabel purred, flashing a quick smile to her two best friends.

"Sam," he said, his eyes fixed on Bianca.

"You do know this is pretty much a gay bar," Bianca said, smiling.

"Yeah, I was just beginning to figure that out. Maybe it was the three drinks I got sent from those guys over there."

He turned and waved at three Brazilian boys, who watched his every move with lustful interest. "It's my first day here, so I'm allowed a few mistakes."

"You here on holiday?" Fabiana asked, as she sipped her drink.

Sam nodded, never taking his eyes off Bianca. He was starting to make her feel uncomfortable. But just a little. He was very cute.

"Traveling alone?" Isabel asked.

Sam nodded again, and then finally stopped gazing at Bianca to look at the other two girls. "Mind if I join you?"

That was it. The minute they said "yes" he was in the seat next to Bianca and wooing her with his charms for the next two hours. Bianca remained distant for at least the first forty-five minutes because she never trusted strangers. But soon her walls began to crumble as she learned more about him. Never married. Recently out of a two-year relationship with his college sweetheart. And working for his family's company, a multi-million dollar pharmaceutical company in Australia. Okay, so his family didn't have billions like she and her stepmother, but he was definitely rich. And she liked that.

As Isabel prattled on about life in Rio and all the sightseeing he must do while visiting, he casually reached under the table and gently took Bianca's hand. He held it for what seemed like an eternity. Bianca didn't know whether to pull away or leave it there. Maybe it was time she just went with it, and stopped questioning everything.

When Sam went to the bar to get another round of drinks, Fabiana turned to Isabel. "I think it's time we go."

"But he's getting us more drinks," Isabel said, pouting.

"I just think we should leave them alone, Isabel, so they can get to know each other a little better."

"No, I don't want you two going anywhere," Bianca said, suddenly panicked.

"He seems like a really good guy, Bianca. You don't have to marry him. Just stay and talk to him for a while, and maybe, if you're really feeling reckless, you can exchange cell phone numbers."

"Am I really that bad?" Bianca said, knowing the answer.

Fabiana smiled and kissed her friend on the cheek. "Call us tomorrow and tell us everything."

"Yes, it seems we're destined to just live vicariously through you," Isabel said, only half kidding.

Fabiana and Isabel stumbled away leaving Bianca sitting at the table alone, debating on whether she should run while she still could, but it was too late. Sam returned, clutching four drinks in his hands.

"What happened to your friends?" he said, looking around.

"They left."

Sam's eyes twinkled. "Guess we're going to have to finish these by ourselves."

Bianca smiled as he set the drinks down on the table and then handed her one. They toasted, and talked some more, and soon she lost track of time. The bar began to empty out as most of the patrons hurried off to Le Boy, the popular gay disco in Copacabana.

She was suddenly very tired, and had a hard time focusing on Sam. He was still talking. About his world travels to Africa, Europe, and Asia. Her head was spinning now. This wasn't good. It was time to go home. She tried to open her mouth to ask a passing waiter to call her a taxi, but her words came out in a jumble.

She tried to stand up, but stumbled, and fell against the table, glasses shattering to the floor of the café. Waiters rushed over to clean up the mess, and somebody, presumably Sam, held her up. He was leading her now, away from Bofetada, down the dark street. Where was he taking her? He didn't know where she lived. How could she be this intoxicated? Isabel and Fabiana had drunk most of the caipirinhas. She just had one when they first arrived and the one Sam had bought for her.

Everything was blurry, but she managed to make out a white van parked at the end of the street. The back doors opened and two men waved at Sam to hurry. He was hustling her toward the van, and she was too drunk or drugged to stop him. What had he put in her drink? She had always heard about locals dropping roofies into the drinks of tourists and luring them away to rob them, but she was the local and Sam was the tourist. This didn't make any sense. As the two men reached out and grabbed her arms, pulling her up into the van, everything suddenly went black.

CHAPTER 5

"Where the hell is he?" Senator Roger Wilkes barked as he clasped the hand of his teary-eyed daughter, Celeste, who was otherwise a vision in her Donna Karan satin, white wedding gown.

Claire Walker-Corley didn't have an answer. Her scattered son was perpetually late for family functions, even a no-show at times, but she had a hard time believing he would forget to show up for his own wedding. The ceremony was scheduled to start at four o'clock. It was five after five. The guests were now up, out of their seats, stretching their legs, quietly gossiping about what might be happening behind the scenes of this one hundred-thousand-dollar extravaganza.

Zak had wanted to elope to Vegas with his girlfriend of two years, but Celeste was the daughter of the junior senator from Oregon. There was no way her father would allow his only daughter to quietly marry without the opportunity to milk the event and land in a few well-placed society pages.

Claire had gone along with all the bells and whistles of the planning mostly because she didn't have to pay for anything, except an understated rehearsal luncheon, which she and her hus-

band Jeb had hosted at their home in Sherman Oaks the day before. The wedding, held outdoors at an exclusive country club
on a hilltop above Malibu, was the responsibility of the senator
and his wife, which was understandably a huge sigh of relief.

Jeb was an airline pilot for American Airlines with a good
salary, but this was why she was thankful she had two sons. It was
the bride's parents who pay for the wedding and reception, and
she was not about to debate that time-honored tradition.

A breeze was picking up and Claire had to hold her hair in
place as she lifted the hem of her burgundy dress, and shuffled
over to Ted, her son's best man, who was nervously chattering on
his cell phone. Claire waited for him to finish before gently taking his arm.

"Any word?" Claire asked quietly.

Ted shook his head, his eyes were bloodshot and bleary, his
face pale. He was obviously nursing a massive hangover. "Sorry,
Mrs. Corley, I just don't know where he could be. I mean, he
never left the hotel. He just went up to his room to . . ."

"Get a lap dance from the stripper you guys bought for him."

"Yeah," Ted shrugged, a little embarrassed. He exchanged
guilty looks with Zak's other best buddy, Anson, who quickly
averted his eyes to avoid Claire's accusing face.

Claire knew her son was wild. He had long ago cemented his
reputation as a party boy, which was why she was so surprised
when he asked the far more conservative Celeste to be his wife.
But she was done questioning her son's decisions. Life was about
learning as you go, and nobody knew that better than she did.

"Do you have a number for the stripper?"

"We used a service. But when I called a few minutes ago, the
number was no longer in service."

"This is so typical," an angry voice spit out.

Claire turned to face her younger son, Evan, the opposite of
his older brother, reserved, quiet, a law student at UCLA. His

whole life was about hard work and responsibility. He took after his father.

"Not now, Evan," Claire said as she waved over her husband Jeb, who was at the bar ordering another Scotch. She could use one too right about now, and she was a little miffed he wasn't getting one for her.

"Are you the least bit surprised?" Evan said as he ripped off his black bow tie and unbuttoned the tight collar of his shirt.

Jeb made his way over, downing the Scotch in one gulp.

"That's not going to help, Jeb," Claire said.

"You try making small talk with the senator's jittery wife when you're sober," Jeb said, chewing on a piece of ice.

"We're going to have to make a decision soon," Claire said. "I don't think he's coming."

"Well, the senator wanted this day to be all over the papers. Be careful what you wish for," Jeb said with a laugh, as he watched some photographers snap pictures of the fuming senator comforting his distraught daughter.

"That guy has a direct line to the president," Evan said. "So don't be surprised if we're all audited next year."

Claire turned to her husband of twenty-four years and said, "I don't want to see you again unless you have a Scotch in your hand for me." Then she took a deep breath, and marched over to the senator.

"Senator . . ." she said, forcing a smile.

"That's a fine son you have, Claire," Senator Wilkes hissed. "Not even bothering to show up for his own wedding."

"Daddy, please, you're just making things worse," Celeste begged, wiping her tears away and hopelessly smudging her mascara.

"I begged you not to rush into this . . ." Wilkes said to his daughter. "I knew he'd just wind up hurting you."

"I think it might be best if we told the guests the wedding has been postponed," Claire said evenly, trying not to upset the senator more than he already was.

"Postponed? It's off, Claire. There won't be any rescheduling," Wilkes said.

"Well, that will be for Celeste and Zak to decide. Once we find him."

"Zak's not deciding anything when it comes to my daughter, of that you can be sure," Wilkes said, suddenly blinded by a flash bulb. "Look at those photographers. They're eating this up, the goddamned vultures."

"You invited them, senator," Claire reminded him in a sweet voice. She was good at being nice and even tempered. It had served her well over the years.

"If my poll numbers suffer for this . . ." Wilkes said, turning his back to the cameras.

"I'm sure your numbers will be just fine. They'll probably spike. People love to feel sorry for public figures. However, if I were you, I would be a bit more concerned with your daughter's well being right now," Claire said, walking away. So much for nice and even tempered. She couldn't help it. She loathed politicians. And there was a tiny bit of her that was happy now that it appeared the senator wouldn't be a permanent fixture at any future family gatherings.

Claire spotted Jeb holding up her Scotch. She practically knocked over some chairs rushing over to him.

"Here you go, honey," Jeb said, handing the glass to her.

"I think it's time we let the guests go home, what do you say, Jeb?"

"I'll go make the announcement," he said, softly patting the small of her back with his large, firm hand and giving her a soft kiss on the cheek.

Claire retreated to a private space behind the atrium to enjoy her Scotch and put this disastrous day behind her.

"You always knew how to throw a memorable party," a voice said.

Claire turned to see Dani Mendez and Tess Monahan, two names from her distant past. When she sent out the wedding invitations, she included her former coworkers because she never thought either one would ever agree to come given their checkered history together.

Dani was a big-deal Assistant Police Chief in San Francisco, and Tess was a widowed socialite gallivanting all over the world. Why on earth would either one of them bother to come to her son's wedding in Los Angeles? But both had accepted, and incredibly were here now.

"I am so sorry. I don't know what to say," Claire said to her old friends.

"What's there to say? The kid smartened up at the last second," Tess said with a throaty laugh.

Dani and Tess. Claire sometimes thought she would never see them again. When they worked together as private detectives in the 1980s, they were an unbeatable team. Dani was the unofficial leader, cool and methodical, so sharp and focused. Tess was always the sexy, wild one, a total free spirit. In fact, if she hadn't given birth to her son Zak herself, she would almost swear he belonged to Tess.

"But you came all this way. I mean, Tess, you flew in from Brazil," Claire said. The ramifications of her son's absence finally began to sink in.

"Paulo's never been to America, and I've been promising him forever that we would come for a visit. This was the perfect excuse. So don't worry about it," Tess said, raising her champagne glass to acknowledge the hunky thirty-year-old Brazilian soccer coach who had arrived as her shiny, beautiful accessory. Like a perfectly muscled lap dog, he eagerly nodded and smiled at his much older lover.

"Isn't he gorgeous?" Tess said, her eyes gazing at him. "And a dynamo in bed."

"She hasn't changed a bit, has she?" Dani remarked with a grin.

"No," Claire said. "Not in the least." She was happy to see them. Both of them. But so much time had passed. Things had ended so badly. She really thought she was over it. But seeing them now, after all these years, some of the old hard feelings began to slowly bubble to the surface.

"Excuse me for a minute, girls," Tess said. "Paulo's starting to have a little separation anxiety." She winked at her two friends, and glided over to her young stallion, who happily threw his arms around her waist and pulled her close to him.

"She used to be into older men," Claire said.

"Yes, but if she still was, she'd be trolling nursing homes for boyfriends. This is a much better way to go," Dani said.

Claire chuckled. It was good to laugh. The tension of the afternoon was almost too much to bear.

"So what do you think happened to him?" Dani said, gently taking Claire by the arm.

Claire shook her head. "I have no idea. I'm pretty sure he loves Celeste. Zak can be flighty and irresponsible, but not like this."

The guests were filing out now after Jeb's announcement. The senator escorted his weeping daughter into the country club for some privacy.

And Claire Walker-Corley stood with her friend Dani as she contemplated the fate of her missing boy. She was starting to get a sickening feeling of dread that her sometimes irresponsible, always unpredictable, son wasn't having second thoughts or last minute jitters. She was afraid something might have happened to him. And it scared the hell out of her.

CHAPTER 6

Dani felt sorry for her friend Claire. She always knew her eldest son Zak could be a handful, but to blow off his own wedding like this. This was bad. Claire never liked to be the center of attention. But right now, there was no avoiding it.

Back in the days of their private detective business, quiet Claire would always prefer to stand behind her two much louder, more colorful cohorts. Dani talked tough, liked to shake things up, throw the arrogant pricks who underestimated the abilities of three female detectives off balance. Tess got them aroused, manipulated them, and used her sexual wiles as a weapon. Claire was the sweet one. She would spend hours meticulously reviewing the mission at hand, and when she did go out in the field, she chose to hide behind some undercover assignment that would allow her to pretend to be someone else.

Dani knew that she herself was the only one of the three who truly missed those rocking, violent, thrill-a-minute days in the eighties. It was resoundingly clear why. Both Claire and Tess went on to meet two wonderful men, and live out the lives they had always dreamed about. But Dani had already been living her fantasy life as a kick-ass private eye. Nothing else could ever come close to matching that adrenaline rush of power and excitement. Deep down she resented her friends for leaving her high and dry, abandoning her just when they were about to hit legendary status. They were a novelty at the time, and no one came close, certainly none of their male competitors, to achieving the same track record. Hell, if they were the hot chicks they were twenty years ago, running around today collaring the bad guys like they did then, they'd probably have their own TV reality show.

Dani watched Claire expertly handle this already painful and uncomfortable situation. She had offended the senator with a rare burst of anger, but she was now working his wife, finding common ground in the fact that they had no control over their children's actions. Dani thought it was a smart way to go. After all, Mrs. Wilkes could relate. Her daughter had chosen to marry a wild boy like Zak in the first place and there was nothing she could do about it. So the poor woman could easily understand Claire's frustration.

Dani spotted a long black stretch limo winding its way up the hill toward the country club. It pulled to a stop, and the bald, black driver in an ill-fitting blue suit hopped out and opened the back door. Dani thought maybe it was Zak, probably still drunk with no concept of how late it was. But it wasn't Zak.

A gorgeous, dark-skinned beauty in a tight black dress, probably a Vera Wang, slid out, her matching shoes making contact with the pavement. Her wavy black hair cascaded perfectly down beyond her soft bare shoulders. It was as if she had just stepped off the pages of *Glamour* magazine. Dani was always annoyed with women who made it look so effortless. She had never been into hair and fashion. A pair of jeans, a ratty T-shirt, a worn pair of sandals, no makeup and she was good to go. How hard did it have to be? It was only after she was promoted to Assistant Chief of Police, when politics began playing a more prominent role in her job, did she start to check out the Clinique counter at Macy's for a little base, some mascara and a light colored lipstick. But she kept her hair short to avoid having to interrupt her day to go visit a stylist.

The young woman walked toward the tented area, a confused look on her face. Where was everybody? Dani watched her intensely. There was something familiar about her, the way she carried herself. And then it hit her when the girl smiled. Tess's stepdaughter. Sure, Tess wasn't her birth mother. But having spent so many years with her after the sudden death of her father, the girl began to resemble Tess in so many ways. Especially that mega-watt smile.

Tess and Paulo were lip-locked and completely unaware of Bianca's arrival.

"Tess!" the girl called out, waving frantically.

Tess looked up, pushed her boy-toy Paulo aside, and raced over, screaming all the way, grabbing her stepdaughter into a warm hug. They chattered and giggled and kissed incessantly. Dani was impressed. Tess had always been so self-centered. When she heard Tess had decided to raise Bianca herself after her husband's untimely death, she had her doubts. Tess a mother? Didn't seem like it would be in the girl's best interest. But according to mutual friends, Bianca had turned out to be a kind, sensitive, and gracious young woman. And that meant a lot considering she was also an heiress worth billions.

Dani's cell phone rang. She reached into her handbag and checked who was calling. If it was anyone from the office, she would let it go to voice mail. She had left all the drama of her work back in San Francisco, at least for a couple of days. This was the one time she had managed to get away, at least for a weekend, all year.

It wasn't the office. It was her son. Dani answered the call.

"Bowie?"

"Hey, Mom," Bowie said, like he always did, although this time she detected something in his voice, something not quite right. She was very close to her only child, and also very intuitive.

"What is it?"

There was a long pause.

"Bowie, what's wrong?"

"I'm at the airport in Mexico City. I've been working a case."

"Are you all right?" Dani braced herself. Her son's business was a dangerous one. She should know. He had followed in her footsteps and become a private detective.

"I'm fine. But I think someone's trying to kill me."

Dani thought she heard wrong. Who would want to kill her son? He had just gotten his license. There hadn't been enough time for him to build up a laundry list of enemies yet.

"I was working a divorce case. Followed the client's husband to Mexico. A sniper started taking potshots at me and my driver. I ducked. He wasn't so lucky."

"Oh my God, Bowie . . ."

"He died at the scene. But I'm okay, Mom, really."

"Do you think it has anything to do with the case you're working on?" Why had she let him get into this business without even raising a concern? She remembered how proud she had been that he wanted to be like her. Now she felt stupid, allowing her only child to put himself in that kind of danger.

"I don't think it's related, but that's just a gut feeling I have," he said.

"Maybe the shooter wanted to harm your driver."

"No. He went down right away. They kept firing and it was pretty obvious they were aiming at me."

"Do you need me to come down there?"

"Stay put, Mom. I'm heading back to Miami. I'll call you when I get there. I just wanted you to know I was okay, in case it somehow got back to you."

There was a commotion near the tent. Dani turned to see Tess having some sort of fit. Paulo was trying to calm her down.

Bianca clasped her stepmother's hand and talked quietly. Dani returned her attention to her son.

"Call me when you get home," she said, still in a state of shock.

"I will. I have to get going, or I'll miss my flight," Bowie said.

"The minute you touch ground, I want a call, you hear me, Bowie?"

"Got it, Mom. Love you."

"Love you, too."

Dani shut off the phone and stuffed it back in her purse. She wanted to bolt right there, hop on the next plane to Miami to be with her son. But she was distracted by Tess's gasping and crying. She walked over and touched Bianca's shoulder.

"Bianca, I'm Dani, a friend of your mother's. What's going on?"

"She's just being overly dramatic," Bianca said, her eyes rolling.

"You're nearly kidnapped and you accuse me of overreacting?" Tess said, gripping Paulo's thick, muscular forearm to maintain her balance.

"Kidnapped?" Dani asked.

"A tourist slipped something in my drink back home. I think he and his friends were going to have some sort of gang bang or rob me or something. But my friend Isabel had forgotten her purse at the café where we were having drinks and when she came back for it, she saw them putting me in a van. She screamed bloody murder, and they took off, leaving me passed out on the street," Bianca said with a shrug.

"No wonder your mother's upset," Dani said.

"There's no reason to be upset. I wasn't raped or robbed. I'm fine. This kind of thing happens all the time in Rio. Mostly to tourists though. I'm embarrassed I let it almost happen to me," Bianca said.

Dani stepped forward and put her arm around Tess. "Are you going to be all right?"

"No," Tess barked. "She's always flirting with the wrong guys, taking unnecessary risks. One of these days she's going to get herself into so much trouble she won't be able to get out of it."

Dani tried not to laugh. Bianca had become a walking clone of her stepmother and Tess didn't even realize it.

"Well, we can be thankful she was not harmed," Paulo offered as he slid his free arm around Tess's waist, pulling her closer to him.

"So, Mom never mentioned you, Dani. How do you know each other?" Bianca asked.

That one hurt. They had shared so much together as a team, and it was as if Tess wanted to put the past in a box and never look at it again. Was Dani the only one of the three to have fond memories of their time together?

Dani opened her mouth to answer Bianca's question, having no idea what she was going to say, if Tess even wanted her to tell the truth. She was saved by the back door of the country club that led into the kitchen slamming open and Claire and her husband Jeb hurrying out. She hadn't even noticed them go inside. Claire's face was pale, her eyes vacant. As they passed, Dani reached out and touched Claire's arm.

"Claire?"

But Claire didn't answer. She just kept walking at a brisk pace toward a waiting car. Jeb stopped and turned to Dani.

"We found Zak," he said solemnly.

"Where?" Dani asked.

"He's in the hospital. Intensive care. Apparently some thugs beat him up." He hurried off to join his wife.

Dani turned to Tess, who was snapping out of her panic attack. Bowie shot at in Mexico City. Bianca nearly kidnapped in Rio. Zak assaulted right here in town. This was suddenly beyond mere coincidence. It made Dani shudder at the possibilities.

CHAPTER 7

Claire's head was spinning as she rode up the elevator with Jeb to the third floor where her son was recovering in intensive care. She felt sick over the fact that she had just assumed Zak was being his usual irresponsible self not showing up for the wedding. Now faced with the truth, a brutal, vicious assault, she wished he had just partied late into the night and overslept.

Jeb gripped her hand as the doors slid open. They walked out into a long, drab hallway with dull gray walls. A sign pointed them in the direction of the intensive care ward. Claire and Jeb marched quickly down the hall where they were intercepted by a young Asian doctor, a white coat flung over his wrinkled turquoise scrubs. He wore glasses, that were bent and barely straddling the tip of his short pointed nose.

"We're looking for Zak Corley," Jeb said.

The doctor nodded. "I'm Doctor Cho. Your son is pretty banged up. Broken nose, fractured rib, some trauma to the head . . ."

"Oh, God," Claire gasped. It was as if she had just been punched in the gut.

"No sign of brain damage as far as we can tell," Doctor Cho said. "We're keeping him in the intensive care unit for observation, but he should be moved to a room first thing in the morning. Whoever was responsible for his injuries left him to die, and he would have if a maid hadn't let herself in to clean the room, and she found him."

"Can we see him?" Claire asked, even though she intended to see her son whether the doctor wanted her to or not.

"He's been awake for about an hour, and asking for Celeste," Doctor Cho said.

"That's his fiancée," Jeb offered. "She and her parents are right behind us."

"You go on ahead then," Doctor Cho said. "And I'll send her in when she arrives. But don't stay too long. Zak needs his rest."

"Thank you, Doctor," Claire said, scurrying into the intensive care ward, Jeb close on her heels.

Claire stopped short upon seeing Zak lying in a bed where he was hooked up to a battery of intimidating and frightening machines, as well as a morphine drip to dull the pain. His face was battered and bruised; a white patch had been secured over his left eye.

Claire fought back tears. She had to be strong for her son.

She slowly and deliberately walked over to his bedside, leaned down and gently took his hand, whispering in his ear, "Zak, honey, it's Mom and Dad, we came as soon as we got word."

Zak slowly opened his one uncovered eye, pulled his mother close to his face and whispered, "What's the return policy on the wedding cake?"

Claire laughed. Zak's humor was intact. That was a good sign.

Jeb said, "Celeste's on her way, son."

Zak frowned. "Her dad must be so pissed."

Claire squeezed her son's hand. "How can he be? It wasn't your fault you were mugged."

"I don't think it was a robbery," Zak said, his voice weak.

"What do you mean?" Claire asked.

"I was set up. The girl I was with . . . um . . . the stripper . . .

Monica . . . she lured me back to my room . . . so they could attack me . . ."

"Attack you?" Claire said, the blood draining from her face.

"I wasn't going to go with her . . . but she was so beautiful . . . and maybe a small part of me wanted one last bit of fun before I got hitched . . . but when I got up there . . ." Zak said softly.

"Did you sleep with her?" a pinched, high-pitched voice asked from behind them.

Claire and Jeb whipped around to see Celeste, now wearing a simple green dress with spaghetti straps, her tear-streaked face smudged with makeup, standing in the doorway. Her father, Senator Wilkes, hovered behind her, glaring.

"Celeste . . ." Zak tried sitting up, but didn't have the strength. Jeb reached over and eased his son back down on the bed.

"Celeste, maybe it would be best if we continued this discussion later. Zak's been through a lot . . ." Claire said, as she withdrew from her son and stood in front of him as if to protect him from his fiancée's building rage.

"And I haven't? I've been humiliated in front of all of my friends and family, and all because my husband-to-be banged some stripper, and got roughed up by her jealous boyfriend the night before our wedding."

"Celeste, that's not how it went down . . . I didn't do anything . . ." Zak moaned.

"I don't care to hear anything you have to say for yourself, Zak. You're a child, and I should have admitted that to myself long before now," Celeste said. "I never want to see or hear from you ever again, you cold, selfish bastard!"

Mustering as much dignity as she possibly could, Celeste whirled around and marched out of the intensive care unit. Her father, the mighty senator, glowered a moment longer, punctuating his indignation, before chasing after his daughter.

Claire was happy to see them go. The self-righteous senator would have made her son's life a living hell as the husband of his precious, spoiled daughter. But she decided not to share that opinion with her son until he was feeling better.

"I thought I'd be treated a whole lot better in intensive care," Zak said with a smile.

"Son, do you have any idea who those men were who attacked you?" Jeb asked, worry lines stretching across his forehead.

Zak shook his head. "Sorry."

"Where did the boys get the stripper?" Claire asked.

"We met a guy in the hotel bar who recommended a service."

"Do you remember what the man looked like?"

"No. We were pretty wasted . . ." Zak said softly. "When the girl showed up she was really hot, and she offered me a lap dance up in her room, and I was so drunk . . . but I changed my mind . . . Then she pushed me and let these two guys in the room . . ."

"It's okay, Zak," Claire said. "Did you get a look at the men who followed you inside?"

"No. It all happened so fast."

Dr. Cho poked his head in the room. "I think Zak should rest now. You can see him again in the morning."

Claire leaned down and gave her son a gentle kiss on the cheek, then she stood erect, as her husband Jeb led her out of the room.

Outside, once the door to the intensive care ward closed, Claire looked into her husband's eyes. "Someone wanted to kill him. Who would do something like that?"

"The only dispute we've ever had was with Mr. Faraday next door because his Doberman never stopped barking, but that dog died four years ago," Jeb said.

Claire knew the last twenty-four years had been blissful and quiet with very little drama. But it was the years before she met Jeb that suddenly came rushing back. So many cases. So many enemies. Her thoughts were interrupted by the elevator doors opening at the other end of the hallway. Dani Mendez and Tess Monahan stepped out, their faces filled with concern.

Claire patted Jeb's cheek with the palm of her hand. "Stay here, Jeb. I'll be right back."

Claire walked down the hall and joined her two old friends.

"How is he?" Dani asked.

"He'll pull through. But somebody sure did a number on him," Claire said. "I just don't understand who would want to hurt my son . . ."

"Sweetheart, there is something you should know . . ." Tess said as she put a comforting hand on Claire's arm.

And it was at that moment that Claire's happy and boring suburban world came crashing down all around her. If the attack on Zak's life had been an isolated incident, she may have been able to convince herself it was just a random attack. But as her friends recounted the near abduction of Tess's daughter in Brazil and Dani's son almost being shot in Mexico she was faced with the truth. Someone was targeting their children. And it was someone from their violent, and high-profile, long-ago past.

"You know what this means," Dani said.

"No, Dani, I don't," Claire said.

"Look, someone is trying to get our attention, and they're doing it by going after our kids," Dani said.

"So we call the police and tell them what's going on," Tess said. "Because I have absolutely no desire to go digging into our past case files to find out who wants to get back at us."

"Tess is right," Claire said. "We're too old for this."

"So you just want to sit back and do nothing, and let whatever thug with a grudge is out there to keep trying until he gets it right? What if the maid hadn't found Zak in time? What if Bianca's friend hadn't forgotten her purse?"

"But it's been so long," Claire said.

"I don't care. As long as someone is taking potshots at my Bowie, I'm not going to rest until I find out who it is and put him down," Dani said.

Claire and Tess exchanged knowing looks. Dani was like a pit bull. She wasn't going to let this go until she got what she needed from them.

"Fine," Claire said. "We figure this out, and then we go back to our separate lives. Okay?"

Claire looked to Tess, who was much less convinced than she was. But Tess loved her stepdaughter, and instinctively knew she had to protect her from any possible harm. "Yes, okay, I'm in."

Dani nodded.

"This is only temporary, Dani. We're not the Rolling Stones, still prancing around the stage even though they're at retirement age," Tess said.

"I understand. A one time thing. For the sake of our kids," Dani said, keeping her unexpressive face in place.

But Claire knew a small part of Dani, a part not so hidden from her and Tess, both of whom knew her so well, was radiating with unbridled joy underneath. The LA Dolls, as they were known in the eighties, were finally back.

CHAPTER 8

Police Commissioner Bruce Talbot looked at Dani with one eyebrow raised. "You want me to get you what?"

"I don't have the resources on my own to get every name. I'm going to need your help," Dani said to her former partner. She and Bruce were paired as beat cops in the late eighties. Both had risen through the ranks. Bruce was now Commissioner and Dani was the Assistant Chief of Police.

Talbot rubbed his forehead as he studied the written request. "Do you know how time consuming this is going to be? I don't have the manpower."

"Somebody's after our kids, Bruce. It's unrealistic to believe it's a mere coincidence." Dani wasn't about to play the mom card and tell Bruce how worried she was, maybe work up a few tears, as much as she wanted to do just that. Bruce would fall for it in a heartbeat, muster up his paternal side, and assure her he would take care of things for her.

Bruce was three years younger than Dani, but he had always been protective of her. He had been in love with her when they first put on the uniform together. At the time, she was a single mother, living from paycheck to paycheck, just focused on feeding her baby since she was never going to rely on the boy's father. Romance was the last thing on her mind, especially with a coworker, and definitely not someone she shared a patrol car with on a daily basis. Dani breathed a big sigh of relief when Bruce met his wife Shelley, a child protective services caseworker they had met while investigating a domestic disturbance involving a custody dispute.

"You just had to bring this to me one month before I'm going to retire, didn't you?" Bruce said, running a calloused hand through his thick gray hair.

Bruce looked tired, Dani thought. It had been a long seven years as Commissioner, and he was happy to finally be stepping down.

"It's been over twenty years since we closed up shop. A lot of these guys we put away have to be out of prison by now," Dani said, locking eyes with Bruce, not willing to leave his office until he agreed to help out. "I just need a list of names so we can run our own little check to see if any are now gunning for us."

Bruce perused the piece of paper in his right hand, and then reached for a Styrofoam cup of cold coffee. He downed what was left of it, winced at the bitter taste, and then looked at Dani. "I'm going to need time, find a couple of people to put on this."

"I appreciate it, Bruce. I know you have your hands full finding a replacement," Dani said, noticing a slight tear in her hose. She hated the fact that she cared, but ever since she had been subtly campaigning for Bruce's job, she figured she had to look her best.

She had been so preoccupied with what happened with Bowie down in Mexico, not to mention Tess and Claire's kids, she hadn't bothered doing her now ritualistic morning once-over in the mirror. Her gray suit jacket was wrinkled, and there was a slight blueberry jelly stain on the left breast of her blouse from the bagel she had on the flight up from LA. Great.

Bruce suddenly couldn't look Dani in the eye. Was he fixated on the jelly stain? Why did he look so uncomfortable?

"Something wrong, Bruce?" Dani asked, not sure she wanted to hear his answer.

"I've been meaning to talk to you about this for a while, Dani, but I've been avoiding it."

"Just come out with it," Dani said. Bruce never had any trouble being honest with Dani. Hell, he confessed his undying love for her all those years ago with a heroin dealer handcuffed in the backseat of their squad car.

"We've been having a lot of meetings lately, me and the powers that be, and you know I've been advocating fiercely for you to be the one who replaces me . . ." Bruce stared at the pile of papers cluttering his desk. He fingered the now-empty Styrofoam cup.

Dani's heart sank. She knew what was coming. Better to deal with it now than later, she thought.

"It's not going to be you," Bruce said with a heavy sigh.

Dani gripped the arm of the chair where she was sitting. Suddenly the jelly stain on her blouse seemed miniscule. She would be lying to herself if she thought she didn't covet the position. It was what she had been working toward for years.

When Bruce was named Commissioner instead of her seven years ago, even though her record stood high above his and so many others, she let it go. Bruce was her oldest friend on the force and she chose to be happy for him. He was married, had three kids in college, and by nature of his gender he was firmly established as a member of the Boys Club. She didn't have those advantages, but still a small part of her hoped that her abilities, her accomplishments, her intelligence would win the day. No such luck. But now, after waiting for so long, knowing Bruce would burn out eventually, leaving the door open for her to take over, it was damn near devastating to find out she was being passed over again.

"It's not because you're female, Dani. There's no glass ceiling politics going on here," Bruce said, trying to convince himself he actually believed what he was saying. "San Francisco is one of the most progressive cities in the country, if not the world. Hell, we're the city that gave Washington Diane Feinstein."

"Then what was it?" Dani said, her mind reeling with possible reasons. She was never good at playing politics, or sucking up to the bosses who could grease the wheels of her career.

"They don't talk openly with me because they know how close we are, but if I were to hazard a guess, I'd say you're too outspoken. You question everything, and I think they're looking for more of a yes-man, if you want me to be brutally honest."

"Is that what you've been, Bruce, a yes-man?" Dani regretted saying it the second it slipped off her tongue. But she was hurting and needed to lash out. Bruce was lying to her. He had a lot of influence and could have fought for her, but he hated confrontation, and undoubtedly rolled over at the slightest opposition to her appointment. Of that she was sure.

"Maybe. I got two kids at Yale and another going to a fancy art school in Boston this fall. I'm not looking to make waves right now before they settle on my retirement package. I'm sorry, Dani," he said, still not willing to make full eye contact except for a few furtive guilty glances.

Dani nodded. It really wasn't Bruce's fault. Maybe she should have kept her mouth shut more, not rattled the cages so much. But Dani was always a scrappy fighter, it was the main reason she had been successful as a private investigator. And it was hard suppressing that side of her as she moved up the ranks. But she knew in her heart that if she were a man, and spouted off as much as she did, she would have been heralded as a born leader and a natural for the position of Police Commissioner.

"I appreciate your candor, Bruce," Dani said. "So who are they going to go with?"

By the look on his face, Dani could tell Bruce was hoping she wasn't going to ask that question.

"They're still looking at possibilities."

This was the ultimate insult. It's not as if they found someone they liked better. They just simply didn't want her. It was like a kick in the stomach.

"You could have waited until they found their pick before you told me, Bruce. Why tell me now?"

Bruce shrugged. "I just thought you should know. Why keep your hopes up? I was trying to do the right thing as your friend."

Dani got up to leave.

"Dani, are you okay?"

Dani forced a smile. "I'm fine, Bruce. I appreciate your concern." She could tell her formality hurt his feelings, but he didn't say anything.

"Shelley's been asking for you. We'd love to have you over for dinner sometime soon," he said, anxious to pave over the obvious bumps of their tough conversation.

"I'd like that," Dani said, keeping the smile on her face firmly in place. "Let's set something up."

"Great. I'll have her give you a call," Bruce said, noticeably relieved that their friendship was at least still intact.

Dani turned to leave.

Bruce waved the piece of paper Dani had handed him when she first entered the office. "I'll have a few of my men get on this right away. We'll get a list to you by the end of the week," Bruce said.

"The sooner the better. Thanks again, Bruce." Dani's face was flushed. Usually she was adept at keeping her feelings in check, but at this moment, she felt as if she was about to cry. She had to get out of there.

She hurried out the door. Damn it. No. She was not going to cry. Not in front of Bruce. Not in front of any of them.

"Hi, Mom," a voice said as she closed the door to Bruce's office and headed down the hall.

Dani took a deep breath and spun around. She knew it wasn't her son, Bowie. It was Eddie Forbes, a smarmy, oily, freshly minted lieutenant that she took under her wing when he first joined the force. At first he had been grateful for her attention. She groomed him and offered him advice, but when he realized a woman wasn't going to get him to the top of the command, he turned on her. He treated her differently, and was no longer one of her allies in the department.

"You know, calling me Mom was kind of cute back when you were a wide-eyed young beat cop, Eddie, but you're older now," Dani said.

"Well, so are you," Eddie said with a sneer.

She wasn't going to lose it. Why give him that kind of satisfaction? But the fact remained she was old enough to be his mother.

Dani's face was tight. She was already upset over her lost promotion. And now she had to deal with this self-satisfied prick. But engaging him would just make it worse, especially now that two of his fellow officers had wandered down the hall to join him, both twenty-something sexist jerks like their good buddy Eddie.

"You're right, Eddie, and mothers always love their sons no matter how disappointing they turn out to be," Dani said with a smile, and then she walked away.

She could still hear Eddie and his boys talking behind her.

One of the officers said to Eddie, "You got some balls calling the Assistant Chief that."

She heard Eddie chuckle. "She can take it."

And then the other officer said, "You know, despite her age and everything, she's kind of hot. I'd still do her."

Dani kept on going. Any other day, she would have stormed back and kicked their asses. But the tears were streaming down her cheeks now and she had to get to the ladies restroom to find some privacy to deal with the question of the day. Was this the life she really wanted?

CHAPTER 9

A thick-muscled arm swung around Claire's neck and tightened against her throat, cutting off her air. Her hands clawed at the man's forearm, but he was too strong for her to even try to pry it loose. She couldn't breathe, and figured she only had a few seconds left to do something before passing out.

Claire drove her heel into the top of the man's foot. The pain forced the man to loosen his vicelike grip, but not enough. He still had a firm hold on her. She then jammed her elbow into his solar plexus, and felt a rush of air from his mouth on the base of her neck. He finally let go, allowing Claire to spin around, grab his hand and twist it up behind his back. She yanked hard, and the man fell to his knees. She then threw her weight against him, driving his face into the mat on the floor and pinning him.

There was an eruption of applause, and Claire let the man go. He lay sprawled on his stomach before raising his arm in surrender. Claire smiled, took his hand and helped the man to his feet. He was a few inches taller than Claire, stocky, with a shaved head and graying goatee. He wore an LAPD sweatshirt and gray sweatpants, and took a dramatic bow before the gaggle of middle-aged women in the room who clapped their hands together in approval.

"It's as simple as that, ladies," Claire said, reaching for a towel draped on a metal chair to wipe the sweat off her face. "The attacker rarely thinks you'll ever fight back, so the one advantage you have is the element of surprise."

The women nodded. One was even writing notes on a pad.

Claire patted the bald stocky man on the back. "You make a very scary attacker, Officer Benny."

Benny gave a sheepish smile.

"But we all know you're an absolute sweetheart," Claire said.

Benny winked at Claire. It was obvious he was attracted to her, but would never make a move because she was a married woman. Claire loved the fact that men still found her attractive, though she would never admit that to Jeb.

"Some of you still owe money for the last two classes, so please stop by the registration office and take care of it," Claire said as she grabbed her light blue sweat jacket and threw it on over her matching sweatpants and white work-out top. Her still-shiny, vibrant blond hair was pulled back in a tight, restricted bun. "Before you go, I have an announcement to make."

The women were anxious to get home and were not really listening as they gathered up their belongings from various corners in the room.

"I guess this is one of those good news/bad news situations. The bad news is this is my last class for a while."

The women stopped what they were doing. There were audible groans.

"I have some personal business that needs my immediate attention," Claire continued. "But the good news is Officer Benny will be taking over for me."

The women lit up. There were a few whistles and catcalls. Benny's face turned red, though it was clear he was lapping up their adoration.

"I thought that might soften the blow a bit," Claire laughed.

A rather rotund and forceful gray-haired lady, obviously resistant to the charms of Officer Benny, stepped forward. "When will you be back, Claire?"

"I'm not sure," she said. "Depends on how fast I can clear up this personal matter."

Claire knew the women were dying to ask what private business she was dealing with was, but they knew she would never tell them. She had always made a point of keeping her private life just that, and never discussed much with her busybody students except the self-defense techniques she was there to teach them. When one asked where she picked up all of these martial arts and back-alley fighting talents, she demurred by claiming to be a rabid *Xena: Warrior Princess* fan in the nineties. But they knew better and constantly speculated on her mysterious past over coffee after class.

"Have a good night, ladies," Claire said, tossing her backpack over her shoulder and heading out of the Sherman Oaks Women's Center. She was halfway to her car when she heard feet clomping up fast behind her. She spun around, ready to use her self-defense moves if necessary.

"Whoa, I've taken enough of a bruising for one night if you don't mind," Benny said with a smile.

"You of all people should know not to sneak up on a woman like that, Benny," Claire said, grinning. "Especially the one who *teaches* the class."

"Sorry, I just didn't want to miss you. I heard what happened to your son," Benny said, suddenly serious.

Claire bristled. She hated anyone knowing her business, but of course Benny would know. After all, he was an officer at the local precinct in Sherman Oaks. They'd answered the call about Zak's attack.

"I'd prefer it if you kept it to yourself, Benny," Claire said, frowning.

"Of course, I would never tell anyone outside of the department," Benny said quickly. "I just want to know how he's doing."

"Better. He's out of intensive care. He's going to come home tomorrow, and stay with us while he's recuperating. In fact, it was he who insisted I show up to this last class. After what happened to him, he wants to make sure these ladies know how to defend themselves."

"So why are you taking a leave?" Benny said, knowing he was risking a tongue lashing about privacy but unable to help himself.

"I need to take care of my son," Claire said.

"I can understand that. Anything else?"

Claire remained stone-faced. She wasn't ready to reveal anything at this juncture. "There are a lot of unanswered questions about why this happened, and I just want to make sure the police are thorough in their investigation," Claire said.

"Well, if you need me to light any fires, get the guys at the department riled up to find these guys, you just let me know, okay?"

Claire squeezed Benny's muscular arm. "Thank you, Benny."

He stood there staring at her. Claire quickly removed her hand from Benny's arm and fumbled for her car door. If she stayed any longer, Benny might do something crazy like try and kiss her.

"Night, Benny," she said, as the automatic lock chirped at the touch of her hand and she swung open the door to her blue Toyota Prius. Once the kids were out of the house, she and Jeb had ditched the gas-guzzling Ford Explorer and downsized for the sake of the planet's future.

"Night," Benny said, eyes still gazing at her face, a wistful air about him.

Claire didn't look at him again as she slid into her car, slammed the door shut and pressed the power button.

As she pulled out of the parking lot, she caught sight of Benny in the rearview mirror, still standing in the same place where she left him. He had to be fifteen years younger than she. Why was he so infatuated with her? She was just an aging suburban empty nester who was married and unavailable, dressed for comfort rather than flash, and had long ago given up primping and polishing her hair and face to impress the opposite sex. If he had seen her twenty years ago in her prime, when she was one-third of a hot team of overpowering estrogen, well, then she would have felt free to flirt back. But she loved her husband Jeb and their life together, and would never jeopardize what they had built together. She had no idea it was going to be something other than a studly thirty-something valley cop that would shake the foundation of her marriage.

Claire was home in less than ten minutes. She parked the car in the driveway and headed inside. The house was dark. Zak wouldn't be released from the hospital until tomorrow. Evan was living in an apartment off campus near UCLA where he was attending law school. And Jeb was a few hours away out over the Pacific piloting a flight from Tokyo to Los Angeles. After disarming the alarm and flipping on a few lights, she put a pot of coffee on, nibbled on a chocolate cookie she had pilfered from the ill-fated wedding a few days earlier, and walked down into the basement.

Claire was an admitted pack rat, holding on to everything, including homemade Mother's Day cards, her sons' dented and scratched mountain bikes from high school, and her husband's uniform and gold-plated wings from when he first became a pilot for the long-shuttered Pan Am Airlines before getting his current gig with American. So it was going to take a while for her to find what she was looking for in this endless sea of memories. But she was determined and within a half hour in a cobwebbed corner of the room underneath a stack of Evan's test papers and school reports, she tugged at a dusty, beat up cardboard box labeled DOLLS.

She dragged it over to the middle of the room and sat down, crossing her legs into the lotus position on a worn beige Ikea rug she had thrown down just to give the basement a hint of warmth. She tossed the bent cover off the cardboard box and began taking out the files and spreading them all around her. This was going to take all night.

Claire flipped open one manila folder, and perused the pages. She couldn't help but smile. It was a case she remembered well. The wealthy wife of a Vegas lounge singer had hired the LA Dolls to find her missing husband, who had failed to show up for a one-night-only gig at the Mirage. They had flown to Vegas on the client's dime, checked into the Mirage, and began sniffing around for clues. Dani was forced to date a mobster with a tight grip on a few of Sin City's casinos; Tess posed as a showgirl to get some inside info on one of the lounge singer's many mistresses; and Claire had a run-in with one of Siegfried and Roy's Bengal tigers long before one mauled poor Roy.

One of the mobster's henchmen caught her rifling through his boss's files and locked her in a cage with one of the big toothy white cats. Her self-defense moves really came in handy that time, and she escaped with just a few scratches. The Dolls ultimately located the missing singer, or pieces of him anyway, in the desert. They discovered he'd double-crossed the mobster by stealing from his fortune in a desperate attempt to alleviate his astronomical gambling debts. What a great case.

But the mobster, released in 1987 on a technicality, died just a few months later. He was gunned down with a mouthful of spaghetti by a rival crime family as he dined at his brother's West Village Italian eatery on a business trip to New York. It was unlikely he or any of his associates was behind the recent attacks on Zak and the other kids. She tossed the file aside and grabbed another.

Four hours flew by as Claire immersed herself in memories from the past. She had spent so many years trying to bury her old life she had forgotten just how much fun they'd all had together. She, Dani and Tess were the original girls gone wild.

Claire pored over more files, more cases, more memories, until she heard the door to the basement creak open.

"Honey, are you down there?"

Jeb was home and he sounded tired. His heavy feet pounded on the steps and when he entered the light she saw her exhausted husband, the sleeves of his wrinkled white shirt rolled up, his blue tie askew, his eyes bleary and his face drawn.

"What are you doing up so late?" he asked as Claire closed another file and added it to the growing stack of discarded cases.

"Just going over some old papers, trying to see if anything stands out," Claire said, bracing herself. She knew her husband didn't think much of her exciting and intimidating past.

"So you think Dani is right," Jeb said with a sigh.

Claire nodded. "I do."

Jeb watched her a moment, surrounded by documents of her colorful career before they met. "If this theory pans out, and I'm not sure it will, I don't want you out there reliving the glory days. I'm just not sure I could handle that."

"Please, Jeb, both you and my thighs know my previous life as an ass-kicking action girl is over," Claire said, laughing.

Claire noticed her husband studying her for a moment. She knew what he was thinking. He didn't quite believe her, which was crazy. She was in her fifties. There was no way she would ever have the stamina to go back even if she wanted to try it again.

"I'm going to bed," Jeb said. "Don't be long."

Jeb disappeared back up the stairs.

The last thing Claire wanted to do was upset her husband. But she couldn't even think about going to bed. She had only just begun reading about all the crimes she had solved. How could she stop now?

CHAPTER 10

"I trust you'll keep this information confidential," Police Commissioner Bruce Talbot said as he handed a red folder over to Dani.

Dani quickly flipped it open and began scanning the pages.

"Of course, Bruce," she said, eagerly digesting the information.

The two were dining at Home, a bustling restaurant, the hot spot of the moment on Market Street, near the Castro district in San Francisco.

"Anybody you might have missed?" she said, studying and memorizing all the names.

"Not likely. We did a thorough search, vetted every case you three worked. As of today, there are sixteen people you put away who are now back on the street," he said, shoveling a forkful of bowtie pasta into his mouth.

It was hard to talk quietly above the chatter of the noisy lunch crowd.

Dani looked up from the pages. "A few of them I can cross off right now. The North Hollywood pimp running his own call girl operation out of a Denny's back in '84 is now a Baptist minister in Calabasas. And this girl, who embezzled fifty grand from her father's mortgage company, is now serving her fourth term on the LA City Council."

"So you ladies are absolutely sure whoever is behind these recent attacks is someone from your past?"

"Pretty sure . . ." Dani said, her eyes returning to the list.

"Women's intuition?" Bruce said, grinning.

Dani looked up at him. "Forget it, Bruce. You're not going to bait me into a typical hysterical reaction to your now-boring and predictable sexist comments."

Bruce laughed. "Okay, I was just hoping to have some fun at this lunch. First time I've actually dined out in a month with everything that's going on at work."

Bruce tore off a hunk of bread and stuffed it in his mouth.

"I'm not going to feel sorry for you. In a few weeks, you'll be a man of leisure, with no worries except which matinee show of The Rock's latest movie you want to go see," Dani said.

"Well, I'm still the man for a little bit longer," Bruce said with his mouth full. "So if you want a few days off to look into these names, I can arrange it."

Dani set the folder down on the table and took a sip of water as Bruce chewed and chewed, trying hard to swallow the cumbersome piece of bread.

"What?" Bruce said, a soggy piece of bread falling out of his mouth and onto the table where he casually brushed it off and onto the floor with one quick hand movement.

"I didn't want to have lunch just to get my hands on this list," Dani said. "I need to talk to you about something else."

Bruce ripped off another unwieldy piece of bread but didn't pop it into his mouth. He kept it squished between his thumb and index finger, waiting to hear what Dani had to say.

"I'd like to take a leave of absence," Dani said.

"Okay," Bruce said. "How much time are we talking about?"

"Indefinitely."

Bruce nodded. He wasn't happy. "I'm assuming this has to do with them passing you over for my job?"

"That's part of it, yes. I'd be lying if I said it wasn't," Dani said. "I'm tired of the sexism and the politics, and I'd like some time to think about what's next for me. You can't blame me for that, Bruce."

"I'm not blaming you for anything. I just want to make sure you're making the right decision. You're very disappointed right now, and I don't want you to let your emotions rule over rational thought. . . ."

"Like most women usually do," Dani said. "You're still not going to get a reaction out of me today, Bruce."

"Damn, I thought that would do it."

They both laughed and then lapsed into a silence that was covered by the din of the busy restaurant.

"You're serious about this?" Bruce said.

"Yes," Dani said.

"They may not want you to come back if I let you go now," Bruce said, raising an eyebrow to see if this might change her mind. "They may force you into early retirement."

"I understand," Dani said. "But I need to do this."

"Fine," Bruce said, popping the now flattened piece of bread into his mouth. "I'll get the paperwork processed today."

"Thank you," Dani said, taking a deep breath and exhaling. She had done it. She was leaving the San Francisco Police Department after twenty years. At least for a while.

CHAPTER 11

There was a startlingly beautiful bouquet of flowers waiting for Tess Monahan as she swept into her favorite suite at the opulent Beverly Wilshire Hotel. Whenever she blew into town, the staff of this five-star establishment kicked into high gear to ensure that Ms. Monahan's stay was a pleasant one. No expense was spared. And the flowers were just the opening act. Dom Perignon champagne, Belgian chocolates, complimentary spa treatments, would all surely follow. Tess was known to stay up to three or four weeks during most of her trips to Los Angeles, and with her suite costing over six grand a night, the owners were always thrilled to see her and bent over backward to make her feel welcome.

An eager to please young bellman rolled a luggage cart piled with seven matching Louis Vuitton bags into the room. After unloading all of them, he tried to launch into a laundry list of amenities the room had to offer. Tess politely told him she was intimately acquainted with everything in the room, and would not require a refresher course. Paulo tipped the bellman a fifty dollar bill and he left with a big smile on his face.

After latching the chain lock on the door, Paulo unbuttoned

his shirt and dropped it to the floor. Tess drank in his taut muscles and glistening brown skin. God, he was sexy. She didn't care that most people whispered behind her back that the kid was only with her because of her money. They would say that about any man she dated. Hell, there was only a handful in the world richer than she was anyway.

She met Paulo at a fundraiser in Rio de Janeiro for a children's charity. The government was threatening to slash the budget for after school activities programs including the arts and sports. Paulo worked at one of the schools as a soccer coach and his job was on the line. Tess's generous donation saved the program and a grateful and relieved Paulo got up the nerve to approach her at the end of the evening to thank her. The chemistry between them was palpable, and two hours later they were sharing a bed. He hadn't left her side since.

Paulo was so gentle, so warm to the touch, so unabashedly comfortable in his own skin for such a young man. He exuded an air of confidence and that was the quality that most drew Tess to him.

He slid his arm around her, and slowly lowered her down onto the bed, climbing on top of her. She stared into his sweet brown eyes. He kissed her, softly at first, then more firmly, pressing his lips over hers. His tongue entered her mouth, and he gripped her tighter. He cupped his hand over her left breast and locked her legs together with his own. So many men were intimidated by Tess's wealth, but not this man, this walking fantasy. He relished in taming her wild spirit.

With his free hand, Paulo traced the outline of Tess's face as he gazed at her. Tess could feel him touching the lines of her face. She had eschewed plastic surgery as she'd gotten older, and sometimes thought perhaps she had made a bum decision. She was still considered a beauty, and because of her celebrity as an heiress, she had been chosen as one of the Fifty Most Beautiful People by *People Magazine* a few years back. She hadn't taken it seriously, but it sure made her more popular than ever on the international party circuit for a while. But she was aging, and up close, she knew she had a few wrinkles and laugh lines. Damn. Why hadn't she gone the facelift route like so many of her friends? Oh well. Never say never.

Paulo seemed to be enthralled with her age. He told her it was her rich life experiences that most attracted him, that and her still-gorgeous figure. She didn't care if he was lying or not because he said it with that sexy Brazilian accent.

The phone rang, and as Tess reached over to answer it, Paulo gripped her arm with his strong hand and pulled it back. He was not going to let the phone interrupt their lovemaking. He liked to show Tess that despite her wealth and age, he could still sometimes be the one in control. Tess let the call go to voice mail, and caressed her young lover's toned arms as he carefully worked at removing her expensive blouse while never taking his eyes off her exquisite face.

When they finished, Tess was spent. She was sweaty and flushed and she convinced herself what she was experiencing was not a hot flash but the warm afterglow of incredible sex.

Paulo climbed out of bed, and padded to the bathroom, still naked. Tess watched his firm young butt as he went. Damn, she would give up all, no make that most, of her money to be that age again and have a perfect body and a perfectly rounded, youthful ass.

Tess pulled the Ralph Lauren white comforter up to her chest to keep warm and reached for the telephone. She pressed three and was connected to the voice mail options. She listened to the message.

"Tess, it's Dani. I'm in LA, and I've got a list of people we need to start looking up. Call me as soon as you get this."

Typical Dani. All business. No "It was great seeing you again." No "I've missed you and Claire so much." And the charge in Dani's voice was electric. She was so excited to be playing detective again. It seemed to be getting Dani off more than the orgasm Tess had experienced with Paulo just five minutes ago.

A pair of strong hands began massaging her shoulders. "Who was it on the phone?" Paulo asked.

"Dani," Tess said with a frown.

"I don't like the idea of you getting into the business of dangerous people, sweetheart," Paulo said, still believing he was in control.

"Well, I like the idea of someone trying to kidnap Bianca even less, so it's not as if I have much of a choice," Tess said, sitting up in bed.

Paulo pouted and Tess smiled to herself. He knew he had no say in this particular situation but liked to pretend he did. Tess always got what she wanted. She was the one who'd wanted to make love, but let Paulo think it was his idea.

"I'm not crazy about reteaming with Dani and Claire. There's a lot of history there that I'm not exactly anxious to relive again," Tess said reaching for her blouse and checking to make sure Paulo hadn't inadvertently ripped off any buttons.

"Like what?" Paulo said, slipping on some red sweatpants.

"For one thing, Dani never forgave me and Claire for abandoning the business and retiring. She was very bitter," Tess said, remembering.

"But that was so long ago," Paulo said, jumping on the bed and lying next to Tess. He slid one bare arm underneath her neck and the other around her waist. He pulled her closer to him. "She has to be over it by now."

Tess nodded. "I hope so. But you don't know Dani. She doesn't let things go so easily. And now that we're back together, I'm worried she might want to start it all up again."

"But that is ridiculous. You have a wonderful life. Lots of money. Many friends. Why would you ever go back to risking your life like that?"

"I wouldn't. I just want to make sure Dani understands that," Tess said, nestling her head against her lover's rock-hard chest.

"Well, I would never allow it," Paulo said, proud of himself for being so emphatic.

Tess tried not to smile and said, "Whatever you say, darling." Let Paulo think she was obeying his commands. The fact was, she had no intention of ever returning to a career she was so happy to put behind her.

She reached underneath the comforter, sliding her hand slowly down Paulo's chest to his stomach and then his crotch. Within seconds, he was back on top of her, smothering her with kisses, preparing for round two. And he was completely under the impression that it was his idea.

CHAPTER 12

"Benito Coronel," Claire said, sliding a weathered file folder across the kitchen table to Dani.

Dani raised her eyebrows. "You held on to our old case files?"

"What can I say? I'm a pack rat. I hate throwing anything away."

Dani took a sip of Claire's freshly brewed strong coffee, another one of her many talents, and considered the name.

Benito Coronel was the ruthless Mexican drug lord they had put behind bars in the mid-eighties. It was their last case. The media attention was overwhelming because Coronel operated as a legitimate businessman in Los Angeles, and when the Dolls discovered that his chain of furniture stores was a front for a multi-million-dollar drug smuggling operation, they, along with Coronel, were splashed across the front pages of the LA papers for a solid week.

They also got a lot of grief from the DEA, which was red faced with embarrassment that three twenty-something hotties were responsible for busting their number one most-wanted criminal. Dani remembered loathing the fact they were media darlings of the moment, simply for the fact that it could possibly compromise any future undercover assignments. They were now recognizable faces! She had no idea at the time it was going to be their swan song as a team.

They never intended to do the DEA's job. It had just worked out that way. It began as a simple missing persons case. Jenna Fowler, a young UCLA psychology student, came to the Dolls for help. Her younger brother, Lenny, a lumbering, borderline retarded boy just nineteen, had recently moved to Los Angeles to be closer to his sister after the sudden death of their parents in a car crash back in their hometown of Kansas City, Missouri. Lenny was directionless, and his below-par aptitude automatically disqualified him from most jobs. But Jenna ultimately found him a low paying, but steady job, at one of Coronel's warehouses unloading furniture from the trucks. He seemed happy to have a purpose, and was thrilled to be contributing to the rent of the apartment he shared with his sister off campus in Westwood.

But then, after Lenny had been at the store for a mere three months, he failed to return home after his shift one day. When Jenna went to the warehouse she was told he hadn't turned up for work. She called the manager of every store in town but got the same answer. No one had seen Lenny since the previous day. She tried to get Mr. Coronel on the phone, but he didn't take her call. Something about a very important sales meeting with some prospective buyers.

Jenna waited the required twenty-four hours, and then filed a missing persons report with the police. The ensuing investigation was an exercise in frustration for the pretty blond coed. She slowly began to realize the police were focused on other cases they deemed more important than the questionable disappearance of a simple-minded furniture mover. They suggested the possibility that he had returned to Kansas City, and even went so far as to imply it was Jenna's fault for not keeping a closer eye on him.

Jenna was not about to let her brother down. She was going to find him. A student in one of her classes told her about a private investigation firm that her parents hired to retrieve some stolen jewelry which they suspected was an inside job. It had taken the detectives a day and a half to produce evidence that his mother's massage therapist, a strapping lothario who dabbled in fencing stolen merchandise, had made off with them. They also returned every last piece unharmed. Jenna eagerly wrote down the number of the firm, and after pooling her meager resources, called to make an appointment. The following morning she took a bus from Westwood to Robertson Boulevard in Beverly Hills to meet with the LA Dolls.

After hearing her story, the girls accepted the case at a fraction of their usual rate and went to work. Jenna told them her brother took the bus to work every day, and after checking with the driver on that route, they discovered he had indeed been on that bus to the warehouse the day he went missing. So unless someone snatched him as he crossed the street from the bus stop to the warehouse, he must have made it to work. Someone had to have seen him.

After their attempts to contact the store's owner, Mr. Benito Coronel, were repeatedly stonewalled by a battery of managers and assistants, the girls decided an undercover operation was required.

The warehouse was filled with drooling, horny Neanderthals, so it was relatively easy for Claire to get a part-time job there as a receptionist. Her access to the warehouse allowed Dani to set a few wiretaps, and before the week was out, they knew they were on the verge of uncovering something big. A few of the workers covertly discussed their moonlighting activities after hours distributing certain pieces of furniture to points all over town.

They dug further and soon discovered that some pieces of the Aztec-inspired furniture, beautifully crafted and built in Mexico, were brought across the border full of heroin. And poor Lenny, whose only goal was to do a good job and keep getting a paycheck, inadvertently stumbled across the operation when he dropped a bed frame and packets of white powder tumbled across the floor.

The girls were able to deduce that when Coronel learned of this, he was brought to the warehouse so he could talk to the boy. After some intense questioning, it unfortunately became clear to Coronel that despite being slow, Lenny did know right from wrong, and was not going to easily forget what he saw. Coronel picked up a wooden table leg from one of his unfinished pieces and bashed in the boy's head. Then he had his goons dump the body in a landfill just outside of the city.

That was the hardest day Dani could remember during her time as an LA Doll. She would never forget waiting outside the science building at UCLA for Jenna to get out of class so she could break the news that her brother was dead.

The Dolls resolved to get the necessary evidence and put this snake behind bars for good.

Tess put on her most revealing halter top and a pair of Daisy Dukes and sashayed into the favorite watering hole of Coronel's men. It took her seven minutes to seduce a six-foot-two muscle-bound, impossibly handsome Latino with jet-black hair and a slight scar down the right side of his face who worked as a liaison between the movers and Coronel himself. Trying to impress the pretty lady, the man, who introduced himself as Ronaldo Soares, bragged to Tess that he was not just some flunkie who lifted fancy coffee tables. He had a much brighter future ahead of him working directly with Benito Coronel. Tess plied him with more tequila and soon finagled an invitation to a party at Coronel's expansive Topanga Canyon property as Ronaldo's date.

The infamous mountaintop retreat. That fateful party when it all came crashing down for Benito Coronel.

As Dani and Claire sat in the kitchen poring over the Benito Coronel case file, Claire put down her coffee mug and said, "I remember that day we showed up in court for the sentencing. He was enraged that we were there. His male ego was so bruised that three women were responsible for his ultimate undoing. Remember what he said?"

"'I won't rest until I see you three bitches dead and buried,'" Dani said, shaking her head. "Nice send off."

"When I happened upon his case, I just had a very strong feeling. It's him. He's the one," Claire said.

"But Claire, he's not on my list," Dani said, pushing a piece of paper over to her. "I had Bruce come up with all the people we put away who are back on the street. Benito Coronel isn't one of them. He's still in prison. He's never getting out."

Claire studied the piece of paper. "Well, he has plenty of people on the outside who he could hire to get the job done."

"But why wait until now? He could have hired someone years ago. It doesn't make any sense," Dani said.

"I don't know," Claire said, staring out the window. "That one just reverberates in my mind. I don't want to say it's intuition, but . . ."

The sound of a car pulling into the driveway suddenly distracted Claire. She stood up, walked over to the window and pulled open the curtain.

"Zak's home," she said, racing for the door leading outside. Dani quickly stood up and followed her.

Jeb and Evan, on either side of Zak, helped him out of the backseat as Claire hustled over to give him a kiss.

"Welcome home, sweetheart," Claire said, kissing his cheek.

"Okay, son, we've got you," Jeb said as he and Evan made their way slowly to the open door to the kitchen. Zak winced with every movement. He was still in a great deal of pain.

A horn blared, stopping them all. A black limousine rolled to a stop in front of the house. A driver jumped out and opened the back door. Tess crawled out and waved at everybody.

"What the neighbors must think," Claire said.

"Who's that, Mom?" Zak said. His voice was still weak.

"An old friend," Claire said.

"Tess. I know. Dad told me all about her. I'm talking about *her*."

Claire turned to see Bianca slide out of the limo behind her mother. She wore a flattering pink shirt and a pair of jeans that could have been painted on her. She looked absolutely stunning.

Claire watched glumly as her two sons didn't even try to contain their excited and intrigued reactions to the gorgeous nineteen-year-old Brazilian model walking up the driveway toward the house. This was the last thing she needed to deal with now.

CHAPTER 13

Claire hadn't been to the Smokehouse in years. Situated across the street from the Warner Brothers studio in Burbank, this decades-old steak joint, with its dark ambience, burgundy booths, and fiercely loyal clientele had been a film industry staple for so long, some of the customers looked as if they hadn't left their tables since 1952.

Claire knew Dani had picked the Smokehouse because they were generous with the size of their cocktails and the LA Dolls lunched there almost every day to discuss whichever case they were working on during their seven-year run as a team in the eighties.

Claire wondered if Tess was going to enjoy this little trip down memory lane, since over the years she had become accustomed to the world's most exclusive restaurants and expertly polished service. But Tess seemed as at home here as if she had been dining on their selections of steaks every week since the Dolls split up over twenty years ago.

An elderly waitress brought their pink drinks, three Cosmopolitans, on a tray. Claire recognized her as a Smokehouse veteran. She probably had started waiting tables there in the sixties, served filet minon to Clint Eastwood and Martinis straight up to Frank Sinatra.

"I remember you three gals," the waitress said in a throaty, scratched, weary voice. "It's been years."

"It's good to see you again, Estelle," Dani said, happy to be remembered.

"Who could forget you three . . . The busboys always stopped working to stare at you. Tables never got cleaned."

The three women laughed.

"Well, you're still looking good. Can't say that about most of the Botoxed bimbos who come in here and want to ignore the fact they're too old to go braless."

Claire was so thankful she was wearing a bra at that moment.

"Enjoy," Estelle said, setting down the Cosmos with a shaky hand and ambling off.

Nothing much had changed at the Smokehouse over the years, except maybe for the prices. Even the men at the bar looked the same. Older, streaks of gray in their hair, and that look in their eyes that told a woman they were on the make despite the fact they all had a wife waiting for them at home. Although Dani loved the cocktails, she always got annoyed when they had meetings here because they were constantly being interrupted by a glassy-eyed businessman who worked up the nerve after a few shots to come over and trot out his best pick-up line. The constant stream of horny men always cost them precious time they could be using to discuss the case. But that was so long ago. The men were now focused on girls far more youthful and with smoother faces that had yet to experience the disappointing revelation that they were not going to become the next Nicole Kidman.

Still, a handsome man perched at the bar, his hammy fist around the stem of his Martini glass, seemed to be gazing right at her. No, Claire thought, he must be looking at some boozed-up wannabe starlet a few tables away. Or at the very least, he was looking at Tess, the most well-preserved of the three of them in Claire's opinion. Dani still looked terrific, Claire thought, but she was just so damn intimidating; a guy would have to be rip-roaring drunk to gather up enough courage to try and talk to her.

The man at the bar winked. Claire casually looked over her shoulder. There was no one behind her except a frail-looking gentleman around eighty, carefully sipping his vegetable soup. The guy at the bar was definitely flirting with *her*. Damn, she thought. Maybe she still had a little sex appeal left in her. Jeb certainly said so. But that was part of his job as her husband. Keep her ego stroked to avoid any unnecessary neurotic melt-downs. There was also Officer Benny who helped out at her self-defense class. He seemed attracted to her. Or maybe it was just her imagination.

"I'd like to make a toast," Dani said, raising her glass. "Here's to the Dolls being back together again."

"At least temporarily," Tess quickly added.

They clinked glasses and each took a sip. Claire winced as she swallowed. Still the strongest drinks in the valley.

"I've always wanted to ask you why you didn't keep the business going on your own after we both left," Claire said, turning to Dani.

Dani shrugged. "I thought about it. I even went and talked to a couple of police academy graduates about the possibility of coming aboard to help me."

"You were going to replace us?" Tess said, feigning outrage.

"I tried," Dani said, "But I knew you two were irreplaceable."

"Good answer," Tess said, taking a large swig of her Cosmo.

"So after moping around for a couple of months, I decided to start from scratch, which is why I joined the force as a beat cop."

"You were pretty mad at us for deserting, weren't you?"

"Hell yeah," Dani said.

Claire could tell there was still some residual anger left in Dani as she considered what might have been.

"I know you wanted the whole white-picket-fence fantasy," Dani said pointedly to Claire before turning to Tess. "And you wanted to see the world."

"And boy, did you," Claire said, laughing as she squeezed Tess's hand.

"I just never knew how much at the time," Tess said.

"Claire never would have left if you hadn't, Tess," Dani said, bringing an abrupt end to the laughter.

Claire could tell Dani knew she shouldn't have said that. There was a long pause. Claire decided she had to speak up.

"That's not true, Dani. I had been running around for seven years, and frankly I was tired of the unrelenting pace. I'm not like you. I don't thrive on excitement and danger."

"That's the old me," Dani said, taking the hint to keep old wounds covered up. "Now it seems my whole life is about politics and career disappointments."

"Why? What's going on at work?" Claire asked.

"Nothing," Dani said, polishing off her drink. "Not worth talking about. Let's get another round." Dani was always the one who could drink both her and Tess under the table. Dani signaled Estelle, who shuffled over to the bar to place the order.

"Well, we certainly did have some pretty wild cases," Tess said. "I got to play dress-up more in those seven years than I did during my entire childhood."

"The worst case ever was when that flight attendant hired us to find out who was stalking her and Dani made us go undercover as stewardesses! Remember?"

Tess chortled with laughter. "Oh, God, how could I forget?"

"Why did you take that case? I hate to fly!" Claire said, playfully punching Dani in the arm.

"Well, I didn't know when I took the case that you were going to have to land the plane," Dani said.

"Who did we end up arresting?" Claire said.

"It was the copilot," Dani said.

"Oh, that's right," Claire said.

"He couldn't stand the fact that the client broke up with him, and became obsessed with her and freaked out at thirty thousand feet when we confronted him," Tess said.

"Well, it was Dani's fault. She was so excited to have figured it out she didn't bother waiting for him to safely land at John Wayne Airport before she confronted him," Claire said.

"No, the worst had to be that low-rent circus out in Riverside that someone was sabotaging. I wanted to go undercover as a glamorous flying trapeze artist or something, but Dani told me I had to be a clown," Tess said.

"You have no balance! You would have killed yourself flying around on some swing a hundred feet off the ground!" Dani said.

"Yes, but those skintight beaded costumes were so elegant," Tess said.

"Well, we would've had to bury you in it," Dani said, chuckling. "I saved your life."

"As I recall, you had a nice consolation prize. That hot ringmaster from Bulgaria."

"Oh yes, he was gorgeous. I must have dated him for close to three months after we solved that case," Tess said, swooning at the memory.

"What about that cheesy beauty contest?" Claire said, putting her hands over her face, embarrassed.

"Oh, God," Dani said, laughing. "That Texas oilman targeting contestants hoping they would drop out so his precious daughter could win the title."

"That was my favorite case. I came in first runner-up," Tess said, proudly cocking her head.

"It was rigged. Every judge knew you were a plant!" Dani said.

"One of the judges told me afterward he would have voted for me anyway because of my killer rendition of 'Feelings' that I sang for the talent competition."

"What I want to know," Claire said, looking straight at Dani, "is how come you didn't pose as a contestant with the two of us?"

"We needed someone behind the scenes keeping tabs on everyone," Dani said. "Besides, I was the unofficial leader. It was my call, and I wouldn't be caught dead in a beauty contest."

"You never did anything that would have made you play up your sex appeal!" Tess said.

"That's not true. Didn't I pose as a prostitute once?" Dani said, trying hard to remember.

"Just once. And that's because Claire was in the hospital with a broken rib after that coked-up pizza delivery-guy rapist tried to attack her," Tess said. "So you didn't have a choice."

"Okay, so maybe I didn't show a lot of skin in those under-cover assignments, but it was my unwavering diligence as team leader that led to us never, ever blowing a case," Dani said.

Claire smiled. "A man yes, but never a case. Right, Tess?" Claire said.

Tess pretended for an instant to be offended, but knowing she was in no position to defend herself, just burst out laughing.

As Estelle dutifully returned with more rounds of Cosmo-politans, the former LA Dolls continued sharing stories and mem-ories and much laughter. What made their business work was the chemistry between them, and it surprised all three of them that it was still there, strong as ever.

It felt good to be back together again.

After a few hours and several attempts by enterprising men from the bar to insinuate themselves into the conversation, Dani, Claire, and Tess paid the bill and stumbled outside to where Tess's limousine driver patiently waited for them.

It was no wonder Tess never bothered worrying about how many cocktails she was served. She didn't have to drive herself anywhere.

After a quick twenty-minute trip back to Sherman Oaks, the driver deposited the now-slurring, giggling ladies at Claire's house.

"Claire, could you send Bianca out?" Tess said, throwing her arms around her old friend and planting a kiss on her cheek.

"I will. Good night, sweetie," Claire said, having almost forgotten that Bianca had stayed behind at the Corley house while her mother went out with Dani and Claire.

"Dani, why don't you spend the night?" Claire said.

Dani shook her head. "I'll be fine. I just need to call a cab." She rummaged through her bag for her cell phone.

Jeb was waiting for Claire in the doorway. He must have heard them. Then again, Claire was pretty confident half the neighborhood had heard them. There was an unmistakable look of concern on Jeb's face as Claire hugged her husband, but mostly she was using him for support. The Cosmopolitans had taken their toll.

"Anything the matter?" Claire asked as her husband helped her into the house.

"No. Nothing," Jeb said.

But Claire knew he was lying. He had seen how much fun the three former best friends were having together, and it worried him. He probably could not articulate why he was bothered by this, but Claire knew. He was afraid his wife missed her old life, and that perhaps a small part of her wanted to use this opportunity to relive, and possibly revive, the good old days.

Once inside, Claire found Bianca and Evan sitting together on the couch, involved in a deep discussion.

"How's Zak?" Claire asked.

Evan reluctantly tore his eyes off Bianca's perfect face. "Who?"

"Your brother," Claire said, sighing.

"He's fine," Jeb said, putting a strong arm around his wife's shoulder. "He fell asleep a few hours ago."

Evan eagerly returned his gaze to the lovely Bianca.

"Your mother's waiting out in the limo to take you back to the hotel, dear," Claire said, still watching her younger son who was so unabashedly smitten.

"Thank you, Mrs. Corley," Bianca said, standing up, her voluptuous figure on full display. It not only drew stares from Evan, but Jeb as well. "It was nice spending time with you, Evan. Good luck at law school."

"I'm sure I'll be seeing you around," Evan quickly said. "I mean, her mother is here for a while, right, Mom?"

"For a little while," Claire said, a gnawing feeling slowly growing in her stomach.

Bianca leaned in and gave Evan a soft quick kiss on the cheek. Nothing too suggestive, but a point had been made. She was drawing him in, giving him just enough encouragement. Bianca was just like her mother.

"Good night, Mr. and Mrs. Corley," Bianca said sweetly as she walked like a runway model out the front door.

Evan gawked at her perfect behind as she left. Damn, Claire thought, he was already a lost cause.

"She's unbelievable," Evan said, more to himself than to anyone else.

And now Claire was seriously worried about her son. The last thing she wanted was for Evan to be hurt, like so many men had been hurt by Bianca's mother. She had yet to know for sure if Bianca was indeed like Tess, who loved the attention of men, but quickly became bored with their constant adoration and eventually moved on to bigger, fresher conquests.

Bianca seemed like a nice enough girl, but the fact remained she was Tess's daughter. And that was the biggest red flag of all. No, Claire thought, she was determined not to let her youngest boy be one of those broken hearts left behind.

CHAPTER 14

Smack Jackson may have been surprised to see a black stretch limousine pull up to his newsstand on Laurel Canyon Boulevard in Studio City, but he was downright shocked when the driver opened the back door, and in perfect succession Dani Mendez, Claire Walker, and Tess Monahan stepped out. In fact, he practically choked on the blueberry scone he had just purchased from the Starbucks down the block.

"I must be dreaming! This is like some tripping eighties flashback," Smack said as the three women descended upon him and showered him with hugs and kisses.

Smack relished his simple, quiet life as manager of a newsstand. It was a far cry from twenty-five years ago when he was the Dolls' Mack Daddy informant, "a real life Huggy Bear" as Claire dubbed him. A former East LA street thug who served time in the seventies, Smack was paroled in 1982, but was still plugged into the entire LA underworld.

He met the girls while they were undercover busting an extortion ring run by one of Smack's former gang brothers. He was the ultimate tipster, always ready with a lead that would help the girls break the case. He was invaluable to them, and Dani paid him handsomely to keep them in the know. Their friends at the LAPD were insanely jealous the girls had such a direct line to the criminal elements in the city, but Smack was intensely loyal to them, mostly because of Claire. Smack had a long line of beauties anxious to date him, but his heart belonged to the soft-spoken Claire. Claire was mostly oblivious to his suppressed feelings, but Dani saw them and exploited them to her advantage. Smack would turn over his own mother if it meant spending more time with Claire.

Dani caught the look in Smack's eye as he clasped Claire's hands and flashed his big, endearing smile. "Claire, baby, look at you. Damn, you haven't changed a bit. Man, oh man, you're still smoking!"

Dani glanced at Tess, who was never comfortable when she was not the immediate object of adoration. Tess managed to keep a smile on her face.

Claire smiled and cupped a hand to Smack's cheek. "You're going on and on, and look at you, you haven't changed a bit."

"Black don't crack and all that," Smack said with a grin. "I'll be fifty-three in August."

"I don't believe it. It's been so many years since we've seen you, and I only live about three miles away," Claire said.

"I thought about dropping by, saying hello, but you've got your life and all, and I didn't want to be hanging around reminding you of the past," Smack said, almost quietly. He still had it for her.

"Don't be silly," Claire said. "Now that I know we're neighbors, we can see each other all the time."

Smack's kind brown eyes lit up at the possibility. "How'd you find me after all these years?"

"It was easy, Smack," Dani said. "I get a Christmas card from your sister every year so I just called her up."

"Yeah, Trina's still a caseworker downtown. She's done us all proud," Smack said with his eyes still fixed on Claire.

Trina also got into trouble during the eighties, and was nearly a sad statistic until Smack and the Dolls busted up the prostitution ring her bad-ass boyfriend had gotten her mixed up with. Smack helped her turn her life around by using the money he made with the Dolls to finance her education. She got a degree in social work and devoted her life to helping kids with similar disadvantaged backgrounds maneuver their way through the system. It was thankless work, but after almost twenty years, she was still going strong.

"You married now, Smack? Got a girlfriend?" Tess said.

"No, I've been waiting for Claire to realize I'm the man of her dreams and show up here professing her love for me," Smack said with a chuckle.

Claire laughed, and playfully punched his arm. "Still with the warped sense of humor."

It was perfectly clear to Dani and Tess, if not Claire, that Smack wasn't joking in the slightest.

"So, you just here to help plan our twentieth reunion dinner, or is there something else going on?" Smack said as he glanced back at Dani, the one he knew would give him a direct answer.

Dani handed him the list.

Smack scanned the names on the piece of paper. "Paprika Lucerne. Haven't thought about her in years."

"She was paroled about seven years ago," Dani said.

"Oh God, I hated that bitch," Tess said, her eyes narrowing.

"Probably because she tried to kill you," Claire said.

Paprika Lucerne was a big-time Hollywood madam the Vice Squad had trouble busting. When a runaway from Seattle turned up dead in a downtown Dumpster, the family hired the Dolls to find out who killed her since the police weren't gung ho to solve the case. She wasn't a pretty blond coed so the press wasn't exactly screaming for justice.

The girls retraced her steps to Paprika, a former bit actress who found a far more lucrative life running her own stable of

85

call girls. She was smooth and thorough when it came to her clients. Other women, especially beautiful rivals, were what rattled her cage, so Tess set up shop as a competing madam to send her over the edge. And boy did it. Her fury over Tess on her turf resulted in a few costly mistakes including attempted murder that sent her to prison for a long time. And when she learned that she had been set up for a fall by not only one, but three beautiful women, her head nearly exploded with rage. Men she could manipulate. Women were her worst enemies.

"Do you know what happened to her?" Dani said.

"I don't talk to my contacts much anymore, Dani. That was a long time ago," Smack said.

Dani folded her arms. She knew he was just saying that, probably because he didn't want his precious Claire to think he was still in touch with the seedier elements in the city. But Smack was a gossip. He thrived on information, which is why he ended up running a newsstand. The irony wasn't lost on anybody.

Smack knew Dani wasn't buying what he was selling. "But I did hear rumblings that she may have set up shop far away from LA in South Florida where people don't know her."

"Miami?" Dani said.

"Very successful now from what I hear," Smack said as he turned to Claire. "But I don't make it my business to know where these hard-timers wind up."

Tess pointed to a name. "What about Akito Tanaka?"

"Released on a technicality a long time ago," Smack said. "Apparently he was cohabiting with his girlfriend when you guys sent the police to arrest him. She let them in without a warrant, but since the house was in his name, all the evidence was inadmissible. His case was finally dismissed."

"Where is he now?" Claire said.

"Oh, Claire, honey, I wouldn't know. I don't make it my business to keep up with Japanese drug lords."

Dani sighed and put her hands on her hips. Smack had no trouble reading her body language.

"Of course I did hear, and mind you, it's just chatter, don't know if it's true or not, but there were rumors he was up in Santa Barbara living the high life," Smack said.

"I'll look him up," Tess said, "He always had a thing for me."

"That was before you sent him to prison. He could be the one who has it out for us," Claire said.

"Well, then I'll be the one to find out," Tess said. "He's been out a while, so it doesn't make much sense why he'd go after us now, but maybe he's just a procrastinator."

Smack snickered at the last name on the list. "This guy? Are you serious?"

Claire looked at the name. "Sonny Anzilotti, the Italian Stallion wannabe."

"He's been out of prison for years. Got married to a big-time movie executive," Smack said. "I carry *Variety* and the *Hollywood Reporter*. It's only right I keep up with the latest entertainment news."

"It's a long shot. But the bastard beat up his girlfriends back in the eighties, and hates women. I think he's worth checking out," Dani said.

"Well, he's obviously changed. He's got a fancy Bel Air address now. A wife on the Top 100 Hollywood Power List. The dude's got it made. Why in hell would he want to risk that by coming after you three?" Smack said, as he turned to take some change from a customer buying the *Los Angeles Times*. "Thanks, buddy."

"I'm with Dani," Claire said. "Anzilotti was a real shit."

Tess raised an eyebrow. She almost never heard Claire use profanity. And it amused her.

"I, for one, would like to see for myself if the little prick is behaving himself," Claire said.

"Guess you can look him up then," Dani said. "Tess has Tanaka and I'll take Paprika Lucerne."

Smack looked at the list one more time. "Benito Coronel. I'm going to need to up my blood pressure medication just thinking about that motherfucker."

"Claire added him. But as far as we know, he's still serving a life sentence for Lenny Fowler's murder," Dani said.

"You really think one of these characters wants to settle a score with you after all these years?" Smack said with a hint of skepticism in his voice.

"We're not sure," Dani said. "But if we don't look at everybody, we could be gambling with the lives of our kids."

"Good enough for me. Just tell me how I can help," Smack said as he gave Claire a flirty wink. "Smack and his Dolls are back in business."

CHAPTER 15

As Dani's United Airlines flight from Los Angeles touched down at Miami International Airport, she knew her reunion with Paprika Lucerne was at the top of her agenda. The challenge had been arranging it. Paprika rarely ventured out in public and was adept at staying out of the limelight. She ran her operations from an undisclosed location, and her roster of girls and clients could only reach her through an ever-changing cell phone number.

Dani's best plan of flushing her out was to create a rival business, and cross into her territory. It had worked once, back in the eighties, and enough time had passed now Dani thought to try it again. Paprika would never suspect the Dolls of trying to fool her twice.

Bowie was waiting for his mother in the baggage claim area, and enveloped her in a warm hug. Dani raised Bowie by herself; his father was relatively nonexistent in both their lives.

Bowie often flew out to San Francisco to see his mother since her job had kept her firmly planted on the West Coast. But now that Bowie's fledgling private detective business needed a lot of attention, his trips to California had tapered off considerably.

Dani was thrilled to see her strapping young son looking healthy and robust, especially given the terrifying phone call she had received after his near miss in Mexico.

"Thank God you're all right," Dani said, more to herself than to her son.

"It's all good," Bowie said, flashing that winning smile he had gotten from his father.

One of her ex's few positive traits, Dani thought.

"So you think this Paprika Lucerne lady is behind the attempted hit on me in Mexico?" Bowie said, as he picked up his mother's carry-on bag and led her out the door to the parking structure, where he had left his sleek blue van, all buffed up and tricked out. Bowie had always liked big toys. Again, just like his dad.

"We're not sure of anything. We're just working off a list of our past cases, hoping to find a connection," Dani said. "Did you get my e-mail?"

"All taken care of," Bowie said, tossing his mother's bag in the back of his van and then scurrying around to open the passenger's door for his mother. "I've laid down all the groundwork you asked for. I gave a couple of her new girls bus fare home, then put out the word that they've gone to work for a new madam in town. You could hear Paprika's head exploding all the way up in Fort Lauderdale."

"I know her. Just as soon as she finds out where I am, she'll send over some muscle," Dani said with a smile.

"You really think she's going to fall for this trick twice?"

"It's been over twenty years. There's no way she'd ever expect us to come all the way down here and try again," Dani said, getting a little charge out of teaming up with her son.

After a twenty-minute drive to South Beach, they drove along a row of retro houseboats from the swinging sixties docked off Ocean Avenue. Bowie pulled his van into a spot just outside a dilapidated single-story houseboat, its off-white paint chipping, and in desperate need of a new roof. Across the bow was painted QE3, named after the opulent Cunard cruise line. Yes, this was the only clue Dani had that her butch, muscular, kick ass private eye son was actually gay.

Once inside, Dani tried to ignore the empty pizza boxes and discarded beer bottles, the stained furniture, and ratty curtains. Of course she would have to be the one who wound up with the gay son who did not acquire the decorating gene.

She tried ignoring the mess, but Bowie caught her wrinkling up her nose a couple of times. "Once I get a few more cases, I'm going to invest in a paint job and a maid," he said apologetically.

"It's nice," Dani said, lying. Bowie knew she was lying but she could tell he appreciated the gesture. He also knew the minute he left for an errand, Dani would not be able to help but do a little vacuuming and dusting and maybe a few dishes. It wasn't that she was a neat freak; she just couldn't see herself staying someplace so disgusting. She was way too old to crash in a post-college bachelor pad.

Dani would have preferred staying at the Delano just a few blocks away, but Bowie had already made it known to the right people that she had opened up shop here on this houseboat, not the ideal location to set a trap but time was of the essence. It wouldn't take long for the greedy madam to send an emissary in the form of a two-ton gorilla to give her a strong message to clear out of Miss Paprika's sacred turf. Dani could only hope Paprika acted soon because the thought of holing up in her son's smelly, unkempt houseboat made her nauseous.

Luck was on her side. But it was the kind of luck that nearly got her killed.

Dani had managed to whip together a nice dinner for the two of them in Bowie's tiny, cluttered kitchen. Some grilled halibut, a light salad and a bottle of Pinot Grigio, which she found among the half-empty bottles of Jack Daniels in her son's makeshift minibar.

She tried not to think of the countless parties her son had thrown here, and what might have transpired. Given her own wild past with Tess and Claire while in their twenties, she had no right to judge.

Bowie ran out to pick up some dessert at a corner grocery store since they both had a craving for something sweet, leaving Dani to clear the scuffed, rickety wooden kitchen table. The small window in front of the sink looked out on the harbor. The moon was bright, almost full, and cast a shimmering glow on the dark, foreboding water. It was serene, quiet, almost hypnotic, and Dani found herself lost in her thoughts as she gazed out the window, her eyes heavy. She was about to fall asleep standing up. Too much wine, she thought.

Then she heard a thump outside. Had Bowie returned already? He had only been gone a few minutes. Another thump and some footsteps. Someone was skulking around outside. She spun around and looked out all the windows. There was a movement in the shadows, like someone hurrying past trying to stay out of sight. Her eyes focused on the front door. It was unlocked. She purposely didn't turn the bolt when Bowie left because he was coming right back. She hadn't planned on Paprika acting so fast. She thought it might take at least a day or two, not a few hours after her arrival. She glanced around for a weapon. She didn't have her gun. She had been counting on Bowie. Where did he keep his gun? The place was a pigsty. It could be anywhere. In an empty pizza box, for all she knew.

She knew she had to lock the door first, and then regroup her thoughts. She quietly walked to the door, went to reach for the lock when suddenly the door swung open violently, clocking her on the forehead. She stumbled back, surprised, and then fell to her knees, dazed. She looked up to see a massive man, at least six feet five, a wide chest, completely bald, dressed in black. He stepped forward, and with a beefy hand, slapped her hard across the face.

The force sent her reeling. She was facedown now, tasting blood from the wound on her forehead. She began crawling away from the man, but knew he was standing over her, watching her, probably smiling. A heavy boot slammed down on the small of her back, pinning her to the floor.

"Who are you?" Dani gasped, pissed at herself for having so easily become the helpless victim. But this thug was so big and overpowering, and she was, she hated to admit, a mature woman in her fifties.

He stepped off her, then crouched down and whispered in her ear.

"Hammer," he said, as he lifted her head with a fistful of her hair. "And I'm here to pound some sense into you."

Dani frantically scanned the room for something she could use. A few feet from her was an empty beer bottle, one she hadn't seen when she'd done her preliminary cleaning sweep before dinner. She couldn't quite reach it.

"Paprika sends her regards," Hammer said, still pulling her hair so tight she thought he was going to rip it out.

She had to get closer to the bottle but there was only one way she could see to do that.

"Tell that skanky whore I don't give a shit," Dani said, hoping for a reaction.

She got one. Hammer drove her head into the floor, drawing more blood.

"Now why did you make me do that?" Hammer growled.

Dani managed to squirm her body just a few inches more before he straddled her and grabbed her hair again. It was all she needed. Her fingertips touched the beer bottle. She gave it a gentle push forward, and the slight momentum caused the bottle to roll back so she could get her hand around the neck. Hammer saw what she was doing but it was too late. She brought it up so fast he had no time to react. It smashed against his face, tiny shards of glass spraying everywhere. He screamed, and raised his hands to his face, allowing Dani the opportunity to flip her body around and knee him hard in the groin. He fell onto his back, his big round chest heaving, his giant hands flailing.

Dani used one of her son's bar stools to balance herself as she stood up. Her head was still spinning from Hammer cracking it against the floor. She staggered over to Hammer, reached inside his black jacket and fished around until she found his gun. She yanked it out, used her right index finger and thumb to open the bully's quivering lips and then slid the nozzle into his mouth. His teeth clattered against the cold hard steel.

"Speaking of Paprika," Dani said, her voice low and even. "I'd love to pop in and say hi. I'm sure she wants to welcome me to the neighborhood."

When Bowie returned with a bag of Mrs. Fields' cookies and a carton of French Vanilla ice cream, he was stunned to find his home even messier than when he left it. A huge bald man sat slumped over in one of his chairs, bound and gagged with duct tape, as he snorted loudly through his nose. And Bowie's mother, a bandage on her forehead, a gun in one hand and one of his half-empty bottles of Jack Daniels in the other, sat on his frayed, dirty couch.

"I hope you got enough dessert for three," she said, before taking a generous swig of whiskey from the bottle.

CHAPTER 16

The following morning, after the police hauled off the mighty Hammer on a slew of charges from breaking and entering to assault, Dani and Bowie, armed with Paprika's address, headed off to pay her a visit. It hadn't taken long for her muscle to talk. He'd been soundly beaten by a woman in her fifties, and that was just a warm-up to what he was to expect from her angry, muscle-bound son with a dragon tattoo on his bicep. The imposing young man didn't take kindly to Hammer roughing up his mother, so the sooner he gave up where they could find Paprika, the sooner he could be safely in the custody of the Miami Police Department.

Bowie drove them in his van to a quiet neighborhood just south of Little Havana, home to many Cuban refugees fleeing Castro's tyranny. Paprika wasn't even Latino, as far as Dani remembered, so this seemed an odd choice for the madam to set up shop. Walking around this neighborhood she would surely be noticed.

When they pulled up to a small, yellow, single-story, modest home in the middle of the block, Dani checked the address again. It was so small. Paprika enjoyed the high life when she was working the Hollywood scene, a house in the hills, a Mercedes, a weekend retreat in Palm Springs. This was certainly a major step down for the former beauty queen.

Dani and Bowie walked up to the door and rang the bell. There was no answer. A dog barked, but it was in the yard next door. Bowie pressed his ear to the door and listened. He looked at his mother and shrugged. They walked around the side of the house, peering into the windows, but the place appeared empty.

Dani was sore. Not just from the attack the night before, but from working out religiously to prepare for her first case out in the field in years. She felt like her bones were cracking. It depressed her to think she wasn't physically in the same shape she had once been. Age had caught up with her, but she wasn't about to acknowledge it. Not in front of her son, who still thought she was as strong and vital as she had always been. Hell, she had taken down a man three times her size just last night.

Bowie stuck out an arm, stopping his mother. He motioned to a window that looked inside a back bedroom. He knelt down, crept in front of it, and then slowly raised his head just high enough to get a good look inside. He gasped.

"What is it?" Dani whispered.

"Oh man, you're not going to believe this," he said as he waved his mother forward. Dani joined her son underneath the windowsill, and then gently raised her head to peer inside.

A woman about Dani's age sat on a king-size bed watching the Home Shopping Network on her plasma television screen. She was gigantic, nearly four hundred pounds. Her black hair was cut short and matted, as if it hadn't been washed in weeks. It was wet from the humidity of the hot Miami weather, and the scattered bangs stuck to her forehead every which way. Her huge nightgown was smudged and clung tightly to her sides. An electric fan worked overtime to cool her immense bulk. She was obviously confined to her bed, unable to move. Through the mammoth amounts of flesh, Dani could barely make out the once-exquisite features of Paprika Lucerne.

Dani stood up and rapped on the window, startling Paprika, who tried to turn her head around to stare at the intruder.

"It's Dani Mendez, Paprika, I'd like to come in and talk to you," Dani said as the once-beautiful madam looked at her with a mix of shock and embarrassment.

Within five minutes of their reunion, when Dani admitted that Paprika had fallen for the same competing madam trick twice, allowing Dani and her son to locate her, the former Hollywood madam seemed resigned to the fact that she was once again out of business.

Prison had not been kind to Paprika. She had sunk into a depression, found solace in food, and was never able to climb back up from the depths of despair. She ended up in Miami because one of her cell mates, a much-in-demand prostitute, had invited her to share a house once she was paroled. With no client base or self-esteem left to keep her going in LA, she took the girl up on the offer, and after a couple of years of wallowing, slowly began to build her business back up again in a fresh location.

"When I heard there was a new game in town, I just went crazy," Paprika said, her voice soft. "This is all I've got left, and I was willing to do anything to keep you from taking it away."

"Who's Hammer?" Bowie asked.

"He just got out of jail. Dates one of my girls. I pay him to do odd jobs here and there. Nice guy actually, but for the right price, he can turn into a monster," Paprika said. "So what now? You calling the police? They can arrest me, but good luck getting me to jail. I haven't been out of this house in three years."

Dani looked around. The cops would have to knock down a wall or raise the roof to get her out of this place. She was that big.

"I just want to know one thing. Claire, Tess, and I really did a number on you back in the eighties, ruined your life, sent you to prison, I just want to know if you're still holding a grudge," Dani said.

"Look at me. I never recovered from what you did. If you're in some twelve-step program and you're here to ask for my forgiveness, forget it," Paprika said, spittle spraying out of the sides of her mouth.

"No, I don't need your forgiveness because I was just doing my job and you tried to commit murder. I only need to know how far you're willing to go to get revenge."

"Revenge? Are you kidding me? Frankly, Mendez, I had forgotten all about you. I'm just trying to make a few bucks in the one business I know, and not slip into a diabetic coma."

Dani nodded. Her mind was at rest. Paprika Lucerne would certainly go to great lengths to protect her call girl operation in South Florida, but she was obviously not out on some mission to bring the former LA Dolls down by killing their kids.

"Thank you, Paprika," Dani said, turning to go.

"That's it? You're not going to call the cops on me?" Paprika said, her eyebrows arched in surprise.

"No," Dani said. "We're not going to say anything as long as Hammer doesn't talk about why he tried to beat me up."

"Oh, don't worry about him. He gets bonuses for every time he keeps his mouth shut," Paprika said, her eyes going back to a fancy juicer being touted on the Home Shopping Network.

"Well, we'll let you get back to whatever you were doing," Dani said, motioning to Bowie. They headed out of the bedroom.

"Hey, Dani," Paprika said, never taking her eyes off the television.

"What?" Dani said, stopping.

"You still look pretty good," Paprika said. "You can always come work for me. I got plenty of clients who go ape shit over the hot older women."

"Let me think about it," Dani said, shaking her head in front of her son at the absurdity of Paprika's proposition, although secretly she was thrilled at the offer.

CHAPTER 17

"I gotta say, Claire, you're just about the most beautiful thing I've ever seen," Smack said, as Claire glided out of the marble bathroom in their lush suite at the Bellagio Hotel in Las Vegas. If she was going to play a vacationing high roller it was imperative she look the part, which was why she had spent the entire afternoon shopping for a new outfit. And this little number, an Elie Tahari Arden Linen jacket and Ashton skirt she picked up in the designer's forum shop at Caesar's Palace seemed to do the trick, at least where Smack was concerned.

It didn't take much for Claire to find out Sonny Anzilotti was gambling here while his wife toiled away greenlighting hundred-million-dollar movies at her film studio back in Hollywood. According to Claire's sources, the Italian Stallion jetted here every week where a room at the Bellagio was always waiting for him, making it easy for him to indulge in his favorite passion—blackjack.

Tess was only too happy to call her old friend, Steve Wynn, chairman of Mirage Resorts, Vegas's biggest builder of dreams, and owner of the Bellagio Hotel, to book a plush suite for Claire while she was in town to check up on Sonny. Tess's endless list of powerful contacts never surprised Claire. Movers and shakers fell over themselves, most of the men anyway, to make sure Tess was happy and to honor any request she might have. Her vast wealth and still stunning beauty was just too much of an enticing combination to ignore.

What did surprise Claire was Smack's insistence on accompanying her to Vegas. He was so convinced Sonny was just a washed-up thug who'd married well. Why did he have to come all this way to see for himself? Claire had to wonder: if it had been Dani or Tess looking into Sonny, would Smack have been so hell-bent on boarding Tess's private jet at the Burbank Airport for the thirty-minute flight to McCarran Airport in Vegas?

She was flattered by his attention certainly, but she was married. There had been a time, early on, when they were both in their twenties, when Claire was attracted to Smack, his handsome face, his swagger, his unyielding confidence. But she was young, and addicted to danger and excitement, and perhaps the kind of men who thrived on chaos. She had changed, and so had Smack. He was almost grandfatherly now. She couldn't tell him that. He'd be crushed. No, the fact that she had Jeb now would keep Smack from trying to alter their friendship by making a pass. At least she hoped that was the case.

Claire's thoughts went to Jeb, who was right now piloting a transatlantic flight from Los Angeles to Hong Kong. She felt deceitful. What would he say if he knew that at this moment his wife was in a Bellagio suite with a former convicted felon-informant about to go down to the casino to try to seduce a lecherous, abusive bully? His patience had been unwavering over the years, but there is only so much one man can take, especially after her constant assurances that this part of her life was over.

Claire gave Smack the once over: a nice expensive suit courtesy of Tess's open charge account at Armani, some alluring cologne, a manicure in the hotel's day spa. He had gone all out. There was no way anyone could ever picture him now on a rusty stool at his Laurel Canyon newsstand, counting out change to an aspiring screenwriter buying the latest issue of *Entertainment Weekly*.

"Man, that poor dude's never going to know what hit him!" Smack said, shaking his head. "You got it going on."

"You're looking pretty hot yourself, mister," Claire said, instantly regretting it as she saw Smack's eyes light up.

Claire squeezed some flab through her blouse on her left side. Just how dumb of a plan was this? Maybe twenty years ago she would have been easily able to draw in the likes of Sonny Anzilotti, but now? She had become so matronly in her mind, and maybe this light and fun Elie Tahari number might make her feel younger, but the fact was she was past menopause. Okay, so Sonny Anzilotti was now older too, but men in their fifties tend to work backward, and find girls in their twenties. But she didn't have a choice. She knew she was the only one of the three who could even try this.

Tess had already worked her way into Sonny's life while he was playing for the LA Rams. She posed as a cheerleader, and grabbed his attention during her first half-time show with a carefully planned wardrobe malfunction, and soon after that carefully planned mishap they were dating, which allowed her to gather up evidence against him in an illegal betting scheme. Dani had a lot of contact with him when she pretended to be a writer for *Sports Illustrated* doing a proposed cover story on him. But Claire had mostly stayed behind the scenes during the case and had limited contact with him. Except when he found out Tess had been lying to him, had played him, and was setting him up for a big fall.

He saw she was wired and went crazy, trying to choke her to death at his apartment in Westwood. Claire had been outside in her Mustang listening when all hell broke loose. She busted in to find Tess pinned up against the wall with Sonny's big hands wringing her neck.

Claire went wild, knowing this was a pattern with the overgrown jerk. She rammed into his back with her elbow, and he jolted forward, releasing his grip on Tess. He spun around and Claire sent a flying kick to his windpipe. His eyes went wide, and he collapsed to the floor. Tess fell into Claire's arms, crying. She hadn't expected such a vicious attack. Sonny had only seen Claire for a few moments. Claire never even testified at the trial. But she had to have made an impression. She was just hoping that it wasn't big enough to ring any bells tonight.

Claire and Smack, arm in arm, playing the happy couple, took the elevator down to the Casino and immediately made a beeline for the high-roller tables. They knew Sonny's game of choice was blackjack, and he always took two spots at a centrally located table. They played for a while, Smack even building up a small pile of winnings, before Claire spotted a familiar man approaching. This couldn't be Sonny. He was fat and bloated, and balding. But it was. It was Sonny. And Claire's first thought was what kind of sordid pictures of the studio executive was he blackmailing her with to keep her married to him?

Sonny was in a tight-fitting black dress shirt that fought, but failed, to make him appear more slimming. His pants and shoes were also black, and Claire could have sworn that there was a black cloud floating just above his head. He muttered a drink order to a passing cocktail waitress, and then took a seat at the same table as Claire and Smack. They played a few more hands, waiting for Sonny to down a few more cocktails and lose some money before Claire gave Smack the signal.

Smack grabbed Claire's wrist and jerked hard. "I said you've lost enough. It's time for bed."

Claire took a sip of her drink. "I'm not done here. I'll be up when I'm good and ready."

"I'm not letting you take out another mortgage on the Aspen house just so you can play some more and get stinking drunk again," Smack hissed, trying to pull her off her chair. "You're coming with me."

Claire yanked away from his grip and hurled her drink in Smack's face. There was an uncomfortable silence. Sonny watched the scene with keen interest.

"You touch me again, and I'll have security haul your black ass out of here and out of my life forever," Claire said.

Smack glared at her, saw that Sonny was about to leap to her defense, then shook his head and stalked off.

"Can I buy you another drink?" Sonny said with a smile. "That little show was better than Celine Dion's."

Claire laughed. "Yes, thank you. Scotch and soda." Claire rarely drank, but ever since the pressures of Zak's ill-fated wedding and playing detective again, she had been less inclined to abstain.

Sonny quickly used the opportunity to haul himself up off his chair, amble around to the other side of the table and slide into the seat vacated by Smack.

Claire was relieved that she hadn't embarrassed herself, and had at least been able to reel him in. Still, this wasn't exactly George Clooney, or even George Clooney's father, the silver-haired foxy guy who used to introduce films on American Movie Classics. This was a shell of a man, a man polluted by alcohol, drugs, and no doubt steroids, who was a long distance away from his glory days of playing pro football. Still, she would take this as a victory.

Sonny made small talk during the next few hands and Claire expertly made up a story of how she and Smack had a successful contracting business in Austin. She even ladled out a nicely re-hearsed Texas accent. She told him how their interracial marriage had kept them on the outskirts of the social whirl for years, but now they were considered a novelty, mostly because they had gobs of money, and were at last welcomed into the fold.

"These people, this high society we so wanted to belong to, they're the type that look up a word in the dictionary that nobody knows, and then use it in a sentence to impress people. I hate people who think they're better than me."

Sonny nodded as if he truly understood. Claire figured he did. His wife traveled in some pretty powerful circles and all those producers and agents probably looked down on him, saw him as a loser, and made jokes behind his back. He had changed so much since his glory days. But of course Claire didn't say any of that. And neither would he. His ego would never allow it.

They played a few more hands. Sonny lost more and more money. He requested an extension of his credit and quickly received it. Claire was guessing his big-time movie executive wife threw money at him just so he would stay out of her hair. That had to be the reason. Sonny may have lost his edge, let himself go, but she was betting he could still be a mean son of a bitch who would make his wife's life utter hell if she tried to get rid of him. It was probably easier just to support him and let him do what he wanted.

Claire was down to her last few chips. Sonny pushed a stack over to her.

"Oh, no," Claire said. "I couldn't."

"Don't worry about it. I got plenty, believe me."

"You must be very successful."

"I'm a film producer. I make movies," Sonny said.

"Really?" Claire said with wide, curious eyes, even though she knew it was a bald-faced lie.

Sonny began listing off titles, taking a chance that Claire wouldn't run back to her computer and look them all up on IMDB and find out he was not connected to any of them in any way. He was, however, consistent in the fact that all of the films were released from his wife's studio under her watch.

He ordered them another round of drinks.

"Have you always produced movies?" Claire said, touching his arm.

"No, I used to be a football player, back in the eighties," he said.

"Really? I've always had a thing for athletes," Claire said.

Sonny perked up. Did he just score? He had no idea Claire only said it to get him to talk more about his high-profile past, get his take on his spectacular and very public downfall. She knew he probably wouldn't fess up about beating his girlfriends or the betting scheme, but she might get an indication if it was still eating away at him, if he still carried a grudge.

She had expected him to prattle on about the glory days, how famous he had been, but he just shrugged as the cocktail waitress arrived with a tray and set the drinks down. He gulped his down and looked at Claire with sad, tired eyes.

"Yeah, well, it was a long time ago. I don't really like to talk about that time of my life," Sonny said.

It was at that moment that Claire knew Smack had been right. Sonny was trying to bury the past and redesign his present, even if that meant making up a whole fake movie producer career. She could have stood up right then and there and walked out. Her job was done. But instead, she sat there having a drink with him, playing a few more hands of blackjack.

It was amazing to her that she actually felt sorry for this man she hated so deeply, who had mistreated so many women, betrayed his friends, who if given half a chance would take her up to his room and have sex with her and not care he was cheating on his wife.

He made his move, gently touching the small of her back with his fleshy hand, proposing a quick night cap up in his room, but she politely declined and headed back up to her suite where Smack was waiting. Smack would want to hear all the details, and they would probably order up room service and watch a movie until they could take the private jet back to Burbank in the morning. She would be back in Sherman Oaks before Jeb arrived home from the second leg of his flight. Because one thing was now perfectly clear. Sonny Anzilotti did not want to kill her children for bringing him down. He was too busy killing himself.

CHAPTER 18

"It's as if time has stopped," Akito Tanaka said, gazing into the seductive, glistening eyes of Tess Monahan-Cardoza.

Tess knew she had him. Hell, she always had him. This strikingly handsome Japanese drug lord called her his Achilles' heel. He was so in love with her during the heyday of his illegal operations, he was blinded by the fact that she was quietly building enough evidence to send him away. And he had been away for twenty years, served his time, and was now a free man.

Tess knew when she rolled into Santa Barbara on one of her husband's yachts and threw an impromptu A-list, champagne-swilling soiree for her friends, Akito would be too curious to see her after all these years not to show up and try to crash. She had left strict instructions to the security team to let him on board with no hassles. The Dolls figured that once he was released, Tanaka would retreat to his palatial home here in the exclusive oceanfront enclave ninety minutes north of Los Angeles.

Tess knew deep down that Tanaka wasn't the one who hired those thugs to try and snatch Bianca in Rio de Janeiro, but on the off chance she could be wrong, she agreed to lure him out with expensive caviar and the chance to reunite after all these years.

What surprised her the most, however, was just how smitten he still was. Even after serving twenty years in prison. Even after Tess appeared at his first parole hearing to explain why he should not be released. He still carried a torch for her. She made sure that she dressed up in her most flattering green-beaded Vera Wang, had a car pick up aging hair guru Jose Eber and deliver him to the yacht in Santa Barbara to oversee her often uncooperative tresses, and stock the boat with the most expensive Dom Perignon she could possibly find on such short notice.

Bianca, her own lush dark hair cascading down below her shoulders, her gorgeous tanned face lit up in the moonlight, and wearing a tight-fitting cocktail dress that even Tyra Banks couldn't pull off, joined her mother to welcome the guests as they arrived in a sea of limousines. When word spread throughout town that Tess Cardoza was in town and throwing a cocktail party, secretaries began to furiously revise their bosses' social calendars.

The idea that her mother was throwing this party to smoke out a suspect thrilled Bianca to no end. She had only recently become aware of her mother's past as a private detective, and couldn't get enough stories. And now, as cohost of the party with her mother, she felt like her mom's partner, a cool, hip crime fighter. Her friends back in Rio would never believe it. Tess had lectured her to just act natural, be herself, and let her mother handle things if Akito made an appearance.

But Bianca just couldn't resist doing her part. She immersed herself in research, Googling Tanaka on the Internet, making notes about his past crimes and present business dealings. She memorized his face and read about his habits. Tess thought her daughter was much more thorough an investigator than she had ever been.

In fact, it was Bianca who first spotted Akito Tanaka in the crowd of guests filing up the plank into the boat. She nudged

Tess nonchalantly, and casually whispered in her ear, "Perp at three o'clock."

Tess couldn't help but smile. Bianca was so into this. She tried not to look in Tanaka's direction. She just kept a bright smile plastered on her face as she greeted the other guests. But it was only a matter of seconds before she felt the burning eyes of Tanaka, like a heat missile, locking on to her.

"Omigod, he's staring at you, Mom," Bianca said in a hushed voice, though her mannerisms were stilted and obvious.

Tess knew she had to get rid of Bianca or she would give everything away, and as luck would have it, that's when Anderson Cooper, with his sexy prematurely gray hair and serious eyes, boarded. Tess and Cooper's mother, wealthy heiress Gloria Vanderbilt were social pals back in the day, and so when the CNN news superstar got an e-mail from Tess announcing her Santa Barbara party, he flew out just for the occasion.

Bianca's jaw fell at the sight of him. Tess knew she had a supreme crush on him, despite the rumors he might be gay, and instantly grabbed the smiling reporter in a bear hug.

"Anderson! Look at you! All grown up and everywhere on the television set! Have you met my daughter Bianca?"

Anderson was polite and gracious and more than happy to have a personal tour of the boat with Bianca, who could barely get any words out at this point. Tess hated using poor Anderson Cooper to get rid of her daughter, but Tanaka was fast approaching, and the last thing Tess needed was her overzealous daughter mucking things up.

Paulo was still down in the master stateroom getting dressed after a rowdy soccer game that afternoon at a private field with a few of Tess's more athletic friends. He had only returned to the yacht forty-five minutes earlier, so Tess knew she still had some time to spend with Tanaka before her protective and jealous Brazilian lover was at her side, making it impossible for her to do any substantive investigating.

Tess had just barely said hello to Naomi Watts, the popular Australian actress, who appeared in a Brazilian film financed by Tess's late husband early in her career, when she heard Akito Tanaka's "time has stopped" line. She looked up to see him gazing into her eyes. And right then, without any further questioning, she knew Tanaka was a dead end.

There was such longing in his eyes, such passion, coupled with a lustful smile as he reached out with his smooth, immaculate hands and wrapped them around hers. She glanced down, and the only thing she could think about was how well preserved he was. Prison had done nothing to wear down his good looks. Time had certainly stopped. But for him unfortunately. Not for her. And she had the pricey face crèmes from France to prove it.

"I was sorry to hear about your husband," Tanaka said, but he wasn't sorry at all. To him, that just meant less competition.

"Thank you. Would you like some champagne?"

"No. I don't drink. And why would I want anything that might dull my senses at this very moment?"

Okay, that was way over the top. In fact, Tess had to stifle a laugh. This guy was too much. Maybe the party was a bad idea. Did she just give license to a stalker?

Tess had to gently extricate herself from his grip, and then began to pepper him with questions. What was he up to? Was he seeing anyone? Tanaka mentioned a few legitimate real estate investments to satisfy her first question. But he gave an emphatic no to the second one.

There was no way Tess could ever get around the idea that Tanaka was the one targeting anyone close to her. Because if Tess knew about one thing, it was men. And she knew he was holding out hope they could pick up where they left off. Except of course for the part where Tess testified against him in court and played a major role in his ultimate conviction and lengthy prison sentence. Tanaka had shown up tonight with one clear-minded agenda. To get back with Tess. Their affair had been brief. She went undercover as an exotic dancer at a club Tanaka frequented when he was a swinging bachelor in his mid-twenties. He fell in love with her faster than you could say Anna Nicole Smith, and set her up in his sprawling seaside condo, unwittingly giving her access to all his illegal dealings including extortion and fraud. Even when Tess personally chased him down as the police were closing in, in a showdown at the Santa Monica Pier, where he fought her, and she karate chopped him to his knees and shoved him into the murky frigid water, he never seemed to get the slightest bit annoyed with her. He knew she was just doing her job. Even with her dramatic betrayal, he was still in love with her. The theory that his anger might have grown and festered in prison to the point where he hated Tess was clearly out the window.

With Akito Tanaka quickly discounted as a suspect, Tess relaxed. She might as well enjoy the rest of the party. When Tanaka asked for a tour of the boat, Tess looked around for Bianca, hoping to pawn her dewy-eyed suitor off on her, but Bianca was still off in her own fantasy world of pretending to be Anderson Cooper's date, so it was left to Tess.

Tess moved quickly, barely stopping in each section as she rattled off the history of the boat, built by Morris Yachts in Bass Harbor, Maine, because nobody else comes close to their caliber of craftsmanship. She hurried through the galley, the dining room, the sauna, and steam room, winding up with a cursory glance at the staterooms.

Tess should have been clued in when Tanaka seemed especially interested in the master stateroom. She had been through this same situation too many times not to suspect what might be coming. But with so many guests upstairs, she never dreamed he would try something so blatant.

Before they were even all the way inside, Tanaka slammed the door shut, spun her around and began pawing her.

"I've waited twenty years for this moment," Tanaka said, almost slobbering.

Tess knew she could take him but she didn't want to inadvertently damage her dress. She loved this dress. So she simply grabbed his wrists and pushed him away as he tried cupping her breasts. She decided she was not going to hit him, or humiliate him in any way. She was just going to extricate herself quietly, leaving him with at least a shred of his dignity.

At least that was the plan.

"What the hell—?" Paulo said, as he walked out of the bathroom, glowering, dressed in a white linen suit that accentuated his flawless bronzed skin.

Tess had completely forgotten about Paulo and the fact that he was downstairs getting ready.

Paulo lunged forward, balling up his fist and cracking it against Tanaka's chin. Tanaka reared back, smashing into the stateroom door and then falling to his knees. Paulo hauled him up by the shirt collar.

"Try something like that again," Paulo hissed, "and you'll be leaving this party over the side with a cement block tied to your feet."

And with that, he shoved him out the door, slamming it behind him. He turned to Tess and the rage in his face slowly subsided.

"I could have handled that myself," Tess said.

"I know," Paulo said, shedding his linen jacket and unbuttoning his shirt. "But sometimes you need to let the man do it. It gives us a sense of purpose."

Paulo had been with Tess long enough to know not to let his passion make him do something crazy, like rip off her expensive dress. He just assisted her in carefully slipping it off, before he threw her down on the bed and climbed on top of her.

Tess decided the party could run smoothly enough without the hosts for at least another twenty minutes or so.

CHAPTER 19

Claire was in major trouble. The flight from Las Vegas to Burbank was delayed by two hours. She had meticulously planned this trip with Smack to scope out Sonny Anzilotti down to the minute. She knew she had to be home and have dinner on the table by the time Jeb walked in that front door from his return flight from Hong Kong. But a mechanical problem kept the private jet grounded at McCarran Airport in Vegas for more than an hour, and as the second hour ticked by Claire decided they should catch a commercial flight on Southwest Airlines.

Claire was starting to sweat. She had promised Jeb she would not let herself get pulled back into this kind of dangerous work. So what would she tell him if he beat her home? She couldn't lie to him. They had sailed through twenty years of marriage without lying to each other. But she also couldn't just come out and say she was in Sin City with a former street informant knocking back a few cocktails and checking out an old adversary. He just wouldn't understand.

Jeb loved their life together. He liked to come home and see his wife, have a nice dinner, make passionate love, and then fall asleep watching Jon Stewart on *The Daily Show*. Okay, they may be in a minor rut, but Claire didn't want to disappoint him.

She had always been a people pleaser. First she worked hard to please her parents, getting stellar grades and going to the right school. Then she stuck it out as an LA Doll to please Dani. And then, of course, it was all about pleasing her husband. No wonder she was so good at undercover assignments back in the day. She could so easily lose sight of herself in whatever role was required as she worked hard to make someone else happy.

Claire nervously checked her watch as the plane taxied in at the Burbank Airport. She and Smack had carpooled, so she had to drop him off at his newsstand on Laurel Canyon first before heading on home to Sherman Oaks. That would take at least twenty minutes. Then there was the matter of picking up dinner and getting it on the table in less than two hours. That was when Jeb was scheduled to walk through the door. She hoped there would be a delay on his end. But those transatlantic flights had an excellent record of on-time arrivals.

Luckily Claire and Smack were seated near the front of the plane, so when the seat belt light went off and the heavyset, balding male flight attendant had pushed open the door, Claire grabbed Smack by the sleeve and dragged him up so they could be the first ones off. She normally would have allowed the elderly couple seated ahead of them to get off first, but they looked slow, and now was not the time for Claire's trademark politeness.

Claire felt bad she had been so silent on the flight home. Smack probably thought she was upset with him or something, but she was single-minded in her resolve to be a good wife, and not bother Jeb with where she had been during the last twenty-four hours.

As Claire raced for the airport's valet stand where they had dropped off her Toyota Prius yesterday, she turned back to see Smack milling around the outdoor baggage claim area. She was already at the crosswalk, waiting for the light to change.

"Smack, let's go! We're late!"

"I gotta get my bag, darling."

Claire's heart sank. "When did you check a bag? I thought we both just had carry-on luggage?"

"My strap broke while you were on line at Starbucks, so I just checked it through so I wouldn't have to drag it around."

This was a disaster. One that would cost her precious minutes. But Claire took a deep breath. What's done was done. And she always operated well under pressure. She could still pull this off. She checked her watch again. An hour and forty minutes until Jeb's arrival. She had already mentally prepared the dinner menu. Pepita-crusted snapper, sautéed vegetables, black beans, and flan for dessert. Jeb loved anything with a Mexican flavor so the choice was obvious. Why take a risk when she was so close to being busted?

The baggage carousel was just firing up and popping out bags. Claire knew that chances were Smack's bag would be one of the last ones out. She whipped out her cell phone and called home. Zak answered. He sounded sleepy. Claire hated to put him to work especially given his physical state, but the doctor said moving around would be good for him, so asking him to set the table seemed like just a big part of his recovery.

"Where were you last night, Mom?" Zak said, yawning.

"Had a girls' night out with Dani and Tess," Claire said. Okay, she never lied to Jeb. But who doesn't fib to their kids every so often just to keep them from asking too many questions and possibly blowing it in front of their father?

After sweet-talking Zak into saving her some time by putting out the plates and silverware, Claire spun around to see Smack pick up his bag with the broken strap. She sprinted through the crosswalk to the valet stand, shoved her ticket along with some cash through the opening in the window to the attendant, and waited impatiently for her car to be brought around. Smack huffed and puffed, trying to keep up with her, his arms wrapped around his unwieldy bag.

"Guess a drink's out of the question, huh?" Smack said in a small voice.

Claire smiled, not betraying even a hint of her near panic. "Another time, Smack. I've got to get home."

Smack's eyes nearly popped out of his head as Claire bombed down Ventura Boulevard, speeding through intersections just as the lights turned red, swerving around slower cars, before almost burning rubber to make a turn on Laurel Canyon Boulevard and depositing Smack at his newsstand.

"Claire, I gotta tell you, this was a rush for me. After all these years, and we got to play together again. Just makes me miss the old days."

Claire kept a smile frozen on her face, but she just wanted him out of the car. She felt silly admitting the truth. That she was acting like some 1950s housewife, focused on getting dinner on the table before Mr. Cleaver got home from work.

"You know, something, Smack," Claire said. "It was a rush for me too." She meant it. She really did. She was so concerned with getting back to her current life she hadn't contemplated just how much fun it was returning to the old one, at least for one night.

"I knew it," Smack said with a sly smile. "It just brought back a lot, you know? You and me made a great team back then and I just wanted you to know . . ."

"I really have to go now," Claire said, interrupting him.

He looked a bit wounded. And Claire felt bad. Smack was a good guy. But the pressure was building fast. She leaned over and gave him a quick peck on the cheek. His face lit up, and that seemed to make up for her rude manners. He almost danced out of the car.

Claire gunned the Prius, did a quick U-turn despite the heavy early evening traffic and sped off north on Laurel Canyon, turning right on Moorpark and then heading west towards Sherman Oaks. She made a quick stop at Trader Joe's to pick up the fish and a bottle of Pinot Grigio. From there, it was only five minutes to the house.

Zak was just finishing setting the table for three when his mother crashed through the door like a hurricane and raced into the kitchen. Within ten minutes, she was sautéing the vegetables, the beans were on the stove and she was rolling the fish in her spicy Mexican flavored bread crumbs. Within a half hour, the wine and the flan mixture were both chilling in the fridge.

Zak watched her curiously as she hurried up the stairs, jumped in the shower and re-emerged fifteen minutes later in a fresh set of clothes and a relaxed smile on her face. Just as she opened the oven door to take the snapper out, the front door opened, and Jeb ambled in, looking exhausted. But just as Claire predicted, he was right on time.

Claire, on the other hand, appeared as if she had just awakened from a long power nap, refreshed and ready to go.

"How was your flight, honey?" she said, kissing him.

"Long," he said, shaking off his jacket and loosening his tie. Claire handed him a glass of Pinot Grigio.

Dinner was on the table within minutes, and Jeb slumped down at the head to nurse his wine, and talk to Claire and Zak.

"Where's your brother?" Jeb asked.

"He said he had some studying to do, but I think he has a date. He's so secretive when it comes to women," Zak said, grinning.

Jeb nodded and then turned to Claire. "So what have you been up to since I've been gone?"

"I flew to Las Vegas for a little blackjack. What do you think?"

Jeb looked at her for a moment and laughed. Claire let out a small sigh of relief. There. She told him where she was. It wasn't her fault he thought she was kidding.

After dinner, Zak moved with a great deal of effort due to his injuries to the living room couch to watch a football game on

TV, and Claire and Jeb retreated upstairs to their master bedroom. Claire turned on the television. It was still twenty minutes until her husband's favorite faux news program with Jon Stewart. She left the channel on the local news. Jeb took a shower as Claire unpacked his bag.

She spied her own carry-on bag, still packed and right there next to Jeb's side of the bed. She was in such a rush, she'd forgotten to unpack it. Right there was evidence of her overnight excursion to Las Vegas. Jeb was drying off and seconds from walking into the bedroom where he would inevitably see it. Claire quickly slid it under the bed with her big toe. Why invite questions?

Despite being tired, Jeb was in an amorous mood. It had been a couple of days since he saw his wife last, and he wanted to show her just how happy he was to be with her again. Jeb, wearing only a white towel, walked up behind Claire and put his arms around her. He began nuzzling her neck, and then turned her around and lowered her down on the bed where he climbed on top of her. They kissed, their lips touching softly at first, before becoming more aggressive. Claire ran her fingers through Jeb's chest hair as he pulled her closer to him, his right hand firmly planted on her buttocks. Claire playfully ripped away his towel and Jeb, with his other hand, worked to free the hook on her pants.

On the television was a report live from downtown Los Angeles where only hours ago a convicted murderer was released after serving twenty years for first-degree murder. Claire didn't listen to it at first, she was too caught up in the throes of passion, but when she heard the name Benito Coronel, her blood ran cold and she immediately stopped making love with Jeb.

"What is it, honey?" Jeb asked, at first thinking he had done something wrong.

Claire's eyes were fixed on the television. Benito Coronel,

with graying hair and deep lines in his face but still incredibly handsome, walked out of the courthouse accompanied by his beautiful, dark-haired lawyer who was young enough to be his daughter.

Reporters crowded in to bark questions. Apparently new DNA evidence from the murder weapon, a table leg from one of the furniture pieces he manufactured, had cleared Coronel. It wasn't a match. He couldn't have killed his mentally challenged employee all those years ago. His lawyer, beaming, explained that it had taken years for her to get the court to agree to the testing, and now justice had finally been served. Her client, having already served his time for drug smuggling, could now be a free man because the judge granted him early release from his murder sentence due to this new evidence.

Jeb didn't have to ask Claire who Benito Coronel was. He figured he was one of the men his wife and the other Dolls had put behind bars.

"So was this guy dangerous?" Jeb said, almost hating to ask because he already knew the answer.

"Of all the people we put behind bars, he was the most vindictive," Claire said with a shiver. "I just can't believe that it's a coincidence that these attempted hits on the kids happened at around the same time he's getting out."

Claire picked up the phone to call Dani.

CHAPTER 20

"The DNA tests from the sweat, and skin blood tissue on the table leg did not match Benito Coronel so it is clear he was not the one who murdered the young man, Lenny Fowler, who worked for him," Maria Consuelos said, sitting behind her large oak desk, a file opened in front of her.

Dani, Claire, and Tess sat across from her in comfortable overstuffed chairs. They exchanged looks before Dani finally spoke up. "That doesn't mean anything. Coronel may not have wanted to get his hands dirty. He could have had one of his goons administer the fatal blow."

"Doesn't matter," Maria said as she meticulously picked a small piece of lint off her smart sage business suit and tossed her long dark hair back. "Mr. Coronel was convicted with evidence suggesting that he personally used the table leg as a weapon to kill the boy. That was the entire basis for the state's case. Since those facts have been proven not to be true with new DNA testing, then the whole case stinks, and the judge felt he had no choice but to overturn the conviction. Sorry, ladies."

"Can he be retried if we come up with some new evidence that shows he ordered the killing?" Tess said her eyes boring into

Maria. Dani could tell Tess hated this lawyer with her fancy Century City office and obvious arrogance. Not so much for her attitude, but more for her youth and beauty that went along with it.

"You can try to bring new charges, but what's the point? The poor man has already served twenty years. Let him enjoy the remaining years of his life in peace," Maria said.

"Lenny Fowler would like to enjoy the remaining years of his life in peace too, but he's dead. He was bludgeoned to death and I still believe your client was behind it if he didn't actually carry out the murder," Dani said. She could feel her face flush with anger.

"I'm sorry for what happened to Mr. Fowler, and I sympathize with his sister, but the reason my client is finally free today is because of that kind of bullheaded thinking. I've read the case file, interviewed most of the investigating officers, the lawyers, and they all seem to agree that you three Charlie's Angels wannabes would have stopped at nothing to see my client put behind bars. The fact that he might be innocent wasn't even a consideration," Maria said as she locked eyes with Dani. "Now that the facts have won out, I hope you ladies are proud of yourselves."

"Mr. Coronel may be a lot of things, Ms. Consuelos," Claire said. "But you can be certain he's not innocent."

"Well, he's obviously innocent of the murder of Lenny Fowler, and I have the test results to prove it."

Maria stood up from her large desk that almost dwarfed her, and came around. She had long, gorgeous, shapely legs that her short sage business skirt showed off in all their glory. And they didn't escape the notice of Dani, Claire, and Tess.

"I think we're done here," Maria said, passing the women and walking toward the door to show them out.

Dani stood up first. She had heard enough. She marched out of the office, not bothering to acknowledge the pretty young lawyer.

"You can get your parking ticket validated at the reception desk," Maria said with a saccharine smile.

Tess stopped and glared at her. "We don't need validation. I own the building." And then she swept out with a flourish. Dani heard the remark from the hallway and suppressed a chuckle. It was a lie, but given Tess's vast wealth, Maria Consuelos didn't dare question it.

Claire was the last to leave. "Thank you for your time, Ms. Consuelos."

Dani shook her head. Claire was always the polite one. Even to a smart-ass, supercilious J Lo with a law degree.

As the ladies walked out of the high-end law offices near the top floor of one of the Century Plaza towers, a lot of the male lawyers and clerks couldn't help but stare. Dani noticed that Tess was enjoying the attention the most.

When they were on the elevator going down, they were finally alone to discuss the demoralizing meeting with Coronel's lawyer.

"She seems green," Claire said. "Why would Coronel hire someone like her?"

"She's not that green. She managed to get him off," Dani said.

"I hated her," Tess spit out, not even trying to conceal her jealousy.

"You don't hate her. You just hate how damn hot she is," Dani said laughing.

"Maybe so," Tess said, not quite ready to admit it. "But I was ready to smack her when she referred to us as Charlie's Angels. I never liked people calling us that. The show was a rip-off of our lives."

"Actually the show premiered before the three of us ever met," Claire offered delicately. "People thought we were trying to model ourselves after them."

"Fine. Whatever," Tess said. "It doesn't change the fact I wanted to hurt that bitch of a lawyer when she said it."

"She did make an interesting point," Claire said.

"What's that?" Dani said as the elevator doors opened and the three women walked across the expansive courtyard towards Century Plaza East where Tess's limousine was waiting for them.

"We were so hell-bent on avenging Lenny Fowler, we might have made a few missteps," Claire said, her eyes downcast.

"Bullshit," Dani said. "Benito Coronel killed that boy. He may have not done the job himself, but he was behind it. You can bet on it. And let's not forget the man was a dirty drug smuggler. There's no telling how many other people he surely slaughtered that we don't know about."

"But maybe if we hadn't been so blinded by Lenny's story, we might not have made the mistakes we made," Claire said.

"What mistakes?" Dani said.

"Benito Coronel is a free man because we never considered the fact that he might have ordered the hit. It was all about nailing him on everything—the drug smuggling, Lenny's murder. When we recovered that table leg, our entire focus became tying it to Coronel. It just got me thinking," Claire said quietly.

"About what?"

"Some of the methods we used back then."

"We didn't doctor evidence," Dani said trying not to get mad. "There just wasn't any DNA testing back then."

"But I do remember a discussion we had when it looked like Coronel wasn't going to get convicted because of the circumstantial evidence, and we found the murder weapon, and you suggested we transfer some fingerprints onto the table leg just to insure he didn't get off," Claire said, keeping her eyes straight ahead, not wanting to look at Dani.

"But we didn't. You two talked me out of it. And Coronel was convicted on the circumstantial evidence. End of story," Dani said.

They reached the limousine. Tess's portly, jovial driver was there with the door open. The ladies climbed inside. The driver shut the door and circled around to the driver's side.

"All I'm saying is," Claire said gingerly, not wanting to set Dani off, "we broke all sorts of rules back in the eighties to bring down the bad guys. I'm just wondering how many we put away who might have been innocent."

There was a long, pregnant pause as all three women considered this. Dani was fuming. She just didn't buy Claire's premise and resented her for even bringing it up.

The driver started up the limo and pulled away, heading north to Santa Monica Boulevard and Beverly Hills. "Where to, ladies?"

Tess, who had remained quiet since they left the elevator, picked up an empty bottle of expensive gin that was nestled in the small bar area and waved it around. "The nearest bar."

That was Tess's way of changing the subject.

CHAPTER 21

Dani thought about what Claire had said during her flight back to Miami from Los Angeles. She sat in First Class, swiveling the ice in her club soda around and around as she contemplated the idea that perhaps Claire was right. Had their methods been reckless? Were they responsible for putting one or two innocent parties behind bars?

Most of the men and women they went after had proven track records when it came to criminal activities. It wasn't a question of bringing down someone good. All of their adversaries were the scum of the earth, and deserved whatever charges were thrown at them. But Claire had softened with age, and was now one of those bleeding hearts who believed in redemption and rehabilitation. Having served almost twenty years with the San Francisco Police Department, Dani felt differently. Cage them and keep them there. That was her opinion. Then and now.

A lot of people assumed Dani was a Bush-loving, diehard Republican. But that wasn't the case. Not that she was a liberal-leaning Democrat. She didn't have much use for politics. She followed her own heart and confused a lot of people with her hard-to-pin-down ideas about the world. She was tough on crime, especially the perpetrator, and she was fiscally conservative, but socially she was very progressive. After all, she lived in San Francisco. And the fact that she had a gay son opened her eyes as well.

Bowie. He was the reason she was winging her way back to Florida after only a day and a half in Los Angeles. Once Dani and Bowie had paid their visit to Paprika Lucerne and crossed her off the list of suspects, Dani returned to Los Angeles to accompany Claire and Tess to their meeting with Maria Consuelos. But after a quick stop at Trader Vic's in Beverly Hills for a fruity drink with her two friends, a meeting fraught with tension over Claire's remarks, Dani had the limo drop her off at LAX so she could catch a flight back to Miami.

Bowie had called her cell seconds before she was ushered into Consuelos's plush office with Claire and Tess, and told her that he was going to meet with his father. Dani knew why.

Aaron Lassiter was a wildly successful real estate entrepreneur in Miami with a mansion on Star Island, a patch of land where money grows on trees. Aaron was also Dani's former lover. She investigated him during her waning days of being an LA Doll. The brother of a maintenance man murdered at an exclusive spa near Carmel, California, hired the Dolls to find out who was responsible. Once they got permission from the spa owners to conduct an investigation, Claire went in as a yoga instructor, Tess as a nutritionist. and Dani as a paying guest. Dani quickly zeroed in on Lassiter, a guest she met during a touchy-feely meditation exercise. She fought her feelings for him the whole way, especially when she began to uncover some disturbing information about his business dealings. Most of his real estate dealings were legitimate. However, there were a lot of nagging questions about his possible mob ties in Florida.

The culprit turned out to be a pretty young massage therapist, who was a regular Glenn Close from *Fatal Attraction*. The maintenance man had engaged in a torrid affair with the unstable girl, and when he tried to break it off for a local waitress he met at a Mexican restaurant in town, she went off the deep end and shot him while he was sleeping.

That cleared Aaron Lassiter. And Dani promptly began a hot and heavy long-distance affair. She knew it was wrong. A former suspect? Bad. Very bad. Sleeping with clients and suspects was Tess's domain, not hers. But she just couldn't help herself. And for the first time since the Dolls opened up shop, Dani was taking days off and flying south to spend time with him.

But the nagging questions continued, and Dani eventually couldn't turn a blind eye to what was going on behind the scenes of Aaron's lucrative business. He was a crook. Plain and simple. And she couldn't reconcile her strong feelings for him with what he was. Like the unlucky maintenance man at the Carmel spa, Dani ended it. At first Aaron winged his way to Los Angeles to implore her not to do anything rash, but she had made up her mind. And she cut him out of her life. He took it like a man. Aaron was the most macho guy Dani had ever been involved with. It was a big reason she was so wildly attracted to him.

They didn't speak until nine months later when Dani had to pick up the phone and call him to let him know he was the father of an eight-pound four-ounce baby boy. She went through the pregnancy alone, at the same time she was dissolving the business, and when she went to work as a beat cop, single motherhood proved challenging and at times dispiriting. But she took no money from Aaron despite his insistence, and only when it was time for Bowie to go to college, did she allow him to help financially.

Bowie's relationship with his father was strained. He spent summers in Miami with him. At first, as a little boy, Bowie loved the annual trek to Miami and its colorful people and culture. But as he hit his teens and worked hard at finding himself, Bowie became less enthralled with Aaron and more distant. Deep down

Bowie knew Aaron would never accept his homosexuality, and it was becoming clear to Bowie that being gay was a large part of who he was.

His mother was entirely accepting despite her hardball opinions, though secretly Dani worried for her son, wondering if he could be happy in the face of such prejudice and small mindedness. But he had grown up mostly in San Francisco, a free spirit, independent, and with his mother's Spanish background and father's black-Irish heritage, incredibly good looking.

As the United flight touched down at Miami International Airport and taxied toward the gate, Dani thought about why Bowie would request a meeting with his father. The two hadn't spoken in several years. But if anyone might have some information about who followed Bowie to Mexico it was Aaron Lassiter. And no bitter feelings would keep him from being the best private investigator he could be and follow any lead, even if it meant talking to his father.

Dani knew she had to be there. She wouldn't let Bowie go through this alone. She also knew just how powerful Aaron was in the Miami scene. Nothing goes on in his town that he doesn't know about.

Bowie had told her that his hunch was the shooters were not locals in Mexico City. He felt he had been stalked and tracked on his own turf even before he got on that plane to Mexico. He didn't have any concrete evidence to back up his theory, just a gut feeling. But Dani agreed with him.

Dani met Bowie at the dock just off Collins Avenue where a charter boat owned by Aaron picked them up and swept them out to sea and towards Star Island. Dani spotted the sprawling, white Lassiter mansion in the distance, towering above the other houses owned by the likes of Rosie O'Donnell and Gloria Estafan.

Once docked, they were driven to the compound, escorted through the expansive property to a large pool that snaked around the entire backyard. Several servants, mostly Latino, were on hand to take drink orders and offer them various lunch items such as poached salmon or a seafood medley. It was all so overwhelming.

Bowie turned to his mother. "Just think, Mom, all this could have been yours."

Dani nudged him, smiling. Like that was ever going to happen.

Aaron Lassiter was a striking man, over six feet tall, with jet-black hair and an angular, handsome face. He was in a salmon-colored polo shirt that matched his lunch selection, and white trousers and sandals. He seemed completely relaxed except for a trace of anxiety Dani recognized in his slightly furrowed brow. He was a little nervous to see both of them after all this time.

He refused to show it in any overt way, however, as he enveloped Dani in a welcoming hug. "My God, still so beautiful. You take my breath away, Dani."

He was always a smooth talker, but Dani didn't mind. In fact, she needed to hear it every now and then, though not as often as say, Tess.

"How are you, Aaron?" Dani said, giving him an affectionate peck on the cheek. "Do I get to meet the new wife?"

"You mean number four? No, she's out shopping. She won't be happy until she's forced me to sell everything I own to pay her credit card bills," Aaron said with faux disgust. He loved his twenty-six-year-old former sitcom-actress wife whom he met at the world famous star-studded Delano Hotel Bar in South Beach. What she lacked in brain power she made up for with her smoking-hot body.

Bowie lingered behind his mother, waiting for Aaron to acknowledge him. He was so focused on Dani, however, he didn't even notice his son at first. Sensing her son's nervousness, Dani stepped aside to allow father and son to greet one another.

Bowie stepped bravely forward, putting out his hand. "Dad, how are you?"

Aaron sized him up. Bowie cut an impressive figure. "Looking good, son."

"Thanks," Bowie said, treading carefully but almost willing to let his guard down.

"Handsome boy like you should have no trouble lining up the ladies."

Dani wanted to kill him. He knew Bowie was gay. She had told him. Bowie had told him. But he refused to accept that his own son would not emulate him in every way, including who he took to bed with him.

Surprisingly Bowie let it go. He didn't challenge his father, or argue with him, or even make some snide remark. He was all business. Dani knew this was the only way Bowie could handle the situation without getting emotional.

Dani jumped in to redirect the conversation. "How's business, Aaron?"

"I'm tired," he said with a sigh. "It's getting to be too much. I want to retire, but with an expensive trophy wife, it's impossible."

"Well, if you didn't have the FBI investigating your businesses year round, it might not be so stressful." Dani couldn't resist the jab. It was payback for the insensitive comment he made to Bowie.

Aaron didn't respond. He just looked at Bowie, a mixture of confusion and disappointment in his eyes. The look was not lost on his son.

"I hear you're a private detective now, Bowie," he said flatly.

"Yes," Bowie said. "I get a rush going after the bad guys." His eyes were locked on to his father's. There was no mistaking his intent either.

Aaron couldn't hold the stare. He turned his attention back to Dani. "You must be very proud."

"I am," Dani said.

The servants fluttered around, offering a tray of sweets, a

cocktail, whatever Aaron's guests desired. Dani and Bowie got tired of politely declining and resorted to just shaking their heads when the next wave came around.

Dani finally got down to business explaining to Aaron about what happened to Bowie in Mexico. He sat there listening, taking it all in before he spoke up.

"I heard there had been an attempted hit on a local private eye. I had no idea it was you, Bowie."

Bowie nodded, thinking about his father hearing the news, but not bothering to pick up the phone to call and see if he was all right.

Dani knew she didn't need Freud to come up with the reason Bowie became a detective. His mission in life seemed to be to try and make up for the sins of his father.

"We were hoping if you heard about it you might have some information for us, anything that might help us find out who ordered it or who tried to carry it out," Dani said.

Aaron thought for a moment. He wanted to help them but he was not about to compromise any of his own illegal operations to do so.

"I don't know who ordered it; I can tell you that much," Aaron said as he popped a chocolate-covered cherry in his mouth from a silver tray that had just been set down next to him. "But I may have a line on who helped carry it out."

Dani leaned forward. "Who?"

"Kid by the name of Doobie Slater," Aaron said.

"Are you kidding? He's a stoner," Bowie said. "He's not capable of driving a car let alone taking a potshot at me."

"Who's Doobie Slater?" Dani asked.

"He's this eccentric surfer dude, hangs out at the beach all day, sells bongs on the Internet, a younger version of Tommy Chong without the washed-up movie career," Bowie said, almost laughing.

"I'm just telling you what my ears on the street heard," Aaron said. "You can believe it or not. But my sources tell me he was somehow connected."

That was all Dani needed to her hear. They had a name. She was on her feet and more than ready to catch the charter boat back to the mainland.

Aaron jumped up and grabbed her hand before she got away. "Dani, I was hoping you'd stay the afternoon. It's been so long. Doobie isn't going anywhere. You two will have plenty of time to reel him in."

Dani turned to her former lover and offered him a mega-watt smile. "I really would love to, Aaron, but we have to go. Bowie has a hot date tonight. A pro football player. Plays for the Dolphins. Don't you have part ownership in that team?"

Bowie couldn't help but giggle. He decided to play along with his mother. "Yeah. A real hottie."

"Which player?" Aaron said with a stunned look on his face.

"Now it wouldn't be fair if we told you, Aaron," Dani said. "There's a little thing called job security. But the next time you pay a surprise visit to the locker room, I'm sure you'll be able to guess. The gays tend to stick out, right, Bowie?"

"Oh yeah, just look for the guy in the shower with the pink triangle tattoo."

And with that, mother and son walked out.

Aaron Lassiter watched them go and Dani knew that he was silently ticking off all the names of the Dolphins players in his head asking himself that age-old question, "Is he gay?"

CHAPTER 22

Jeb had a few days off before his next LA-to-Hong Kong flight, so he decided to make the most of it and take his wife out for a nice dinner. Eat, an upscale restaurant in Hollywood at the corner of Sunset and Gower, seemed like a nice choice. It had a lovely outdoor patio and the food, pricey California cuisine, was light and tasty.

Claire jumped at the chance for a night out. After all that had been happening over the last few weeks—her son's aborted wedding and physical assault, the uneasy reunion with Dani and Tess, and the last-minute trip to Las Vegas with Smack where she had to drudge up a lot of memories and go back undercover—the idea of some steak and red wine with her husband sounded absolutely heavenly.

Eat was big with the entertainment industry, having gone through many incarnations over the years with various owners, but it was a staple with the Hollywood crowd, especially since it was situated right next to a production facility, the Sunset-Gower studios, where many television shows were filmed. When you stepped out to retrieve your car from the valet, the majestic, iconic Hollywood sign was just off in the distance to your right.

Claire and Jeb were seated on the patio and offered menus by the perky wannabe-actress hostess. Claire smiled as the hostess lingered a bit too long, trying to figure out if either she or Jeb were producers or studio executives who might be instrumental in helping her career get off the ground. When Jeb mentioned to Claire that the pilot's union at his airline was about to enter contract negotiation talks, the pretty hostess was off like a shot to seat someone more important.

Claire perused the menu, and of course she went to the desserts first. She was always about having something to look forward to. There was a chocolate mousse that looked delectable. Then she scanned the entrees, settling on a tri-tip sirloin special that caught her eye.

Jeb was going over the wine list when Claire saw a man and woman being led to the patio. Sonny Anzilotti. Here at the same restaurant. Claire swallowed hard. This was not good. She had just seen Sonny in Vegas a couple of days ago. And now he was back in town, playing the dutiful husband to his aging, yet well-preserved wife.

They were seated at a table directly facing Claire and Jeb. Claire quickly raised her menu up to hide her face. The last thing she needed was Sonny recognizing her. What were her options? She could ask Jeb if they could move, but that would only raise questions, and the commotion of signaling the hostess and asking for another table might draw Sonny's attention. She couldn't very well keep the menu up in front of her face all night. She would have to order her dinner some time and then it would be a tug of war with the waiter who would inevitably try to take her menu away. She had to think fast. She and Jeb had both been looking forward to this meal out all day, and she was about to ruin it. She felt terrible. But the risk of staying and being spotted was too great.

Sonny was ordering a drink from a passing waiter while his wife chatted on her cell phone. Claire had seen pictures of the woman in the *Los Angeles Times*. She was featured in the calendar section almost on a weekly basis since she was one of a handful of women in the movie industry with real power. She appeared smaller than Claire had thought, very delicate and almost fragile. She looked fantastic in her Donna Karan power suit and her hair was immaculate. But now was not the time to admire the woman. She had to get out of there.

"Jeb, I'm not feeling well."

Jeb had put down the wine list and was now on to his menu. He looked up surprised. "What is it?"

"I'm nauseated," Claire said.

"That's awfully sudden," Jeb said, with concern in his voice but looking a bit confused. His wife never got sick.

"Would you mind if we just went home. I'm so sorry," Claire said.

Sonny's wife was still talking on the phone. Probably negotiating to get Denzel or Russell in her next movie. Sonny had nothing better to do than glance around the restaurant to see who was there. Claire turned to her right and raised her linen napkin in an awkward, obvious effort to conceal herself.

"Honey, what is it?" Jeb said.

"Nothing, let's just go. Do you mind?"

"No. Not at all," he said as he stood up and went over to put a comforting arm around his wife, who still had the napkin up to her face. A few diners looked at them curiously, but Sonny was still oblivious.

Jeb took the napkin from Claire and tossed it on the table. The gesture surprised Claire, but she figured he didn't want to walk off with it since they hadn't ordered anything and weren't leaving any money.

Jeb escorted Claire toward the exit, but the problem was they had to pass right by Sonny Anzilotti's table. Claire kept her head down, feigning another wave of nausea, hoping she would glide by without Sonny even noticing. No such luck. Just as they passed, his eyes fell on her, and Claire swore there was a hint of recognition. She could feel him spinning around in his chair and staring at the back of her as Jeb led her outside. Jeb stopped long enough to explain to the hostess that they were leaving and would not be having dinner. Claire used the opportunity to glance back and at that moment she made direct eye contact with Sonny, whose eyes were fixed right on her. She quickly looked away and rushed out the door ahead of Jeb.

The minute they were outside her heart sank. She realized they would have to wait for the valet to bring around the car. Jeb handed the ticket to a small Mexican man in a white shirt, black slacks and a green vest, who took off running down the street to retrieve Jeb's car. Jeb stroked Claire's back gently, trying to comfort his wife, and it made her feel just awful. He was so loving and so protective and right now she was lying to him. What happened to her rule of never lying to Jeb? She was now making a habit of it.

"It is you," a voice said from behind them. "I knew it."

Claire and Jeb turned around to face Sonny. Claire didn't know what to say or how to handle this without blowing it. She just offered Sonny a confused look, hoping he might have had a few cocktails already and she could convince him she was not who he thought she was.

"Where's your husband?" Sonny said, eyeing Jeb.

"I am her husband," Jeb said, too quickly for Claire to say anything.

"Really? You don't look anything like the husband I met in Las Vegas the other night."

Jeb turned to Claire. "What is he talking about?"

"I haven't the foggiest idea. He's obviously confused me with someone else," Claire said.

"No, it's you. I'm sure of it," Sonny said, stone-cold sober. "What happened to your Texas twang?"

Just then, the valet pulled up with Jeb's car. But there was no quick getaway from Sonny, especially since Jeb wanted to clear this miscommunication up right now.

"Look, buddy, I don't know who you are or what you want, but you've obviously made a mistake," Jeb said.

"No, I don't think so," Sonny said with a smile. "If this is your wife, ask her where she was two nights ago."

Jeb looked at Claire, hoping she would deny this man's crazy story about her being in Las Vegas. But Claire hesitated just a moment too long, and suddenly it became clear to her husband that the paunchy, bleary-eyed former athlete in front of him was telling the truth.

"And what about that shit-for-brains husband of yours who caused a scene right in front of me so I would come to your rescue? What's this all about, lady? Why were you scamming me?" Sonny demanded to know.

Claire was at a loss for words. Anything she said would either confirm Sonny's accusations or piss off her husband big time.

"Claire, say something," Jeb said.

Sonny nearly gasped. The name Claire had set a bell off in his head. "Claire. I knew a Claire once. And a Dani. And a Tess."

Jeb froze. It was all suddenly crystal clear.

"Of course! I didn't recognize you! I haven't seen you since you attacked me in my apartment back in the eighties! What do you want from me? Why are you still hounding me?"

Claire didn't answer. She just got into the car and shut the door before the valet had the chance to do it for her.

Sonny was now yelling at Jeb. "Tell that bitch to stay away from me! I've done my time! She's got no right to keep harassing me! Next time I'll call the cops and have her ass tossed in jail for stalking!"

Jeb shoved Sonny aside and walked around the car to the driver's side. He tipped the valet a few dollars, got in and sped off with Sonny screaming obscenities at Claire.

Jeb drove up to Franklin Avenue and hung a left, heading for the Hollywood Freeway North and home to Sherman Oaks. He gripped the wheel tightly, his knuckles white. Finally, he turned to his wife.

"Feeling better?"

Claire didn't respond. She didn't have to. There was going to be a fight and she wasn't in any position to defend herself. It wasn't so much she was back out playing with the girls. It was more about the lie. And there was no wiggling out of that one.

They drove the rest of the twenty minutes home in utter silence.

CHAPTER 23

Dani arrived in the predawn hours of a misty morning on the soft white sands of Miami Beach, near the all-night clubs and busy restaurants of South Beach. Only now, just after 5 AM, the area was deserted except for Dani, whose arms formed goose bumps from the cutting, chilly wind. She knew if she had any chance of talking to Doobie Slater, now would be the time as the surfers arrived for their daily ritual of riding the waves. Bowie had made some calls to a few of his local contacts to find out where Slater and his pals hung out, and was able to pinpoint this stretch of beach and a rough time of when he usually showed up.

Unfortunately, Bowie got a high-paying client anxious to find out who in his employ was embezzling money, a case that just might be that elusive watershed assignment that would put his new business on the map. The client wanted Bowie to meet him for breakfast, so that left Dani on her own to search out Slater.

Dani hugged herself to keep warm. She didn't think to wear a sweater. Her thin aquamarine wraparound skirt blew in the wind, flapping so hard she was afraid it might fly away. Dani sipped a steaming Starbucks hazelnut latte and sat down in the sand to wait.

A half hour later a beat-up yellow Jeep Cherokee squealed into the parking lot adjacent to the beach. Three fluorescent surfboards stuck out of the back. A trio of young guys, around mid-twenties, piled out and began lifting the boards out of the vehicle. Two were roughly six feet, bulky, with buzz cuts. They looked like brothers. The third, a small, wiry guy with long jet-black hair pulled back in a ponytail, a green tank top hanging on his bony frame, and giant Pacific Sunwear orange shorts that he nearly drowned in, grabbed the candy-apple red surfboard and jogged ahead of his buddies down the beach.

Dani instantly recognized him as Doobie Slater. Bowie had a contact fax a photo of him to the houseboat, so Dani was able to get a look at him ahead of time. She quickly stood up and intercepted him.

"Doobie?"

He looked at her with half closed eyes, and with a slow, southern drawl, said, "Who wants to know?"

"I'm Dani Mendez, a private investigator," she said, getting a slight charge out of identifying herself as a detective after all these years.

Slater stiffened a bit, but maintained his lackadaisical demeanor. "Well, good for you." He started walking away, but Dani grabbed the back end of his surfboard, jolting him and nearly causing him to lose his balance.

"Let go of my board, bitch," he said, trying to muster up as much menace as he could.

Dani wanted to laugh. He wasn't too convincing as a thug, which made her second guess Aaron's information.

"I will once you tell me who you work for," she said evenly.

He yanked the board away from her and glared at her. "I don't know what the hell you're talking about. I don't work for nobody. Just the surf gods, baby."

By now Slater's two buddies had noticed Dani talking to their friend. They were ambling over in her direction. If they got involved, the discussion was over. Dani had to work fast. She had already decided she wouldn't try to con Slater into talking. A more direct approach was required.

"I'm going to ask you once. Did Benito Coronel hire you to shoot a private detective named Bowie Lassiter down in Mexico?"

Dani studied his reaction. There was a slight flinch as his mind raced on how to respond to this, if at all. She knew at that moment he was somehow mixed up in the plot against the Dolls.

"You're one crazy old bitch," he said.

Suddenly Slater swung his board around like a baseball bat. Dani acted fast, diving to the sand before she could get slammed in the head. She heard Slater chuckle as she rolled over and sat up. A spray of sand hit her in the face. Despite his diminutive size, Doobie towered over her, and angrily pointed a thin bony finger at her.

"I'm warning you, stay out of my business."

"I'm not going anywhere until you talk to me," Dani said defiantly. She'd dealt with plenty of young punks. She wasn't going to be intimidated by this one.

Doobie raised his board over his head like he was going to slam it down hard on her. Dani locked eyes with him, daring him. He was frustrated she wasn't afraid of him and wasn't backing down.

"Look, talking out of school could get me killed. So the last thing I'm going to do is run my mouth off to one of the Golden Girls."

He bounded off down the beach toward the water. His two buddies hustled to join him. All three dropped their surfboards, climbed on, and began paddling out to sea.

Dani scrambled to her feet and sighed. She knew what she was going to have to do, and she hated it. She had to go out there in the water and keep badgering him until he told her something useful. She hadn't surfed since she was in her early twenties. Her first time out, someone saw a tiger shark swim past just a few feet away from her and that was it. She lost interest in the sport completely. She saw a small surf shop with boards to rent a hundred yards down the beach that was just opening up for the early morning rush.

Dani jogged over and tossed a wad of bills down on the wooden counter. The sleepy-eyed attendant counted out the money, and then satisfied, pointed to a bright pink board. Talk about standing out. Dani realized she hadn't brought a bathing suit. Underneath her wrap was some expensive silk panties. And she didn't have a bra on so swimming in her white Calvin Klein top wasn't an option. The last thing she wanted was to start an impromptu wet T-shirt contest. She asked the attendant if he sold ladies swimsuits and he gestured over to a corner where a rack held colorful swimwear barely staying attached to their hangers in the gusty wind.

Dani quickly perused the selection. Her heart sank. There was not a one-piece in the bunch. All bikinis. This was a disaster. She was north of fifty. Her bikini days were over in her mind. The idea of parading around in one nauseated her. But if she didn't buck up and swim out to confront Slater again, the whole morning would be a bust. Of all days for Bowie to have to meet a client. She could have sent him out there. The attendant watched her, an amused look on his face. He knew she was debating the idea of actually buying one.

And they were all so tiny. They covered her private parts and that was just about it. Dani cursed silently as she searched through the rack for the least revealing one she could find. She settled on a bright multicolored Blue Sky number. At least it wasn't a thong, but it was still microscopic, and would show off her many physical imperfections that had come with age. As she paid the attendant, she thought how nice it would look on one of America's Top Models, but a middle-aged woman? Oh, God. Sometimes her devotion to solving a case frightened her. She was always up for taking risks. She'd go up against an armed robber or serial rapist any day. But wearing a bikini? Not for the faint of heart.

The attendant allowed her to change in the back, mostly because he wanted to see her come out. This would certainly give him something to laugh about all day. Dani balled up her wraparound skirt and T-shirt and stuffed them in her bag. When she emerged she was surprised when the attendant didn't crack a joke or bust up in hysterics. He was simply staring her up and down. Probably from shock, she thought. But then he whistled. This poor kid probably had cataracts or something.

Dani grabbed the bright pink board that clashed hopelessly with her loud bikini and ran down to the surf. The sun was coming up, and she easily spotted Slater and his pals already catching their first wave. She tossed her board down, climbed on, and began paddling furiously out to join them.

The two bulky brothers wiped out, but Slater managed to ride the wave in before jumping off and swimming back out, dragging his board with a rope slung over his left shoulder. He didn't see Dani at first so she was able to come up behind him without him trying to swim away from her.

The brothers saw her first. They exchanged impressed looks, and yelled a few catcalls. Dani looked behind her to see if Heidi Klum was doing the breast stroke nearby before realizing the muscle twins were actually pointing at her. What do you know? She wasn't completely humiliated as she expected to be. One of the brothers cupped his hands around his mouth and called out, "Hot!"

Dani didn't even try to suppress a smile. She was flattered and enormously relieved. But she was also focused on business. Slater spun his head around to see what his friends were reacting to and a frown instantly appeared on his face at the sight of Dani.

"Oh Christ," he spit out, and splashed water at her with the open palm of his hand, as if that might deter her.

"Talk to me, Doobie," Dani said.

Doobie couldn't help but ogle her near-naked body like his two surfing buddies. "I told you, lady. I want to stay alive."

"Do you want to stay out of prison? I've done some research on you and it turns out there are a few warrants out for your arrest. Drug trafficking for one."

"Give me a break. I sold pot to a few friends. No big deal."

"Well, what about attempted murder?"

"I didn't try to kill nobody."

"Were you in Mexico in the last few weeks?"

"Nope."

"I don't believe you."

"I've been here every morning with my two buddies over there. Go ahead and ask them."

"I'm sure they're both very reliable witnesses. Have you ever heard of Bowie Lassiter?"

"Who?"

"Benito Coronel?"

"Lady, are you on crack? I said I'm not talking to you. Hell, I've never even been to Mexico City."

"I just said Mexico. I didn't say Mexico City. It *was* you who took a shot at my son."

"No!"

"You killed an innocent man, the driver of a boat, who just happened to be in the line of fire, did you know that?"

"I didn't shoot nobody!"

"Then you know who did. How much did you get paid?"

"I'm done with you."

Doobie tried to paddle away from Dani but she followed him. A giant wave reared up behind them and Doobie hopped up on his board and rode it in to shore, mostly as an effort to put some distance between himself and Dani. Dani wasn't having any of it. She stayed flat on her board, swimming with the wave, before gripping the sides of her board, standing up, her arms out, and shakily surfing after Doobie before the wave consumed her. Just before she went under, she heard a crack as if a board split in half. It surprised her enough that she opened her mouth and took in some salt water, and when she swam to the surface she was coughing and trying to catch her breath.

She swam toward shore until she was able to touch her feet on the sand, and proceeded to wade the rest of the way in, dragging her pink surfboard by a tenuous piece of rope.

That's when she spotted Doobie Slater lying facedown in the sand, the remnants of the crashing waves rushing over his limp body. Dani dropped the rope and splashed over to him, kneeling down and turning his body over to examine him. His eyes were lifeless, staring at her in a mixture of confusion and shock, the last reaction he would ever have. There was a dark stain that was still spreading along the chest of his green tank top.

Dani rolled up the shirt and saw a black hole in the middle of his chest, right through the heart. Someone had shot him. The crack she had heard before going under had been from a gun.

Dani searched up and down the beach and saw a figure, a man, running away from the scene. He was too far away to even attempt to chase after him. It would be a wasted effort. And the sun was blinding her so she couldn't make out any distinctive clothing or features. In fact, she wasn't even one hundred per-cent sure it was a man.

Doobie Slater had been right about one thing. Talking could get him killed. And Dani knew they must be on the right track now if someone was willing to commit murder to keep secrets concealed. And despite the fact he might have taken a potshot at her son, she felt terrible that she may have been the reason he was now dead.

CHAPTER 24

W hen Tess's private Lear jet landed at the airport in Puerto Vallarta, Mexico, she immediately put in a call to Paulo, who was staying back at her suite at the Beverly Wilshire in Los Angeles. Paulo was angry that she did not allow him to accompany her on this last-minute side trip to reunite with Ronaldo Soares, Benito Coronel's chief bodyguard with whom she had once had a brief, but intense, affair in order to bring down his boss. She had basically used him to secure an invitation to Coronel's Sunday afternoon party at his Topanga Canyon estate and she was responsible for his ultimate arrest and conviction, along with most of the drug czar's stable of ragtag mercenaries. Tess could only imagine the amount of hate he must have in his heart for the Dolls, especially for her since she had been the one who played with his feelings and humiliated him with her betrayal.

He was the one who brought Tess to the party. It was because of her Coronel's whole operation had gone up in smoke. And one day Coronel could come looking for him for some kind of payback, so he'd gotten the hell out of Dodge.

Tess had mixed feelings about paying him a visit after all these years. Smack had done some digging and discovered Ronaldo

149

had fled to Mexico after being paroled, and had opened up a bar on the beach. He had been keeping a low profile for the past five years and probably wanted to keep it that way. But Tess knew she was the one who had to find out for sure, like she had with Akito Tanaka in Santa Barbara, if he was the one carrying out some elaborate revenge plot or if he was still working for Coronel and following orders.

Tess changed into a yellow sundress, similar to the one she'd been wearing all those years ago on that fateful day when the Dolls crashed Coronel's party, before she deplaned and climbed into the waiting limousine that would take her to town.

During the short fifteen-minute ride from the airport, Tess couldn't help but smile when she thought of Paulo. He was so young, strong, and pigheaded. He had thrown a fit when she refused to allow him to come with her, and he was still pouty when she left the suite for LAX. He wanted to be with her, to protect her in case anything went wrong, like he had in Santa Barbara with Akito Tanaka. Or at least he thought he had protected her. Tess was perfectly capable of taking care of herself. Tess knew if she showed up at Ronaldo's bar on Paulo's arm, she would never be able to talk straight with him. He would be too self-conscious and nervous with a musclebound, and jealousy prone, Brazilian staring him down.

When the limo rolled to a stop in front of a dank, dingy, crumbling old building a few blocks from the beach, Tess at first assumed the driver was lost. But her driver was a local, and knew exactly which bar she meant. This had to be the place. It was a dump and there wasn't even a sign out front. Tess told the driver to wait. She wasn't going to be long. And then she got out and pushed open the faded green wooden door with chipped paint and walked inside.

There was no one inside. Not even someone tending the bar.

"Hello?" Tess looked around. There were just a few tables and a row of six bar stools. This business venture wasn't exactly going to make Ronaldo a rich man. But maybe the bar was just to keep him busy, to give him something to do so he could try to forget the many years he spent behind bars.

Tess wandered over to the serving station. At least the bar was fully stocked. There was a window off to the side where if you stretched your neck hard enough you could see the glistening ocean where the tourists flocked for some sun. Tess slid up onto one of the stools, deciding to wait. A few minutes went by before she heard the door behind her open and a deep familiar voice penetrate the air.

"Is that your limo parked outside?"

Tess didn't turn around but, rather, sat facing the window. She knew it was Ronaldo. "Yes."

"It's blocking the street. Nobody can get by. You're going to have to tell the driver to move."

Tess swung around on the stool so Ronaldo could get a good look at her. "Why? Are you expecting a rush of customers soon?"

Ronaldo, his mouth agape, was at a loss for words. He recognized Tess immediately, and for a split second Tess thought she had given the poor man a heart attack because he clutched his chest and tried to talk, but no words came out.

Tess was struck by his appearance. His six-foot-two massive physique still projected strength, but his face was entirely different. His eyes were watery, and his skin ravaged by pockmarks and deep wrinkles. She could only guess alcohol had sped up the aging process considerably. In fact, at first she wasn't even sure it was him until she saw the identifiable scar down the side of his right cheek.

"What are you doing here?" Ronaldo finally managed to get out, his hands shaking. Tess couldn't decide whether it was from nervousness or too much time had passed since his last drink.

"I came to see you," Tess said as she got off the stool and walked over with her hand out to shake.

He didn't take it. He just stared at her as if this were some kind of dream that he would wake up from at any moment.

"Why?"

"I just want to make sure you've been a good boy since you got out of prison," Tess said, smiling.

She half expected him to slap her across the face, but he just stood there, his mind reliving the past. Her sudden appearance was almost too much for him.

"I don't understand . . ."

"Someone's coming after us and we want to know who," Tess said, not wanting to waste time playing games with the man.

"And you think I'm the one?"

"No, not necessarily, but I just wanted to be sure."

"You want a shot of tequila?"

"Like old times? Sure."

Ronaldo's hands were still shaking as he crossed behind the bar, salted two shot glasses and poured from a bottle of Jose Cuervo. He put one down in front of Tess and kept the other in his meaty fist. Tess raised her glass and downed it in one gulp before slamming the shot glass down on the bar. Ronaldo quickly followed suit, never taking his eyes off her. But his hands momentarily stopped shaking.

"I got out a while ago," Ronaldo said. "If I wanted to come after you for revenge I would have done it then."

"Makes sense," Tess said. Ronaldo went to pour her another shot, but she put her hand over the glass and politely shook her head.

"I've been trying very hard to put the past behind me and just live my life. That's why I came home to Mexico. I got family here, it's quiet, and I can make a little money with The Blue Parrot."

"What's The Blue Parrot?"

"You're sitting in it. That's the name of my bar."

"You should think about getting yourself a sign out front—then maybe people might actually come inside."

Ronaldo gave her a half smile. "I have a small but loyal clientele."

"I'm sure you've heard your old boss has been released from prison?"

"Yeah," he said as he poured himself another shot of Jose Cuervo. "We get CNN down here."

"Have you been in contact with him?"

Ronaldo chuckled. "Oh sure, we e-mail each other all the time. We'll be best friends forever."

"So that's a 'no'."

"After I brought you to that party, he wanted nothing to do with me. I wrote to him from prison during his trial, begging for his forgiveness, hoping he wouldn't have me killed, but he never answered. I was already dead to him. And can you blame him for feeling that way? I got conned by you, and it cost him his whole empire."

"We would have gotten him another way if it hadn't been through you. It was just a matter of time."

"He doesn't see it that way. I fucked up big time."

"But now you're trying to live on the straight and narrow."

"If you call saturating the livers of a few locals with tequila the straight and narrow then, yes, I'm doing things differently these days."

Tess looked around at the run-down, sad little establishment. "You could make a lot more money if you went back to being a bodyguard, live a better life."

"Like I said, I'm done with all that. Nobody would hire me anyway. Besides, my dad died a couple of months ago and left me a little money. I won't be partying with Lindsay Lohan anytime soon, but it's enough for me to get by."

"Well, I'm happy for you, Ronaldo. I'm glad you've found some peace," Tess said, and she meant it. "What about Coronel? Do you think he's capable of putting his past behind him now that he's out?"

"Are you kidding? Never. If someone's out to get you, then the first person you should be visiting is him. He will never ever forget what you did to him."

Tess knew he was right. It was becoming more and more clear that Benito Coronel and whoever was currently working for him were the ones they needed to focus on and fast before they tried something else.

Tess turned to go, but Ronaldo reached out with his red, splotchy hand and took hold of her wrist, not roughly but gently.

"I got a room in the back. We always did have a spark, huh, Tess?"

Tess wasn't angry or scared. She felt bad for him. He had fallen so far, become so pathetic. And just like Akito Tanaka, she knew she could take him out if he got too fresh with her. Besides, her driver outside was packing a gun and Ronaldo knew she could call him in at any moment.

Tess fought the urge to verbally cut him down to size, make some kind of insulting remark about his manhood, but she didn't have the heart. He was just a lonely and sad man who was trying to scrape together a hint of what he once was.

"Sorry, Ronaldo, but I'm seeing someone," Tess said, casually removing her wrist from his grasp and turning to go. She was halfway to the door before she turned around to face him one last time.

"Since you recently came into a little money you might want to use some of it to fix this dive up."

Ronaldo broke out into a smile. "I'll think about it. But why mess with success?"

Despite the toll of liquor on his face, he still had a winning smile and Tess caught a glimpse of the heartbreaker he used to be. And then she slipped out the door to her waiting limo.

CHAPTER 25

"What's this?" Jeb said picking up a brochure from the kitchen table as Claire loaded the breakfast plates into the dishwasher.

Claire froze. She didn't mean to leave the brochure out in plain view. "It's from a real estate company. There are some open houses today I thought I might check out."

Jeb cocked an eyebrow. "Really? Are we moving?"

"No. I mean not right away, but the boys are on their own, and once Zak is fully recovered he's going to be moving back into his apartment in Hollywood, and I thought it wouldn't hurt to look around and see what's out there. This is an awfully big house for the two of us. I just want to see some smaller homes that are out there and available."

Jeb eyed her suspiciously. "Great. I'll go with you."

Claire flinched and Jeb caught it.

"You don't want me to go?" he said.

"Of course I do. You just hate open houses and I don't want to hear you complaining all afternoon that you'd rather be on the golf course."

"I just figure I should at least see the house I'm going to be moving into, don't you agree?"

Claire nodded as she quickly poured some liquid detergent into the dishwasher, closed the door, and turned the knob.

"Remember, Jeb, this is just a preliminary search and I'm basically having some fun today. So promise me you'll be good and just let me look."

"I can be ready in five minutes," Jeb said as he bounded up the stairs. Claire watched him go. She was so certain he had a golf date with his buddies today. Maybe he did, but didn't trust her. Especially not after the run-in with Sonny Anzilotti at Eat Restaurant. Maybe he thought she was up to her old tricks and not being completely truthful with him. Once again he was dead on. They hadn't spoken about what had happened at the restaurant the night before. Claire hoped Jeb had decided to let it go. He knew why she was up to her old tricks after all these years. She would never be doing it if the lives of her kids weren't on the line. She thought he might want to talk about it some more, but Jeb wasn't a talk-it-out kind of guy. And in this one instance, Claire was grateful for that. But when he figured out what she was really up to today, that might change. And it worried her.

Jeb was in the car in four minutes, wearing a nice navy blue polo shirt and tan khaki pants. Claire got in the passenger's side and told him the first address on her list. He didn't press her on the drive over to Encino and a nice residential side street off Ventura Boulevard. He wanted to hang back and see how things played out. Claire knew it was only a matter of time before he caught on to what was happening, but this was important and she had to do it.

They pulled up to a sprawling single-story ranch-style house with a southwestern flavor.

Jeb's eyes went wide. "This is bigger than the house we have now!"

"It's beautiful. Let's just go inside and take a look."

"Why? We can't even afford it."

"Jeb, please, you promised to let me have fun."

Jeb turned off the car. "Okay, let's go."

They got out and strolled up the cement walk to the front door, passing a Sotheby's real estate sign wedged into the front lawn with a picture of an older woman, in her fifties, with big wavy brown hair and an electric smile. Underneath the photo was the name Abigail Foster along with a phone number and Web site.

Claire knocked on the door, and within seconds, it swung open and they were greeted by the same woman who was beaming on the sign.

"Abigail? I'm Claire Corley. We spoke earlier this morning."

"Yes, hello, Claire. Lovely to meet you. Please come in," she said waving her inside.

"This is my husband Jeb," Claire added as she stepped across the threshold into the foyer.

Jeb and Abigail shook hands and exchanged pleasantries before Abigail shut the door behind them and commenced with the tour.

"This is one of my favorite listings. It's a rambling four bedroom/two-bath contemporary with a grand open floor plan, vaulted ceilings with skylights, wood-type floors, wood-burning fireplace, central air and heat, kitchen with newer stainless steel appliances, breakfast bar and eat-in area. The backyard is a private oasis with a huge covered patio, above-ground therapeutic hot tub, and wait until you see the tropical landscaping with charming bridge-covered water pond," Abigail said as she led them through each room.

"We were looking for some place a little smaller now that our sons are out of the house, but this is just so beautiful," Claire said.

"This would be the perfect home to live in and grow old together," Abigail said.

Jeb fingered the brochure, looking for a price. He actually liked the place.

"I've visited your Web site many times. You always have the best listings," Claire said.

"Thank you," Abigail said as she showed off the expansive master bedroom suite.

"Have you been selling houses long?"

"Almost twenty years," Abigail said.

"Jeb, why don't you take a look outside," Claire said turning to her husband and flashing him an innocent smile. He instantly knew she wanted to get rid of him, but didn't know why. He decided to roll with it for now, and ambled out the sliding glass door that led to the bridge-covered water pond.

Claire did not want him knowing that Abigail Foster was Benito Coronel's wife. Claire knew that when she called the agent she had to introduce herself with her married name Corley, not Walker, which she might recognize from her husband's trial. Abigail herself was now going by her maiden name. She undoubtedly had to completely reinvent herself after her husband's conviction. Claire remembered that she was a former beauty queen, Miss New Mexico, or one of those southwestern states, but didn't make the top ten in the late seventies Miss America pageant. But she had won Benito Coronel's heart and lived the high life until the LA Dolls brought him down.

When Coronel was sentenced to prison, she lost everything. She managed to hold on to the Topanga Canyon property, because Benito was insistent, but it quickly fell into disrepair and she moved out, renting an apartment somewhere in the valley. After that, she seemed to disappear until she began popping up in real estate listings as Abigail Foster.

Claire was pretty sure Abigail had little or no contact with her ex-husband, whom she divorced in the early nineties while he was serving his sentence. But Dani felt it was worth one of them having a talk with her to see if she might provide some pertinent information.

Claire watched Jeb poking around out by the water pond and

shook her head. "I'm hoping to find a place that's big enough so we can escape each other. We tend to get on each other's nerves if we spend too much time together."

She was lying. If anything, she and Jeb were apart too much of the time. But she wanted to steer the conversation in a specific direction.

"I understand. I've lived alone for quite some time now, and have gotten used to it. I'm not sure I could ever go back to sharing space with a man."

"Are you a widow?"

"No. Divorced."

"I've seen you recently," Claire said, looking her up and down.

Abigail laughed. "I'm sure you have. My face is plastered all over the valley. I have forty listings at the moment."

"No, in the newspaper, and it wasn't the real estate section. Where was it?"

Abigail's big smile faded away and she cleared her throat. "I wouldn't know."

"It was just a few days ago. Was your ex-husband in the news for some reason?"

Abigail knew it was only a matter of time before the client would put it all together. She didn't want to lose a sale because she wasn't honest so she finally relented. "Yes. My ex-husband is rather well known."

Claire pretended a light bulb went off in her head. "Benito Coronel, yes, of course. That's where I've seen you. They had a picture of you next to the article about his release."

Abigail continued with the tour, leading Claire into the guest room suite as she talked. "One of the penalties for marrying a notorious criminal. You're associated with him for eternity even if you've closed that chapter of your life and started over. They keep dragging you back in, mentioning your name, showing your picture. At first I was mortified and afraid it would hurt my business. But ironically, more people come to me because of my connection to the whole Coronel business. They think it's glamorous, or something they can tell their friends over dinner. 'We just bought a house from the ex-wife of Benito Coronel.' "

"Have you spoken to him since he was released from prison?"

"God no, I want nothing to do with him. He cost me everything. After we divorced, I purposely lost all contact with him. I was afraid he was still carrying on with some of his illegal activities behind bars, and I wanted a clean slate, a fresh start. Frankly, I never want to see him again."

"I read that they cleared him of some murder charge. That must have been a relief. He was many things, but at least he didn't murder someone."

Abigail scoffed. "That was just one incident in a long line, I'm afraid. And it just happened to be the one they pinned their case on. Trust me, Benito is behind many untold crimes in the past that would keep him in prison for several lifetimes. I want no part of it."

Claire studied her. She was saying all the right things, especially for someone protective of her successful real estate business. She was direct in her opinion of her ex-husband and convincing in her resolve to remain estranged. But there was one problem. Her eyes. At the mere mention of Benito Coronel's name her eyes seemed to melt just a bit, hardly perceptible, but Claire who knew how to read people, could tell there was real pent up emotion behind her perky saleslady persona. And it wasn't anger. It was love.

Claire would bet she still had feelings for her ex-husband in spite of her adamant denials. Abigail was working too hard to distance herself from Coronel. She knew women who did that. Put up a good front but then call him the first chance she got. Abigail had built up a thriving business on her own, without any help from her ex-husband, but the game had changed. He was a free man, and possibly Abigail's ticket out of the workforce and back into the good life if he was still secretly running a profitable enterprise as they all suspected.

"So you were once married to Benito Coronel?" Jeb said, surprising both women. He had walked back in from outside and the two women had been so engaged in conversation neither one of them had noticed.

Claire looked at her husband. He wasn't happy. And she didn't blame him.

"Yes, but enough about that," Abigail said, trying her best to move on. "Wait until you see the dining room."

Abigail shot down the hall, her heels clicking on the hardwood floors.

Claire took Jeb's hand. "I know you're mad, and I'm sorry I wasn't up front with you, but I think she's still in contact with him. It's just a feeling I have . . ."

"I don't want to hear it," Jeb said, yanking his hand away and following after Abigail. Claire was left standing alone in the guest room suite. Her husband was pissed off again and it was all her fault.

CHAPTER 26

It was an excruciatingly long ride back to Sherman Oaks, and Claire initially made every effort to pile on the apologies, but Jeb was having none of it. He was steaming, letting the anger grow inside of him. She hated the way he dealt with his emotions sometimes. They had to talk this out, or he might have a heart attack.

"Jeb, you of all people should understand why I'm doing this."

"I know, I know, you're worried about Zak and Evan and some creep from your past exacting his revenge. I get it, okay? It's a noble cause but that doesn't mean I should just keep my mouth shut and hope you don't get killed in the process. I understand you protecting the boys, but how can I protect you?"

"I've got a lot of experience and I'm very careful . . ."

"This is a side of you I don't even know. You barely talked about it when we met. It's like I'm suddenly living with someone I don't even know."

"This is only temporary, Jeb. Believe me."

"Why should I believe anything you say, Claire? You've been lying to me nonstop lately."

He had a point. And Claire didn't have an answer.

"Tell me something. And be honest. Deep down, do you enjoy this? Are you secretly happy to be back doing this? Does it give you some kind of rush?"

Claire hesitated because to some degree it did, but she didn't want Jeb for one moment to believe he might lose her to the excitement she had been experiencing again since her reunion with Dani and Tess.

"No. Not exactly," she said.

"There you go lying to me again."

"Jeb, stop it."

He pulled the car into the driveway and jumped out.

"Jeb, don't be like that," Claire said as she got out and followed him.

Jeb stopped suddenly as they both heard shouting coming from inside the house. Claire and Jeb exchanged concerned looks, and then hurried up the stone-lined walk toward the front door.

Claire entered first, rushing through the foyer into the living room, just in time to see Evan give his brother Zak a powerful shove. Zak dropped his crutches, and fell backward, landing on the couch. Evan reared back with his fist, his face flushed with anger. Zak, still weak from his injuries, threw his hands up in front of his face in an attempt to protect himself.

"Evan, stop!" Claire cried, shooting across the room and grabbing his arm. "What the hell are you doing?"

"You wouldn't believe what that bastard just did," Evan spat out, his furious eyes still boring into his older brother.

"I don't care. You have an unfair advantage. Zak's hurt," Claire said as she pulled her son's fist down with all her might.

Jeb was now in the room, eyeing both boys, a puzzled look on his face.

"Oh, yeah, poor hurt Zak. He's not strong enough to defend himself. Well, he sure as shit was strong enough to make a pass at *her*."

Evan pointed at Bianca, who hovered in the corner of the room, her arms wrapped around herself, wishing she was anywhere else but here.

Claire hadn't even noticed her when she came into the room with all the excitement. She couldn't help but think Tess's beautiful young daughter was responsible for her sons brawling in the house. She didn't realize she was glaring at the poor girl until Bianca spoke up in a quiet, tiny voice. "I'm sorry, Mrs. Corley. I'm so, so sorry."

Jeb picked up the crutches off the floor and then crossed to the couch. He helped Zak stand up. "Okay, would one of you mind telling us what happened?"

Evan shook his mother's hand away, and stalked to the other side of the room, like a boxer returning to his corner to regroup. "Bianca and I had lunch and she suggested we stop by to see how Zak was doing. I just went upstairs to pick up some books I left here the other day, and when I came back down he had his paws all over her."

Zak let out a sigh.

Jeb whipped around and gave him a hard look. "You got something to say?"

"He's so dramatic. He always has to make such a big deal out of everything. I got a little dizzy and lost my balance. Bianca was just helping me," Zak said with a slight smile which infuriated his brother.

"Look at him. He's smiling!" Evan screamed. "He's a fucking liar!"

"All right, now calm down, both of you," Claire said. "Evan, I think you might be blowing this out of proportion."

"No! He always does this! I meet someone nice, and he has to move in on her, stake some kind of claim, show me that he's the stud of the family! I hate it! I hate him!"

Zak shook his head and then turned to Bianca. "I'm sorry about all this, Bianca. The last thing you probably wanted to see today was a ridiculous family feud."

It stung Claire that Zak was more concerned about Bianca than anybody else in the room. It reminded her of Tess, and how people, men especially, always were focused on her comfort and well being at the cost of everybody else.

A cell phone chirped, and Bianca reached into her clutch purse, pulled her phone out and answered it. "Mom?"

Evan turned his back on everyone in the room. Claire thought he might be crying and was too embarrassed to show it. She walked over and gently put a hand on his back, but he shrugged it off.

Bianca shut her phone and slipped it back in her purse. "My mother is back from Mexico. She's a few blocks away. I should go wait for her outside."

Bianca quickly bowed out of the bitter scene before either Evan or Zak could react or even say good-bye. Claire watched her go, relieved. Perhaps now they would be able to settle the situation.

"Okay, do you think we can be a little rational now that she's gone and you don't have to show her how manly you both are?" Claire said.

"That's Evan's whole problem," Zak said. "He's just afraid he's not man enough!"

Evan sprung across the room and plowed into his brother before either Claire or Jeb knew what was happening. Evan began pounding at his brother's face with his fists. Jeb jumped in between them, hauling Evan away by grabbing a fistful of his shirt collar. But Zak, fed up with his brother's angry attacks, bunched his hand up into a fist and took a swing with all his strength. But his aim was off and the blow landed smack in his father's right eye.

Jeb stumbled back and both boys immediately stopped fighting.

"Christ, Dad, are you all right? I didn't mean to . . ." Zak said, hobbling over to his father and putting his arm around him.

Claire marched over to Evan and got right up in his face. "I want you to leave right now, and don't come back until you've cooled off."

Evan didn't have to be told twice. He stalked out the front door, slamming it behind him.

Claire picked up the crutches and shoved them at Zak. "And you keep your mouth shut. I've heard enough out of you."

She positioned herself under Jeb's arm and led him into the kitchen where she sat him down at the table and then opened the refrigerator and pulled out a big package wrapped in white paper. She tore it open revealing a big juicy steak and then slapped it over her husband's wounded eye.

"I'll just have to come up with something else for dinner," Claire said, rubbing Jeb's shoulders as he held the steak over his eye.

"Don't think all this kindness is getting you off the hook for earlier," Jeb said. At first she thought he was joking, but then realized he was not.

Claire's head was spinning from this day. Her nerves were frayed. And she was at the breaking point. She couldn't take much more. That's when she heard a clicking sound outside and looked out the kitchen window to see Tess running across the cement toward the back of the house in her high heels.

Claire flung open the screen door and walked out to intercept her before she came inside.

"Claire, Bianca just told me what happened. Can I do anything to help?"

"Yes, you can turn around and get back in your limousine and get out of here."

"Bianca feels terrible. She feels somewhat responsible."

"Somewhat?"

RICK COPP

Tess gave her a curious look. She hadn't seen Claire this cold in quite a while and she knew where her mind was going with all this. "Bianca did not encourage this in any way, if that's what you think."

"How would you know? Were you there?"

"I know my daughter."

"And I know my sons. And I know you."

"What's that supposed to mean?"

"It means this, Tess. Back in the eighties, I let you go after men I cared about because we were a team and I wanted us to stay together. But that was then. This is now. And I have no intention of allowing your daughter to steal my sons."

"This is about Dan, isn't it?"

Dan Hunter. A name that Claire had long buried in the past.

"No, this is about you," Claire said. "You were always so good at shaking your ass and pitting men against each other. I used to think you just did for the assignment. But then I realized you liked it. You were doing it for kicks."

"That's not fair," Tess said, trying not to show how hurt she was.

"It's true. And it seems your daughter is taking her cues from you."

Tess was on the verge of tears now. She turned around and ran off, her heels clicking loudly on the pavement before slowly fading away. Claire turned and went back into the house to check on Jeb.

In the past, Dani always mediated the fights between Claire and Tess, and worked hard to relieve the tension and encourage reconciliation for the sake of the business or the assignment at hand. But Dani wasn't around today. And frankly Claire didn't care. She was finally able to tell Tess exactly what she thought without having to apologize for it.

CHAPTER 27

Dani wanted to run the red light, but Claire warned her about the electronic camera situated above the intersection that would surely snap a photograph of her breaking the law if she dared to try it. Twenty years ago there weren't any high-tech methods of nabbing aggressive drivers, and Dani got away with a lot more, especially on the case where she posed as a taxi driver to find out who was sabotaging the cars and hurting the drivers. But times had changed and she didn't feel like forking over a couple of hundred dollars just to ensure she didn't lose the Mazarati she and Claire were tailing.

"Don't worry," Claire said, donning some Armani sunglasses to block out the glare of the blinding midday scorching sun. "Traffic's moving at a crawl. We won't lose her."

Dani craned her neck to try and see past a Federal Express truck that had just changed lanes and was now directly in front of them. Dani tried pulling out into the left lane, which was moving a little faster, but no cars would let her. They kept bunching up close together making it impossible to merge.

"God, I don't miss LA traffic. It's just gotten worse," Dani said, forcing her way into the left lane not caring if she bumped another car because she was driving a rental.

Dani and Claire had staked out the West Hollywood Realty Office where Abigail Foster worked after Dani's flight from Miami had landed, and they waited until she emerged for lunch. Dani had called the office earlier that morning pretending to be a prospective buyer for one of her properties, and was told Abigail had meetings all morning, and a scheduled lunch, but would be able to show the listing in the late afternoon. Dani had been working on the hunch that Abigail was still in contact with her ex-husband, and wanted to keep tabs on her until they could definitively nail down her relationship with her ex-husband, who now, in Dani's mind, was almost certainly behind the attacks on their kids.

Abigail swerved her Mazarati from lane to lane, at one point nearly clipping a tour bus barreling towards Beverly Hills in search of stars' homes. She was obviously late meeting someone. Dani did her best to keep up, but now the Federal Express truck was slowing her down.

Claire rolled her window down and poked her head out. "I think she's turning down Robertson."

They were heading west, and there were a row of restaurants and shops south of Beverly Boulevard where someone like Abigail might arrange to have lunch.

Dani managed to steer into the turn lane, but had to wait for the green arrow before she gunned it, squealing the tires slightly. But they were heading south now, and were still able to see the Mazarati in the distance.

"I bet she's meeting him at the Ivy," Claire said.

"Too obvious," Dani said.

"Since when did Benito Coronel ever care about being discreet?"

Claire silently gloated when they saw Abigail Foster pull the Mazarati over to the valet stand outside the Ivy.

"Okay, what now?" Claire said, turning to Dani.

"Call Tess. She knows the owner of the Ivy. Tell her to get us a table a safe distance away so we can watch."

"No," Claire said glowering.

"Claire, come on, just let it go. You two have been friends a long time," Dani said, frustrated that even after all these years she was still trying to keep the peace.

Claire didn't respond. She just sat there behind her big Armani sunglasses, staring straight ahead.

Dani knew she was going to have to handle this. She picked up her cell phone off the dash and speed-dialed Tess. She was at the Beverly Wilshire when they last spoke, relaxing in a bubble bath, the place where she claimed to come up with her best ideas.

Dani got Tess's voice mail and told her to call her back just as soon as she could. She shoved the phone in her pants pocket and pulled in behind the Mazarati, which had yet to be driven away by one of the valets.

"Well, we might as well go inside and try to get a look at who she's meeting," Dani said getting out of the car. Claire followed her.

They walked up to the hostess stand where a Paris Hilton look-alike in a snappy print sundress greeted them with droopy eyelids and a half smile that said, "You're not Brad Pitt so I'm looking right through you."

"Reservation?" she said in a flat voice.

"Yes. Mendez. Dani Mendez," Dani said confidently. Claire turned away, not wanting to laugh.

Paris perused the list and then gave Dani another bored look. "I don't see it. Are you sure it's for one o'clock?"

"Yes, I'm sure," Dani said.

Paris went back to the list again to recheck. Dani used the opportunity to scan the tables inside. She spotted Abigail Foster sitting alone at a corner table looking over the menu. There was no sign of her lunch companion.

Paris huffily pushed the reservation list away. "I'm sorry, it's not here and we're completely booked for lunch."

At that moment Dani's cell phone rang. It was Tess. Dani answered it. "Tess? Hi. We're at the Ivy. We need a table." She handed the phone to Paris.

Paris scowled as she took the phone. "Yes? Who is this?" In a flash, the girl broke out into a wide grin and her eyes perked up. "Ms. Monahan! How are you? No, I didn't get the pilot at the CW. But I did get a recurring role on *Ugly Betty*. I know. It's such a cool show. What can I do for you today?"

Paris flashed Dani a fake smile as Tess chattered away. "Yes, absolutely. I hope you come see us soon. You're welcome." Paris handed the phone back to Dani and scooped up two menus. "Right this way, ladies."

She led them to a table on the opposite side of the restaurant from Abigail, but they had a clear view. Dani and Claire waited for just a few minutes before a yellow Mustang pulled up out front and a woman got out. They only glimpsed the back of her long jet-black hair as she sashayed inside. Once she rounded the corner of the hostess station, they would get a good view. To their shock and amazement, Paris escorted Maria Consuelos, Benito Coronel's lawyer, looking smashing in a smart pink suit jacket and miniskirt. Leave it to LA lawyers to look like models. Abigail stood up to greet her, and the two women kissed each other on both cheeks before sitting down and leaning in towards one another for an obviously private conversation.

"Well, this pretty much confirms Abigail Foster was lying. She's so chummy with her ex-husband's lawyer she has to be in some kind of contact with him."

"You're probably right. We'll stick with Abigail and I'll call Tess back and have her meet us here. She can follow Maria around, just in case."

Dani was getting excited. They were finally getting somewhere.

But she noticed that Claire was making no move to call Tess. Dani sighed and pulled out her cell phone again to call Tess at the Beverly Wilshire. She worried that all this unresolved tension between the three of them was going to hinder them from getting to the truth.

CHAPTER 28

When Tess agreed to keep tabs on Maria Consuelos, she had no idea she would be driving an hour east of Los Angeles to Riverside, California, to the Glen Ivy Natural Outdoor Hot Springs and Day Spa. Of course, she wasn't doing the driving herself. She was in the plush backseat of her limo, flipping through the current issue of *Vanity Fair* and sipping a Cosmopolitan. It was well after two o'clock in the afternoon, so she didn't feel it was too early for a cocktail.

The driver reported to her that Maria had just entered the spa as he drove around to find a parking space. Tess, meanwhile, checked in with Dani on her cell phone and told her where she was and that she was going in for a Vitamin Repair Facial and hopefully some information they could use to help prove Maria's client Benito Coronel was targeting their kids.

"Now hold on, Tess, I know you. You'll get so wrapped up in your facial and massage, and God knows what else, you'll forget why you're even there."

"That's where you're wrong, Dani," Tess said huffily. "I'm getting the Vitamin Repair Facial because not only will it re-texture and repair environmentally damaged skin, but it's also an exfoliating masque that will keep the Consuelos woman from recognizing me and will allow me to move freely about the spa without the fear of being identified."

Dani couldn't argue with her logic. Tess was a master of rationalizing just about anything to her advantage.

Tess told her driver she would be at least a couple of hours, depending on when she could get close to Maria Consuelos. She then got out of the limo, leaving him behind to read about Kate Hudson's exciting Hollywood life in Tess's discarded magazine.

The Glen Ivy Day Spa was situated on eleven acres near the base of the Santa Ana Mountains. The grounds were expansive and beautiful, decorated with majestic palms, cascading bougainvillea, and sparkling water.

Tess only had to give her name to the receptionist and all hell broke loose. The attendants rushed to greet her and the owner was immediately called. No appointment was necessary because everyone who knew the name Tess Monahan knew that it was possible she would drop at least a few grand on spa treatments, products, and services on this sweltering hot California afternoon. With Tess's arrival, the Glen Ivy Hot Springs and Spa had hit the mother lode.

Tess was worried the royal greeting might alert Maria Consuelos to her presence, which she couldn't let happen. Maria would surely recognize her from their meeting in her Century City law office a few days ago. And she certainly knew Tess's name. Who in the world didn't?

So Tess kept her eyes open as she was escorted by a short, pleasant-looking Thai woman to the spa, past the grapefruit trees that lined the serene and peaceful mineral hot springs waterfall.

Once inside, Tess shed her clothes and slipped into a luxurious white robe and silk slippers, and was led to a private room where she awaited the woman who would apply her facial masque. A nervous-looking young woman with sandy-blond hair, freckles, and a shy smile walked into the room and said hello to Tess in a shaky voice. She introduced herself as Summer and told Tess that she was new to the spa and hadn't worked on such a high-end client, which explained her jittery demeanor. Tess could tell that Summer expected her to be demanding and difficult, so the girl was surprised and somewhat relieved when Tess warmly received her. The girl relaxed a bit, and started applying the masque.

"Busy day, Summer?" Tess said, trying to engage the girl in conversation.

"Kind of quiet actually," the girl said as she rubbed the green cream all over Tess's face. "A few regulars are here, but we expect a weekend rush tomorrow. You picked a good day to come."

"Yes, it's very peaceful."

"You're not going to believe how this facial will improve your skin elasticity, tone, and texture. You have to experience all the treatments when you come to work here. My favorite is the sea kelp clay wrap. Have you tried it?"

"No, maybe once we're done here."

"For women like you, I recommend the Apricot Walnut Body Polishing. Aged skin cells are massaged away with our own Apricot Body Polish. You'll feel moisturized and revitalized, believe me."

"Women like me? You mean older women?" Tess asked, suddenly liking Summer a lot less than she had moments before.

"Oh no, any age, I just meant women who visit a lot of spas," Summer stammered, praying she wouldn't be fired for such a glaring faux pas.

"You know, I thought I spied a friend when I was checking in. She might be a regular," Tess said. She knew the spa staff were strictly forbidden to discuss other guests, but Tess figured Summer was new to the place, and probably was desperate to make up for the insensitive remark about Tess's age.

"Oh? Who's that?" Summer said, not even hesitating.

Tess was right. The girl was putty in her hand.

"Maria Consuelos," Tess said.

"Oh yes. She and her friend drive out here from LA at least once a week. Maria's very nice. I worked on her my first day on the job just a few weeks ago."

"I was hoping to say hello. Is she getting a facial?"

"No, she and her friend love the Grotto. In fact, they're in there right now," Summer said as she finished applying the masque and began to gently massage Tess's shoulders.

"What's the Grotto?"

"Oh you'll love it. It's an underground cavern where they do the most incredible skin treatment."

"How long are Maria and her friend going to be there? If there's time after my facial and before my Brazilian Plus Waxing, I'd love to drop in and say hello."

"Oh, they usually stay there for at least an hour."

Tess nodded and now waited for Summer to finish her work. Soft Enya-style music wafted through the air as Summer gently placed a warm damp cloth over Tess's eyes and quietly left the room. Tess knew she had at least ten minutes before Summer would return to finish the facial, so she slipped off the table, opened the door slightly to make sure the coast was clear, and then hurried out toward the Grotto.

Tess glided past several women relaxing in the Quiet Room and followed the arrows past Club Mud, California's only therapeutic red clay mud bath, and to a slow-moving elevator that took her underground to the Grotto, where an attendant awaited her.

The attendant was a strapping hunk, and Tess almost forgot why she had come down here in the first place. He was tan and wore a skin-tight, white tank top that accentuated every rippled ab. Tess nearly melted on the spot.

He tenderly took her by the arm and led her to a private area where he began covering her skin with a rich, light green body moisturizer of sea kelp, aloe vera, and other elements.

Tess looked herself over in a mirror and thought she resembled the She Hulk from the comic books. The attendant pointed her in the direction of the hydrating chamber where she sat down and allowed the rich moisturizer to work its magic. There was no sign of Maria Consuelos.

After only a few minutes, Tess wandered into the multi-head shower and washed off the green coating, carefully making sure her face masque disguise was still intact. Then she headed into the mist chamber. There she saw Maria Consuelos with her friend, an older redheaded woman with sharp features and an intense gaze. She was about ten years older than Maria and they sat close together talking in hushed tones.

Tess sat down nearby and put her head back against the cavern wall, pretending to take a quick catnap. She knew she was running late, and that Summer would soon return to the facial room and find her missing.

Maria and her friend were enjoying a cup of Glen Ivy tea and a crisp green apple as they discussed an obviously very serious topic.

Tess closed her eyes and strained to hear what they were saying. She surmised from the bits and pieces she was able to pick up that the redheaded woman worked in a doctor's office; she heard the name Dr. Featherstone, apparently the man treating Maria's father for some serious condition.

Tess nonchalantly pulled her cell phone out of the pocket of her white robe and flipped it open, pretending to check her text messages. But what she was really doing was snapping digital photographs of the two women. Satisfied she got some decent shots, Tess slipped the phone back in her robe and closed her eyes again, trying to hear more of their conversation.

The women suddenly stopped talking and Tess popped open one eye to see them looking at her. Tess wasn't worried. The masque would hide her identity. But Maria was staring now, as if she recognized Tess. But that was impossible. Tess reached up and felt her face. The masque was completely gone. The mister in the room had melted it away, and her face was now in full view.

"I know you," Maria said curtly as she rose and crossed over for a closer look.

Tess resisted the urge to cover her face with her hands. That would have been a dead giveaway. She just held her head high.

"You're one of the LA Dolls," Maria gasped as it suddenly hit her. She reached out and grabbed Tess' wrist. "What are you doing here?"

"I'm sorry, do I know you?" Tess said, almost groaning at the lameness of her response.

"Maria Consuelos," she said haughtily. "You came to my office a few days ago. Are you following me?"

"Don't be ridiculous," Tess said, standing up. She was ready to bail. "I spend half my life in spas. This is just a coincidence."

Tess yanked her wrist from Maria's grasp. The redheaded lady watched the scene curiously. She couldn't wait to see what happened next.

"I have to get back. I'm having a facial," Tess said, spinning around and heading back towards the elevator.

"Come back here," Maria said, chasing after her. "I thought I saw you taking photographs of me with your phone!"

Tess glanced back. She couldn't believe it. The girl was running to catch up with her. Tess picked up the pace, passing the puzzled attendant and scurrying onto the elevator. She had blown it big time. What would Dani say? Tess wasn't used to all this cloak and dagger business anymore.

Luckily the elevator doors closed just as Maria rushed up to them. Tess let out a sigh of relief. That was a close call. If Maria went to the spa manager to complain, what could she possibly say? Billionairess Tess Monahan was stalking her? The notion was outlandish, even if it was true.

When the elevators slid open after what seemed like an eternity, Tess glided off, pretending she hadn't just been through an

180

uncomfortable scene down in the Grotto. She checked her watch. She still had about three minutes before Summer would come back. She was passing Club Mud where several guests were wallowing in the therapeutic red clay mud baths when someone rapidly came up behind her and yanked her hair.

Tess yelped, shocked at the sudden pain and childishness of the gesture. She turned around and Maria Consuelos glared at her. She must have come up the stairs to confront her.

"Sweetheart, this isn't the third grade," Tess said icily. "There are other ways to get my attention. And it's not a smart move for a lawyer to physically assault someone in front of witnesses."

But Maria didn't seem to care. She pointed an accusing finger at Tess. "I know you're following me. I want to know why!"

The guests in the mud baths were riveted to the scene. Tess didn't want to aggravate the situation by engaging the girl, so she just shook her head at Maria and turned to go. Maria rushed forward and swiftly grabbed a fistful of Tess's white robe, pulling hard enough so Tess lost her balance and stumbled into the wall. This bitch was looking for a catfight. And the audience in the mud bath seemed to want one too.

"You really shouldn't have done that," Tess said.

"Oh yeah? What are you going to do about it?"

Tess hadn't been in a physical altercation since that case at a beach dance club in Marina Del Ray in the early eighties, a leftover from the disco era, where the Dolls went undercover to ferret out a killer targeting members in a dance class. Tess posed as an instructor and her budding romance with one of the suspects, her suave, gorgeous Chilean male counterpart ignited the fiery temper of a waitress in the club who happened to be carrying on with him too. Of course, the minute he met Tess, the poor waitress was history. She waited until Tess was alone and then attacked her as she was choreographing a bit to a Katrina and the Waves song she wanted to teach her students. Tess mopped the floor with the girl. But now, twenty years later, Maria Consuelos was bigger than Tess and at least twenty years younger. She wasn't one hundred percent sure she could take her. So why try?

Maria ran at Tess, fists in the air, and Tess simply stepped aside in a signature move Claire had once taught her. Surprise your opponent. Maria stumbled, allowing Tess to grab Maria's arm and twist it back, and then she slid her foot in front of her and pulled Maria forward. She tripped over Tess's foot, losing her balance, and Tess casually placed her hands on the girl's butt and upended her into the mud bath. The couple that was already in the bath jumped up as Maria hit the mud face first.

Maria's redheaded pal appeared, having followed her friend up the stairs. Her mouth was agape as she watched Maria splash around in the thick, oozing mud. She was desperately trying to stand up.

Tess walked out, passing the redhead, and said, "You really should try it. The mud exfoliates the skin, draws from the pores, and absorbs the impurities to release the waste from the skin. The glow you get afterward is heavenly. Trust me. She'll thank me for this."

And with that, Tess got the hell out of there before someone called the cops.

CHAPTER 29

Dani downloaded the photos Tess had e-mailed her from her cell phone and printed them from Claire's home office. Tess had decided to drive straight back to the Beverly Wilshire Hotel. She said it was because she was neglecting Paulo, but Dani knew better. She didn't want to show her face at Claire's house and possibly set off another altercation.

Claire entered with two cups of green tea and handed one to Dani before studying the pictures from the Glen Ivy Spa.

"The woman with Maria Consuelos is named Olivia Caldwell. Tess checked the registry when she paid her bill, and she works at Providence Medical Center for a doctor by the name of Featherstone," Dani said.

Claire shrugged. "Doesn't ring a bell."

"He's apparently treating Maria's father for some kind of illness."

"That doesn't help us at all with Coronel. Did Tess find out anything else?"

"No. Just that Maria has an awful temper and that she's still not half bad when it comes to defending herself."

"Well, then it sounds like a wasted trip, but I'm sure her skin is flawless now from all her expensive beauty treatments," Claire said, sipping her tea.

Dani sighed. She could hardly believe these two were at it again after all these years.

"Claire," Dani said throwing her a reproachful glance.

"You're right. I'm sorry. I'm done being bitchy," Claire said, flopping down on the plush blue-striped couch that sat adjacent to her cluttered glass-top desk.

"When we had dinner a few years ago, you told me you had buried all the old grudges," Dani said.

"I did. Or at least I thought I did. That was when Tess was traveling around the world, throwing A-list parties, hobnobbing with royalty, and completely out of my life."

"But now she's in your face, and so is her stepdaughter, who might as well be a carbon copy of her."

"I know Bianca is a sweet girl, and it makes me feel terrible that I don't trust her, but she was raised by Tess, and I'm so afraid she's just like her."

"Tess never meant to hurt you."

Claire blew on her tea to cool it down and gave a sideways look to Dani that said, "You've got to be kidding me."

"I'm serious," Dani said. "I'm not defending what she did; I'm just saying she didn't realize how much Dan meant to you."

She was referring to Dan Hunter, a Mark Harmon look-a-like, at least in the late eighties during his *St. Elsewhere* years, who helped the Dolls investigate a wealthy San Francisco family after the mysterious death of their patriarch. The case came to them about a month before the Benito Coronel affair, so it was close to the end of their run as the LA Dolls.

The father, Edward Hunter, had died from a heart condition, though later after the coroner's report it appeared his death was sped up by a fast-acting poison. Dan, the youngest son, feared one of his brothers or sisters was responsible because they were anxious to get their hands on the family money.

Since there were rumors that the real estate mogul had fathered an illegitimate daughter, Claire showed up at the family estate in Nob Hill pretending to be her in order to shake things up and get a good hard look at all the grieving children. Tess went to work as a secretary at the family's offices and Dani kept the fort down in Los Angeles, digging up what she could on all the financial dealings and personal secrets of the family's six children. What began as a routine case for Claire became complicated when she began to fall in love with the genuinely nice and startlingly good-looking Dan. The feeling was mutual, and they began a secretive affair that Claire did not dare tell Dani or Tess about. It was her first professional breach of ethics. She knew Dani's hard and fast rule of never, ever getting personally involved with a client.

But Claire couldn't help herself. She really thought Dan was the one. She was gearing up to admit the truth to her fellow coworkers when she walked in on Dan and Tess kissing passionately in the family's pool house.

Tess had also become enamored of Dan while working in his office, and the two embarked on a similarly steamy affair, which was typical of Tess, so it just made it that much harder for Claire. Tess did this all the time. To her Dan was a pleasant diversion, worthy of a little fun until the case was solved and they were on to the next assignment.

What Claire hadn't counted on when she confronted Tess was Tess's claim that she too had developed serious feelings for their client Dan. Dani was apoplectic that both her partners had broken her number one rule. One she would later break herself with Bowie's father Aaron Lassiter.

When the women brought Dan in for an emergency meeting, he was like a love-struck teenager, claiming to have deep feelings for both of the women and unwilling to choose between them.

Claire desperately wanted Tess to back off for once. Just give him up and then Claire could finally realize her dream of quitting the agency and getting married. But Tess refused. She said she loved him just as much as Claire, if not more. She wanted Dan to make the choice because deep down she knew he would choose her, the more glamorous, sexy, exciting Doll. Claire could never compete with Tess and never thought she would have to until that moment.

Claire quit. She couldn't take it. She just walked out. In the end, Dani discovered that none of the children had murdered their father. It was his business partner who had embezzled millions from the company, and was about to be exposed by Mr. Hunter. But solving the crime didn't matter. Claire was out and Dani was desperate to do damage control. Claire never knew if Tess continued to carry on with Dan. Dani assured her that Tess ultimately did the right thing and walked away from Dan. But Claire never knew if it was of her own volition or Dani's strong-arming.

After much begging and wooing on Dani's part, Claire returned to the agency and made up with Tess, who had already moved on to a slick French race car driver pushing a new power drink as the Dolls began a smuggling case involving an auto show. But things were never the same between them, and the team suffered for it. It was only a month later when they accepted Jenna Fowler as a client, never dreaming taking down Benito Coronel would be their last case and that when it was over they would break up for good. Claire met Jeb, the man of her dreams, and finally lived out her fantasy of a quiet suburban life, with two boys and all the trimmings. Still, Tess's betrayal gnawed at her for years. And she was never able to let it go completely.

The last thing Dani ever expected was for those simmering tensions to bubble up again. After all, Claire was happily married now. She never dreamed they would resurface over a rivalry between Claire's sons for Tess's daughter's affections. This was not going to end well.

Claire wasn't used to displaying her emotions in front of people. She liked to be in complete control. But with the past blasting her in the face again it was becoming increasingly difficult. She smiled at Dani, signaling to her that she was fine and preferred the discussion be over. Dani picked up on the cue and studied the photographs again, hoping to find some clue they had overlooked.

Evan wandered in the room and gave his mother a peck on the cheek.

"Hi, honey. Did you drop by to beat up your brother again?" Claire said, only half kidding.

"He's taking a nap right now. I'll wait for him to wake up before I smack him around some more," Evan said grinning. "What are you two doing?"

"A little detective work," Dani said.

"Don't tell your father," Claire quickly added.

Evan chuckled and then strolled over closer to Dani to look at the photographs. "Naked women. Awesome. I should chuck law school and become a private eye. Looks like a hell of a lot more fun."

"They're wearing towels, you just can't tell from all that green gunk covering their bodies," Dani said, laughing.

"Hey, I know her," Evan said.

Dani and Claire exchanged surprised looks. Dani pointed at the woman with Maria Consuelos. "Her name is Olivia Caldwell. Where do you know her from?"

"Not her. The other one. Maria somebody, I think,"

"Yes. Maria Consuelos. How do you know her?" Dani said.

"She came to speak at my law school. She was representing her firm, some big Century City outfit. They were looking to recruit associates. I thought she was really hot. Still is apparently," he said with a wolfish grin.

"She represents a man we put away, and we have her under surveillance because we're hoping she might provide some information about what he's up to now," Claire said, not wanting to divulge the truth to her son, that it was likely the man had marked Zak for murder.

"I remember there were rumors going around about her when she came to speak. They were calling her Meadow Soprano because her father used to be some kind of big time mobster," Evan said.

Dani stared at Evan. "So her father is a criminal?"

"Yeah, she refused to talk about it, but we later found out that the reason she became a lawyer was because her father had been railroaded to prison on some false charges and she wanted to get him out," Evan said.

Dani turned to Claire. "You remember any mobster types named Consuelos?"

"No," Claire said.

"Consuelos is her married name," Evan said matter-of-factly.

Claire couldn't believe it. Her son had this information all along and they had no idea. "Do you remember her father's name? Was it Coronel? Benito Coronel?"

"Yeah, that's it," Evan said.

Dani nearly dropped her ceramic cup of green tea.

CHAPTER 30

"I can't tell you what an honor it is having you visit me personally, Ms. Monahan," Matt Consuelos said, coming around his desk and taking a seat in one of his expensive tan leather Sparta chairs that sat opposite his matching sofa where Tess lounged with a bottled water.

"I've been reading a lot about you, and I have to say I'm impressed," Tess said, crossing her legs. She had worn a skirt a little on the short side for a woman her age, but what the hell? Her gams were still in amazing shape from all her private dance classes with Baryshnikov. Dani disarmed men using a gun. Tess preferred using her legs.

Matt leaned forward and slapped a serious look on his face. "My wife reads *People* magazine religiously and sometimes I'll leaf through it after she's done."

He clearly didn't want to give Tess the impression he had time to read a gossip magazine, though it was obvious he was an avid reader.

"Congratulations on being named one of the Fifty Most Beautiful People. It was a lovely picture of you, absolutely stunning."

Tess nodded, pretending as if she barely remembered the distinction, though she bought up more copies than there were beautiful people when the issue came out.

"Anyway," Matt continued, trying to stay on point. "I remember the article mentioned you spend most of your time traveling around the globe attending parties with heads of state and world-famous rock stars and supermodels. Why are you taking an interest in local Los Angeles politics?"

"I care deeply about the state of the world, Matt, I truly do," Tess said as she reached out with her hand and tapped his knee with her finger, "especially global warming. I believe the only real way to effect change is on the state and local level. We can't leave it to the administration in Washington to pass the necessary legislation nationally to cut down on the pollutants we're constantly sending up into the air. Anyway, California is where the national trends begin. It's always been that way, and so I want to start supporting congressional candidates with strong environmental records that I can really get behind, and you fit that bill."

In Tess's research, she had read that Consuelos had attended a state-sponsored environmental summit earlier in the year. She had no clue whether or not he was a serious advocate for cleaner air, but it was something to hang her visit on, and even if he wasn't, she had her checkbook at the ready and he wasn't about to turn her away. Even if he was a shill for the oil companies, he would have kept that big smile plastered on his face for as long as she decided to stay in his office.

"You know, despite the fact that I'm a Republican, I did go see Al Gore's movie a couple of years back and I thought it was really good," Matt said. "And I'm looking into buying a Prius real soon. You wouldn't believe how much it costs to fill up my Hummers."

Matt noticed Tess's face drop at the mention of a Hummer. "I only have two. The Governor has a whole fleet. I used to admire him for that, but of course then I became enlightened. And I applaud your efforts to support candidates like me who care about the air our children are going to breathe twenty years from now."

Debbie, a sprite little thing with a killer body, popped her head in, "I have a marketing manager from Exxon Mobil on the line, do you want to talk to him?"

Her timing couldn't have been worse.

Matt shook his head. "I said I didn't want to be interrupted."

"Oh, right. Sorry," Debbie said with a pouty frown before backing out of the office.

"They're probably calling with another threat. They target politicians like me, who take them to task for their environmental policies," Matt said in a lame attempt to cover what was probably a lunch date or corporate retreat invitation.

Tess tried hard not to laugh. "I understand completely."

"Now, how would you like to become involved with my campaign?" Matt said.

Tess thought Matt Consuelos was a handsome man, with smooth dark skin and an impressive head of jet-black hair that was slicked back with just a bit too much product. But he dressed the part of an up-and-coming city insider and probably had a bright future.

"Well, obviously, I don't have time to roll up my sleeves and make buttons and placards like I did when I was a much younger woman, but the advantage of being a woman of a certain age and one with means is that I can always just write a check."

Tess opened up her bag and pulled out her checkbook. Matt watched her in amazement as she took out a very expensive looking emerald-green marble fountain pen and began scribbling out a number.

Matt clasped his hands together in anticipation. Tess Monahan was a very rich woman and he was chomping at the bit to see how much she was going to fork over to him.

Tess finished filling out the check, looked it over and then handed it to him. He did everything possible to contain his excitement. She was donating ten grand.

Matt was struck dumb. Tess didn't even know if it was legal in California for a single individual to donate that much. And frankly, she didn't care. The look on his face was priceless.

"I think that will do for a start," Tess said.

"Start?" Matt said with an incredulous look on his face.

"When I get behind a candidate, I really get behind a candidate," Tess said, taking a sip from her water.

"Well, it seems I'm blessed to have such a generous benefactress. I thank you, Ms. Monahan."

"Please. Call me Tess."

"I hope this means we will be spending a lot more time together."

"Yes. In fact, I have a pretty big boat I tool around in and sometimes I dock it in Marina Del Ray. I think that would be the ideal location for a five hundred dollar a plate fund-raising dinner, wouldn't you agree?"

Matt looked as if he was going to explode with joy, but he worked extra hard to keep his emotions in check. "Why yes, I think that's a wonderful idea."

"There's just one thing we need to discuss."

"Of course. Anything."

"Your wife."

"My wife?"

Matt's face flickered a bit. He had no idea where she could possibly be going with this. But if she wanted him to jump into bed with her, odds were he wasn't going to hesitate.

"I have many friends who know a lot of people, and when I announced my intentions of supporting you financially, they expressed some concerns."

"Concerns about my wife?"

"Concerns about her family."

The lightbulb went off in his head and he suddenly went into overdrive. "Ms. Monahan, I mean, Tess, you must believe me, I know Maria's father has had a shady past . . ."

"Shady past? He was convicted of murder and drug smuggling."

"Well, if you've been reading the papers and watching the news, you know he has been cleared one hundred percent of the murder charge. As for the drug smuggling, he served his time and is now a free man."

Matt studied Tess intently and she made sure she looked as if she weren't buying it.

"Besides, she has virtually no contact with her family," Matt quickly added, fearing he might lose Tess and she would cancel the check before he had a chance to cash it.

"I find that curious since she seems to be representing her father in his legal case. They were both on the local news recently in fact when he was released," Tess said, enjoying watching Matt Consuelos squirm.

"Yes, that's correct. But she only did it out of family loyalty. Trust me, Tess, this is a clean campaign and we have no ties to Benito Coronel. In fact, we're prepared for my opponent to try to dig up some dirt and attempt to connect me to Coronel's past, but we have a whole team ready to refute it."

"I just don't need my money tainted by scandal."

"You have my utmost assurance that will not happen."

Debbie, the sprite assistant, reappeared in the doorway. "I just got a call from downstairs. There's a problem."

"How many times do I have to tell you I don't want to be interrupted?" Matt said in a scolding voice.

"Yeah, but this is serious," she said, stepping in the room and whispering in his ear. "They're towing your Aston Martin."

"What?" Matt bellowed as he jumped out of his expensive chair.

"The valet guys in the parking garage tried to stop them, but they showed them some legal papers. Apparently you haven't made a lease payment in four months."

Matt's face fell. He shot a look over to Tess, who raised a troubled eyebrow. "This has to be some colossal mistake. I have never missed a payment. I'll show you out, and then I can take care of this matter."

"I was hoping to discuss some C2 emissions cutback proposals, but if you don't have the time . . ." Tess said throwing in just enough haughty attitude.

"No, no, please, stay right here, relax, Debbie will get you another water. I'll be right back."

He was out of the room like a shot. Debbie reached for the now empty bottle of water in Tess's hand but she shook her head. "I'm fine."

"Okay," Debbie said with a smile. "If you need anything, just holler."

"I will, dear. Thank you."

And then she wandered out, finally leaving Tess alone. Tess got up off the couch and kicked the door closed with her foot. The staff wouldn't dare disturb her. She was too rich and too important to their boss.

She had told Smack to keep Consuelos occupied for at least fifteen minutes. That would be all the time she needed to go through his date book and computer files for anything of interest to the investigation.

Smack had a buddy in Burbank with a tow truck, and for a couple of hundred he was able to rent it for the day. Claire's Pilates instructor had her sister, who worked at a leasing company, come up with some fake papers. Smack would stall in showing Consuelos the papers, but when he would finally relent, Consuelos would see that his last name was spelled wrong, and that Smack clearly had the wrong guy and the wrong Aston Martin. Smack would call Tess's cell when Consuelos was on his way back up to the office.

Tess punched a few keys on his desktop, and found a Time & Chaos computer program that kept records of all his appointments and phone numbers. She did a quick scan. She was coming up with nothing. Just a bunch of potential fat-cat donors, some college buddies, Maria's numbers, and an endless list of professional contacts, none of which raised any kind of alarm. She did a fast check of his calendar. A lot of questionable political activity but nothing linking him to Benito Coronel. He obviously worked very hard to keep his political aspirations entirely separate from his criminally tainted in-laws.

Tess withdrew a compact disc from her bag and inserted it into the computer. She hastily began transferring the data onto the disc, where she could peruse it at her leisure once she was safely out of the building. Her cell rang. She checked the ID. It was Smack. Consuelos was on his way back upstairs.

Just as the disc completed the transfer, she noticed a name in the Time & Chaos address box that she had missed before. Paprika Lucerne, the former Hollywood madam who had moved her call girl operation to South Florida. Dani had already cleared her. So what was she doing in Consuelos's computer? And what was her relationship with Benito Coronel's son-in-law?

CHAPTER 31

"Well, there is only one way I can think of to find out what the connection is between Benito Coronel and Paprika Lucerne," Bianca said as she took a small bite of her Black Salmon with Chipotle Squash and Mango Rice she had ordered from the Beverly Wilshire's room service. For a tiny wisp of a girl, Bianca sure did love to eat.

"And what's that?" Tess asked, eyeing her daughter warily.

"I need to take the jet down to Florida and go undercover as a hooker," Bianca said matter-of-factly, as if the sheer will of announcing her decision would stop her mother's forthcoming objections.

"You've got to be kidding me," Tess said, dropping her fork. She hadn't ordered any dinner, but requested an extra fork so she could nibble off her daughter's plate, a habit she had developed in her dieting heyday when Bianca was twelve, and it drove the poor girl crazy. She could never have a meal all to herself.

"It's not a bad idea," Dani said, sitting at a desk across the room. She had arrived at the hotel just a few minutes earlier to discuss their next course of action after Tess called her to report what she found in Matt Consuelos's address book on his computer.

"No way, Dani, I would never put my daughter in that kind of danger. She has no training. And I can still see the bump on your head from Paprika's muscle boy. Absolutely not. Discussion over," Tess said, stabbing again at her daughter's salmon.

"So you don't think I can cut it as a prostitute?" Bianca exclaimed, genuinely insulted.

"I think you'd make a wonderful hooker," Tess said, pausing for a moment to ruminate over the implications of what she just said, but then quickly recovering. "That's not the point. As a responsible mother, I am not allowing you to get involved in this situation."

"I already am involved in this situation. Somebody tried to kidnap me in Rio," Bianca said, hurling her fork down on the table to drive her point home.

"Tess, we don't have a lot of choices. I can't go back down there because Paprika just saw me and would be instantly suspicious," Dani said.

"Well, obviously we do have one option. When I joined Paprika's stable in the eighties undercover, I wore a blond wig and lots of makeup. She'd never recognize me now, even though I haven't aged a bit. Isn't that right?"

Tess paused, waiting for someone to agree with her. Bianca knew the discussion would not move forward until she confirmed her mother's appraisal that she hadn't aged a bit.

"Yes, Mother," Bianca said with a sigh.

"Tess, honey, you know I love you dearly, but trust me, you're a bit long in the tooth to be posing as a high-class call girl," Dani said as gently as possible.

Tess reared back like a tiger just poked in the ribs with a stick. Her mouth dropped open and she roared, "What?"

The fact of the matter was Tess probably could have pulled it off. Dani remembered what Paprika had told her. She had a list of clients who liked hot older women, and Tess most certainly filled the bill. But the problem was she would stand out. What they needed was a girl who could blend in with the other late teen and twenty-something girls who made up the majority of women working for Paprika. Bianca would be the ideal candidate, there was no doubt in Dani's mind.

Dani guessed that Claire would be all for Bianca winging her way to South Florida for an undercover assignment as well, since it would take her away from her two sons, at least for the time being. Unfortunately, however, Tess was having none of it.

"I've made up my mind. Bianca is not going near Paprika Lucerne and that Mack Truck that works for her," Tess said picking up a spoon and helping herself to a generous helping of her daughter's mango rice.

"Mom, why don't you order some dinner for yourself?" Bianca said, more than a little annoyed.

"No, I'm not hungry," Tess said, moving on to her daughter's chipotle squash.

"We would have her wired so if anything went wrong, Bowie and I could move in before anything could possibly happen," Dani said, taking one final shot.

Bianca's face lit up. It all sounded so exciting to her.

"I'm through discussing this," Tess said, pointing her fork at Dani for emphasis. "It's not happening."

"Fine," Dani said. The matter was over as far as she was concerned. She would rendezvous with Claire and they would discuss what to do next. But she had to know if there was some sinister connection between Benito Coronel and Paprika Lucerne, and if it was in any way connected to their investigation. Two days later she would have her answer, but it would come at a cost.

*   *   *

Dani was roused out of a deep sleep a couple of days later by the ringing of her cell phone. She had forgotten to turn it off when she went to bed. She was staying in Claire's guest room for a few nights. Dani checked the digital clock on the dresser. It was four in the morning. She couldn't imagine who would be calling this early.

She opened the phone and said in a groggy voice, "This is Dani."

"Dani, I think I'm in trouble," a hushed voice said.

"Who is this?"

"Bianca."

Dani sat up, now completely awake.

"Where are you?" she said, fearing the answer.

"Florida."

Dani could have predicted this. Bianca was just as stubborn and bullheaded as her mother, and once she got an idea into her head she wasn't about to let it go.

"Tell me you didn't," Dani said.

"I did. I had to. I wanted to help with the investigation."

"You wanted to be a kick-ass action hero like your mother."

"Yeah, maybe that had something to do with it. Listen, I don't have a lot of time to talk. I overheard you telling Mom about Paprika's operation and so I copied down her address and staked out her house. I saw some of her girls leaving, and followed them to a bar where I struck up a conversation with them. Within two hours they took me back over to Paprika's and she hired me on the spot."

Dani wasn't the least bit surprised by that. Bianca was a stunning girl and Paprika probably saw dollar signs.

"Where are you now?"

"In an apartment in South Beach. A couple of the girls invited me to stay with them until I found my own place."

"Bianca, I want you to get out of there right now and catch

the first plane back to LA. This isn't how we do things. We never go out in the field alone. We always have backup."

"Bambi, who are you on the phone with?" a female voice said with a southern drawl in the background.

"My boyfriend back home," Bianca said convincingly. "He's trying to talk me into coming back."

"Hang up!" the girl in the background said with a laugh.

"Who's Bambi?" Dani asked.

"I had to have a cover name. I called myself Bambi Salazar. Isn't it great? Bambi Salazar's a famous porn star back in Brazil. I figured no one here would know her name."

Dani would have laughed if she wasn't so worried. Tess was going to go bananas once she learned what Bianca had done and she would without a doubt blame Dani for somehow encouraging her. She had to get her out of there safely.

"Listen, Dani, while I was over at Paprika's house today, her bodyguard Hammer, who just got out on bail, went for cigarettes, and Paprika was busy buying some Suzanne Somers exercise bar off QVC, so I had a chance to go through her books."

"What did you find?"

"Matt Consuelos. But he's just a john. He's down here a lot, apparently he's got family in the Miami area, and he always requests Priscilla, one of the girls I'm rooming with. When I asked Priscilla about him, she said he's a regular. Nothing more. I don't think he has any serious link to some kind of conspiracy against you three. But there's another guy who used to come down to Florida with Matt all the time, a really good-looking kid, but he hasn't been around in a while. Priscilla thought he might be Matt's brother-in-law."

"Coronel's son?" Dani said, her mind racing.

The Dolls knew Coronel had two young children at the time of his arrest in the eighties. Abigail had kept them out of the limelight during the height of the trial. In fact, Dani had forgotten all about them until they found out Maria was Coronel's daughter. What about the son? Where was he? Was he out there somewhere carrying out a revenge plot on behalf of his father? It all made sense. If they found him, they might find the key to solving the case.

"Any idea how we track him down?"

"There was a cell phone number. I tried to call it but it is no longer in service."

"And I don't think Matt or Maria will be eager to offer any contact information. We'll have to find him some other way. Okay, Bianca, you've done a good job," Dani said. "Now I need you to get out of there."

"I'm going to wait until the other girls go to sleep and then I'm going to leave. Don't worry. I was going to slip out today, but there was a slight complication."

"What do you mean?"

"Well, I'm new but they've already sent me out three times."

Dani gasped. The implications of what Bianca meant suddenly hit her. "Dear God, tell me you didn't . . ."

"No, don't be ridiculous. The first two guys were happy with just a hand job . . ."

"Oh God," Dani groaned.

"But the third guy today, he wanted more, and I kept skirting the issue and I think he might have complained to Paprika. I'm not sure. But I couldn't bolt right then and there, so I've been waiting for the right opportunity."

"I want you to put the phone down right now and get the hell out of there," Dani said. "Your mother's going to kill me."

There was a knock at the door in the background, and Dani heard the girl with the southern accent answer it.

"Bambi, it's Hammer. He wants to talk to you," the girl said.

"Bianca, listen to me, you do not go anywhere alone with him. He's a dangerous man."

"Don't worry. I have everything under control," Bianca said.

But she didn't. Bianca was in way over her head. And Dani was helpless because she was clear across the country.

"Hold on, I'll be right back," Bianca said as she put down the phone.

Dani strained to hear what was happening. She could hear Hammer's gruff, gravelly voice. At first they seemed to just be talking but it grew into an argument and then there were sounds as if some kind of scuffle broke out, and finally someone hung up the phone. Dani was in a complete panic.

She speed dialed her son, praying he wasn't out of town on his current case and that his phone was on. After a few rings, Bowie picked up and Dani breathed a heavy sigh of relief.

"Honey, are you in Miami?"

"Yeah, I just got home. I've been out all night dancing with friends. Why?"

Dani quickly explained the situation and Bowie promised to take care of it. He told his mother he would call back when he had some news and then he left for Paprika Lucerne's house.

Dani sat on the edge of the bed, her hands clasped together, rocking back and forth for over an hour. She briefly considered calling Tess and filling her in, but what good would that do? Tess would just spiral into a panic attack. Why put her through all that? There was nothing she could do. It would be better to wait until Bianca was out of harm's way before admitting the truth.

She thought about waking Claire, but she and Jeb had been arguing earlier and finally went to bed just after midnight. They were sleeping in the same room so that was a good sign. Dani certainly didn't want to disrupt that. So she sat on the bed alone. Waiting. Worrying. And desperately hoping it would turn out all right.

One hour stretched by. And then two. Still no word from Bowie. It was going on seven in the morning. Claire would be getting up soon to make breakfast for Jeb. He was off from work for the next couple of days.

Finally, after what seemed like an interminable amount of time, Dani's cell phone rang and she quickly answered it.

"Bowie?"

"I'm here, Mom."

"Where's Bianca?"

"With me. A little shaken up, but she's okay."

Bianca took the phone. "You didn't mention how cute your son is, Dani," she said in a flirty voice. "Figures he'd be gay."

Bianca put on a brave front, but Dani could tell even from far away that she was a puddle of nerves. But at least she was safe.

Dani found out later from Bowie that Hammer had dragged Bianca back to Paprika's for a confrontation with the madam. They had checked out her story, and Bianca being an under-cover novice, never seriously thought they would do that. They knew she was lying to them, and after Hammer slapped her around a little, she admitted the truth, expecting them to release her once they discovered she was the daughter of the great Tess Monahan. It only enraged them further, and though they didn't talk in front of her, it quickly became clear to Bianca that they were plotting her disappearance for good.

Hammer grabbed her and hustled her out the front door to his car, undoubtedly with the plan to shoot her and dump her body in the Everglades. But Bowie had arrived in the nick of time, and after a wrestling smack down, the much younger, far more lithe and athletic Bowie buried the less agile Hammer. Bowie then quickly whisked Bianca away. They were now driving back to Bowie's houseboat, the QE3.

Bowie took the phone from Bianca and promised to drive her straight to the airport later that day so she could catch a flight back to Los Angeles.

Bianca had told her mother she was visiting friends in San Diego, which explained her absence. She wasn't expected back until tomorrow anyway, so it was possible that Tess would never have to know any of this. But Dani knew concealing the truth would eventually backfire. Somehow it would come out, from Bowie or Bianca, or even the pilot of Tess's jet who flew her down there and then raced right back before Tess realized her plane was missing. Anyway you cut it, Dani would be the one who suffered the wrath of her highly emotional friend.

Dani had breakfast with Claire and Jeb in Sherman Oaks and then drove over the hill to the Beverly Wilshire to talk to Tess.

As expected it did not go well. Tess was furious with Dani. She blamed her for not backing her up in front of her daughter. They should have been a united front, but Dani suggested wiring Bianca, letting her waltz right into trouble. Tess was so angry, Dani thought she might bundle her daughter on her jet and fly immediately back to Brazil. Damn the stinking investigation. She would just surround herself and her daughter with an army of bodyguards, who would keep them safe. And to hell with Dani and Claire. But Tess didn't. She gave Dani a tongue-lashing all right, but their roots were too deep. She wasn't going to desert them now. But the team was in turmoil. Claire was mad at Tess. And Tess was mad at Dani. And it would be their greatest challenge to keep the team together to solve this one last case.

CHAPTER 32

Claire stood in her bedroom looking herself over in the full-length mirror inside her walk-in closet. Not bad, she thought. The white lab coat that she borrowed from her neighbor down the street who was a gynecologist was a perfect fit. And the professional name tag she had Evan design on his computer just made her disguise all the more authentic. A pair of horn-rimmed glasses and her hair pulled back in a bun completed her transformation. Dr. Walker-Corley was ready for duty.

It was a hasty cover arranged through some old contacts she had at the Saint Providence Medical Center in Burbank, where Benito Coronel was showing up for appointments with Dr. Featherstone. Dani believed that if Coronel was really sick, maybe even dying, that it might play into the timing of his revenge plot. If he had only six to eight months to live, he would want to clear up any business, and exacting revenge on the women who sent him to prison would be tops on the list.

Dr. Dara Boland, the gynecologist neighbor, was leaving for a three week vacation to Bali with her contractor husband, David. Claire managed to drop in with a coffee cake the morning before their flight out of LAX, and filled her in on the attack on Zak and the attempts to kill the children of her two former partners. Dr. Boland was riveted, and more than a bit disturbed given the strong bond she had with her own children, both attending Ivy League schools back east. She asked Claire how she could help, and Claire was more than happy to suggest lending her a lab coat and the keys to her office for just one day since she would be away. Dr. Boland's office was two doors down from Coronel's physician and Claire could easily come up with a story that would explain her sudden presence. She would be a doctor with her own practice in Tarzana who offered to oversee some of Dr. Boland's more immediate cases while she was away on vacation. It was a plausible scenario and would get her close to Coronel's medical file without raising too much suspicion.

Dara Boland got a charge out of her tenuous involvement with a real-life private detective investigation, though Claire tried hard to downplay it. The last thing she needed was for word to get back to Jeb at the next neighborhood block barbecue. Why worry him more than he already was? Dara promised to keep mum and Claire accepted the lab coat in exchange for her freshly baked coffee cake.

Claire was about to take off the coat when she sensed some movement behind her. No. It couldn't be. She turned around and her worst fears were realized. It was Jeb. He was supposed to be out golfing all day. Claire hadn't even noticed it had started to rain outside, which had unfortunately cut his usual eighteen holes down to nine. And for the first time since she could remember, her husband hadn't joined his friends at the nineteenth hole for a drink. Just her luck.

"Mind telling me what you're wearing?" Jeb said with a stern look on his face.

"It's a lab coat," Claire said weakly.

"I can see that. I hope you've got that on because you want to play doctor with your husband."

Claire laughed. Jeb didn't. He was waiting for an explanation.

"Okay, I'm going to be straight with you . . ." Claire said.

"Good. That will be a refreshing change."

"That's unfair."

"I don't think I'm being unfair. I think I've been exceedingly patient with you. More than most husbands would be."

Claire couldn't argue with that. But it was clear Jeb's patience had just plain worn out. "Look, Benito Coronel has been seeing a doctor in Burbank, and I want to know what it is he's suffering from because it could have some relevance to the case."

"The case? Listen to yourself, Claire. You're talking like it's 1985. Nothing I said made a bit of difference to you the other day, did it?"

"What do you want me to say? You're right? You are. There. I used to be in a dangerous business. And now I've been pulled back into it. But how many times do I have to tell you the only reason I'm even doing this is because our sons' lives are at risk?"

"So call the police! Enough is enough, Claire. I'm not going to stand by and watch you get yourself killed. I want you to tell Dani you're out of it."

Jeb turned to make a dramatic exit. But he stopped short when he heard his wife say in a firm voice, "No."

He slowly turned around and stared at Claire. He was doing a slow burn. "What?"

"I have to do this."

"You *want* to do this."

"You don't get it, Jeb. I was perfectly happy with my life before Dani and Tess walked back into it. You of all people should know that."

"All I know is that if you walk out that door and continue with this nonsense, I may not be here when you come back."

Claire nearly gasped. Jeb had never gone this far, never gotten this angry, at least to the point where he made such a threat. She was mortified and scared and furious all at the same time.

"I don't consider someone trying to kill our son nonsense,"

Claire said, sweeping past Jeb and out of the room. She made a point of slamming the front door behind her.

Outside Claire got behind the wheel of her car, trying desperately not to give in to her fast-rising emotions. She was fighting back tears and trying to stay calm as she backed out of the driveway.

Was Jeb bluffing? It certainly didn't sound like it. But she was driven now, feeling as if she was getting closer to the truth, and she couldn't stop before the job was finished and she knew for certain her sons were safe.

If Jeb was packed up and gone when she returned home, she would have to deal with it then.

CHAPTER 33

Claire barely had time to unlock the office and set her Starbucks down before the curious onlookers were strolling by, trying to get a glimpse of her. Everyone on the floor knew Dr. Dara Boland was away on vacation, so the early morning buzz was all about who this stranger was who was in her office. It took roughly five minutes before a handsome middle-aged doctor, graying at the temples, but still fit and with a tanned face that made him look years younger, poked his head in and smiled, showing off the whitest teeth Claire had ever seen.

"Can I help you?" he said, in a deep baritone voice that just added to his robust masculinity.

"Claire Walker-Corley," she said with a smile, quickly laying out the cover story of filling in for Dr. Boland with a few patients while the good doctor took a much-deserved rest.

"Well, let me be the first one to welcome you," the man said, shaking Claire's hand. "Bill Featherstone from next door. Cardiologist."

Heart doctor? Did Benito Coronel have some kind of heart condition?

"Well, there are a few things you need to know if you're going to fill in for Dara. She and I have lunch every Wednesday, and guess what, it's Wednesday, so if you're filling in for her then I expect you to meet all her obligations."

He was smiling. God, he was terrific looking. And no wedding ring. That raised alarm bells. The last thing Claire needed was a gorgeous single doctor romancing her. She was here to do a job. And it was a terrible idea to break bread with another man only hours after a big blowout with Jeb.

"I've got a very full day of patients. I'm afraid I won't be able to get away," Claire said.

Dr. Featherstone shrugged, and playfully pouted in a mock show of devastation. It made Claire laugh. This guy was certainly a charmer.

"Well, I'm right next door if you change your mind," he said. "And if you have any questions, if you need to know where to get the best cinnamon buns around here, you just let me know."

"A heart doctor pushing a pastry?" Claire said with a wink.

"Hey, if I push oatmeal and whole wheat toast with no butter then I'm out of business," he said. And with a grin, he disappeared.

Claire knew she had to work fast. It wouldn't take long for people to notice there were no patients showing up for appointments. If she was going to get a good look at Coronel's records she would have to do so in the next hour and then get the hell out of there. But just how she was going to pull that off was the big question. Dr. Featherstone's office was bustling with activity when she wandered over.

The pretty, young Hispanic receptionist gave her the once-over when Claire strolled in and asked to borrow a couple of magazines for the office. The girl appeared suspicious of Claire, especially when she returned a second time and asked to use their restroom since she couldn't find the key to Dr. Boland's bathroom. The girl let Claire through, and directed her down the hall to the left.

Claire studied all the rooms, passing an office where she caught a glimpse of Dr. Featherstone pressing a stethoscope against an elderly man's sagging bare chest. There was a lab to her left where the redheaded woman, Olivia Caldwell, who was friends with Maria Consuelos, drew blood from an older female patient. To her right was the X-ray room. And at the end of the hall across from the restroom was the file room. That's where she would get her answers. She casually turned around to see the receptionist eyeing her, so she immediately went into the bathroom and shut the door. She waited a few seconds before she silently opened the door and poked her head out.

The receptionist was on the phone. This was her chance. She scooted across the hall to the file room and locked herself inside. If anyone found her, she was in major trouble. She figured she had about three to five minutes before that nosy receptionist would start looking for her. She quietly began opening drawers and sifting through the files. Dr. Featherstone was very popular. He had what seemed to be an endless list of patients. Probably most of them women who were bowled over by his good looks and soothing bedside manner.

Claire rifled through the files. Whoever was in charge of the system was disorganized. The files were alphabetized, but a lot of them were misplaced. It took her longer than she expected to find Coronel's file. It wasn't under C or even B for Benito. It was stuffed in the back.

The file wasn't as thick as Claire expected. In fact there were only a few pages. Claire sat down at a desk and flipped it open. It was immediately clear that Benito Coronel's heart was just fine. In fact, overall his health was pretty good for a man his age. And the first prescription listed was for Viagra. She almost burst out laughing. Benito Coronel's secret medical condition and these visits to Dr. Featherstone were all because of erectile dysfunction? Claire understood why Coronel would want to be so secretive about it. He was a proud, macho Latin man. It would kill him if word got out he needed help getting it up. There were also issues with his cholesterol, which would explain why he was consulting a cardiologist. He was being monitored for acutely elevated triglycerides and was trying to find the right balance of medications that wouldn't harm his liver, which would explain the number of visits. So there was nothing immediately life threatening and there was no reason Coronel needed to clean up any unfinished business, so that theory was out the window.

Claire was about to close the file when she noticed one more notation on Coronel's medical records. He had a low sperm count. Dr. Featherstone scribbled on the side of the paper that this had been the case since Benito Coronel was a young man. He was incapable of impregnating a woman.

Claire sat back in her chair, stunned. If that was the case, then there was no way he fathered Maria Consuelos. She was not his daughter.

Someone tried opening the door to the file room. Claire leapt out of her seat and hurried over, unlocking and opening the door.

The receptionist stood there, a file in hand, glaring at Claire. "What are you doing in here?"

Claire glanced across the hall to see the open door to the bathroom. "Oh there it is. I thought you said down the hall to the right."

"No. Left," the receptionist said, peering around Claire to see if she had disrupted anything in the room.

"I'm sorry," Claire said, talking fast. "I thought the bathroom might be in the back of the file room so I was looking around for it."

"Why did you lock this door?" the receptionist asked. She was not going to give up until she had a satisfactory answer.

"Claire," Dr. Featherstone said as he ambled out of his office and he saw her. Saved by the eye-catching doctor.

"Yes, Bill, what can I do for you?"

The receptionist wasn't going to let Claire off the hook so easily. "Excuse me, Dr. Featherstone, but this woman was in the file room with the door locked."

The doctor didn't even hear what she said. "That'll be all, Eva, thank you."

He brushed past the receptionist and took Claire's hand into his own and steered her back down the hall towards his examining room.

He spoke in a low tone. "I have a patient, Mrs. Levitz. She's here now and I thought you might take a quick look at her."

Claire's mouth dropped open. No! This couldn't be happening. "Bill, I'm not a cardiologist, I'm a gynecologist."

"I know. She's complaining about some vaginal irritation, and I thought since you're here you might be able to give us a preliminary diagnosis."

"What's she doing coming to you?"

"Well, I'm also a general practitioner. I just specialize in hearts."

Claire was in a near panic. The last thing she was going to do was poke her nose inside a strange woman's vagina. That was way beyond the call of duty. But if she resisted, then Bill might start listening to his suspicious receptionist. She was inside the exam room before she could come up with any kind of excuse and smiling at a forty-something woman with a nervous look on her face.

"This is Dr. Walker-Corley, Martha, she's filling in for Dr. Boland next door. Describe to her what you told me."

The woman prattled on about her itching and discomfort and Claire kept a frozen smile plastered on her face. She was about to make a run for it. The next thing she knew, the woman was lying down on the table and Claire was examining her. This had to be illegal. She would be arrested if anyone found out she was a fake. What was she going to tell Dara when she got back from Bali? If she came clean now, she could get her neighbor in deep trouble for complicity. Claire had to be convincing, but what if she said something or prescribed something that worsened the woman's problem? She could get sued.

Finally, the cute doctor came to her rescue again. "Sounds like dermatitis to me. My wife had the same thing. Is that what you think?"

"Absolutely," Claire said, relieved. "Yes. Dermatitis."

"Is it serious?" the woman asked, her face filled with terror.

"Oh, no," Dr. Featherstone said, and Claire hastily agreed. "It's very common and can be caused by anything that irritates sensitive skin such as detergents used to wash underwear, soaps, perfumes . . ."

"Even bubble baths and shower gels," Claire tossed in to sound authentic. The tension was now draining out of her body. She was going to get out of this prickly situation relatively un-scathed.

"Is there something I can take to relieve the itching?"

Dr. Featherstone looked to Claire. "What do you suggest, Doctor?"

Claire was stumped. She mentally reviewed the contents of her medicine cabinet hoping something would come to her. "I would suggest a cortisone ointment," she said and held her breath.

"I concur," Dr. Featherstone said with a nod.

And with that, Claire was off the hook. Dr. Featherstone scribbled out a prescription then tore it off his notepad and handed it to the patient.

"Well, if that's all, I have other patients to attend to," Claire said, knowing full well the office next door was empty.

"Thank you, Dr. Corley," Featherstone said with a winning smile. "And if you change your mind about lunch, you know where to find me."

Claire nodded and then scurried down the hall past the scowl-ing receptionist and back out into the waiting room, where she ran smack into a man who had just swept through the door to the office.

"Oh excuse me," Claire said, and then stopped, startled. It was Benito Coronel.

He had aged quite a bit since the eighties obviously, but he was still a handsome man. He looked at her and studied her face as if he was reaching back into his mind to try and figure out why she appeared so familiar.

"Do I know you?" he said in a scratchy, tired voice.

"Not unless you've been to the gynecologist recently," she said with a strained laugh.

Claire couldn't believe this was happening. If he suddenly remembered her, realized who she was, it was all over. The thick glasses and hair in a bun was helping, not to mention the twenty years of life gone by reflected in her face. But Benito Coronel had stared at Claire in that courtroom through two whole days of testimony. And despite the time that had passed, he was still sharp and observant. There was a good chance he would see through her paltry disguise at any moment. She had to get out of there.

"Have a good day," she said as she scooted out the door. She didn't look back and she hoped and prayed that Coronel would give up trying to figure out why she looked so familiar, and then get distracted by one of the magazines in the waiting room while he waited to see Dr. Featherstone.

Claire hung up the lab coat in the closet, locked up Dr. Boland's office and bolted for her car in the parking lot. Coronel had obviously let the matter go. Luck was on her side.

CHAPTER 34

"They had a very rocky marriage," Smack said as he took a bite of his cheese omelet and chased it down with some orange juice.

"How rocky?" Claire asked, acutely aware that her own marriage was teetering on the brink of collapse.

Claire had met Smack for an early breakfast at the 101 Coffee Shop on Franklin Avenue in Hollywood, an iconic diner attached to a Best Western Hotel and made famous by Vince Vaughn and Jon Favreau in the red-hot nineties independent movie *Swingers*. Claire was almost a half hour early meeting Smack on this overcast Los Angeles morning because she couldn't stand the tension and silence at home with Jeb. She had back-burnered their fight, choosing to deal with it later, and that only exacerbated the situation. So when they awoke, and went about their morning rituals with mere grunts of good morning, Claire just wanted to get the hell out of there.

Smack had been following Matt Consuelos ever since Tess had met with him and unearthed the connection with Paprika Lucerne. Smack was an expert at cozying up to valets and doormen, striking up conversations with hotel bellhops and restaurant busboys, chatting them up and always walking away with valuable information. It was his signature talent. So when he slid into the corner booth and greeted Claire, she knew he would provide something useful.

And a rocky marriage between Matt and Maria Consuelos was a good starting point.

"He spends a lot of time in Florida, that's where he's originally from. Miami," Smack said. "According to his secretary, a nice lady, well put together, who I just happened to meet the other night while shopping at the Grove, his parents still live down there."

Smack gave Claire a playful wink, who was amazed at his gift of gab and uncanny ability to get people to talk.

"Matt's stuck in an unhappy marriage, so when he escapes to Florida to visit his family he calls upon Paprika to provide a few of her girls to make up for what he's missing out here when he's with Maria," Claire surmised, taking a sip of her coffee. "What about Maria's brother who seems to have vanished off the face of the earth?"

"Maria met Matt through her brother Pedro. They were buddies in high school and a couple of hard-partying jocks."

"So the brother doesn't have a problem with Matt cheating on his own sister?"

"Doesn't seem that way since they often flew down to Miami together and on occasion even hired Paprika's girls at the same time," Smack said.

"So you think Paprika's connection to the Coronel family is by way of the son, not the father."

"Yeah, which is why I'm thinking Coronel's phantom son Pedro is who we need to focus on. There's very little information out there about him. And that may be due to the fact he wants to keep a low profile in order to avenge what we did to Daddy Coronel."

"So Matt and Maria Consuelos are out of it."

"Not necessarily."

Claire gave Smack a look. "Matt's a hound dog, no doubt about that. He pays Paprika Lucerne a fortune to keep him happy when he's in town supposedly visiting his parents. Maria is under the false impression that her husband is just a devoted son who can't get enough of his mommy."

"So Maria has no idea her husband is a cheating louse?"

"No. And she doesn't seem to care. She's too busy sneaking around on him."

"Really? Do we know with whom?"

Smack gave Claire a disappointed look. "Now would I make you drive all the way over the hill to meet me here at our favorite spot if I didn't have something good to give you?"

"You spoil me, Smack," Claire said with a smile.

"Kid by the name of Lucas Ridley. I followed Maria Consuelos from her law office in Century City. They met at a quiet spot in Westwood and then disappeared into the W Hotel, where apparently they go once or twice a week according to the valet who used to date my sister."

"Who is Lucas Ridley?"

"Wiry kid, lots of energy from what I can tell, and a brother," Smack said.

"Once you go black, you never go back."

"I've been trying to tell you that for years, Claire. But you had to go marry that smooth-talking white dude," Smack said laughing.

Claire wanted to tell Smack that she may not be with the smooth-talking white dude for much longer, but that was for another time. She decided to stay on point. "So what else do we know about Maria's boyfriend on the side?"

"You know I always save the best for last because I like to build up the drama for you, Claire. The kid works at a police crime lab. Not too high up. Just an assistant. But he does come in contact with all the blood samples shipped out to be tested for DNA."

Claire sat back in the booth, stunned. This was big. Really big. If Lucas Ridley was having an affair with Maria, who just happened to be Benito Coronel's brand new attorney, if not his daughter, then she may have been able to wrap him around her little finger and convince him to tamper with Coronel's blood sample before it was shipped to the testing facility. The results would clear Coronel of the crime in which he was convicted. It wouldn't match the blood and sweat found on the murder weapon. And nobody would suspect Ridley because on the surface he would have no motive or cause to help Coronel.

"Maria orchestrated the whole thing to get Coronel out of prison. And she used the Ridley kid as a dupe," Claire said.

"Ridley's no dupe, believe me. Have you seen that girl in her short skirts and bouncy hair? That boy knew exactly what he was doing," Smack said. "So what do we do now?"

"You try to find out what you can about Coronel's son and how we might be able to locate him. I'm going to call Dani about this Ridley character."

Claire was getting excited. Pieces of the puzzle were slowly starting to come together. She hated the fact Jeb was right. She was enjoying this.

CHAPTER 35

Dani had staked out Lucas Ridley's apartment building in Valley Village for three hours before she saw him saunter out in a brown leather jacket and jeans and carrying a motorcycle helmet. He was tall and sexy and Dani could see why Maria would be drawn to him with his laid-back demeanor.

Dani got out of her car and crossed the street to intercept him as he climbed on his Kawasaki Vulcan 2000 that was parked at the curb in front of his building. Another Kawasaki bike was next to it, an Eliminator 125, bright blue, very hot. Dani used to drive motorcycles in the eighties, and even jumped a few, believe it or not. The Dolls were investigating the murder of a hot young extreme sports athlete at a motocross event, and Dani trained for weeks so she could join the racing team. She managed to convince the gang she could fit in but luckily she never had to do any competitive racing during the course of the case.

Ridley was putting on his helmet as she approached. "Excuse me, Lucas? I'm Dani Mendez. I'd like to talk to you."

He looked her up and down. He obviously liked what he saw but kept up his rough exterior. "About what?"

"Maria Consuelos."

"Never heard of her."

"Are you sure? Does she use another name when you two secretly meet at the W every week?"

Ridley didn't even flinch. "Lady, you got the wrong guy. Now get lost."

Another young African-American man walked out of the building in a colorful black and yellow jacket and carrying a helmet. He gave both Ridley and Dani a curious look as he put the key in his bike, the Eliminator.

"Man, we got ourselves a Milf, don't we, Lucas?"

Lucas scowled.

Dani turned to the other kid with a questioning look.

The kid broke out with a wide grin. "Never heard of a MILF? It's an expression, baby. It stands for Mothers I'd Like to Fuck."

"Charming," Dani said, not knowing whether to be flattered or to deck him. She decided to turn her attention back to Lucas Ridley.

"Lucas, I'm a police officer," Dani said neglecting to add that she was out of her jurisdiction and could basically do nothing. "And we know you tainted the blood samples that were tested and cleared Maria's father Benito Coronel."

Dani held her breath. It was all speculation. They had no proof. They were just putting pieces of the puzzle together and hoping for some kind of reaction that would indicate whether they were on target.

She got it. Ridley fired up his bike and took off down the street. He was making a run for it, leaving his friend behind. Dani thought for a split second about running back across the street and getting in her car to give chase, but that would be a waste of time. Motorcycles weave in and out of traffic with ease, and she'd lose him at the first stop light. No, if she was going to catch him she was going to have to do it on a motorcycle.

"Sorry, kid, I have to borrow your bike," Dani said, shoving the kid hard. He stumbled back and fell to the ground, and before he could get back up, Dani straddled his Eliminator 125. She revved it up, and squealed off after Ridley, the kid in the black and yellow jacket running down the street after her, screaming obscenities.

This was insane. What the hell was she doing? She wasn't wearing a helmet and would probably get herself killed. She also hadn't been on a motorcycle in over twenty years. But it all came back to her as she whipped through the streets towards the 101 Hollywood Freeway like some wild-eyed Motorcycle Mama. She prayed Ridley wouldn't speed onto the freeway, because with a sea of cars barreling along at sixty miles an hour, switching lanes at random, it would be a minefield of potential accidents.

She was closing in on him and he finally noticed her in his rearview mirror. At first he slowed down, believing it was his buddy trying to catch up, but when she was only a few cars away, he saw her hair whipping in the wind, unprotected by a helmet, and he panicked. He raced through a red light toward the free-way on-ramp, forcing two oncoming cars to hit the brakes and collide. The smash-up drew the attention of a police car that was turning onto the main street, and suddenly the flashing lights went on, and the cruiser, with two officers inside, pulled in front of Dani to give chase. Oh great. This was just what she needed. The cops involved.

Ridley zipped up the on-ramp to the Hollywood Freeway heading south toward downtown. Dani kept close behind the cruiser, trying not to draw too much attention to herself. In front of her, she saw one of the officers on his radio, obviously calling in backup. This guy caused an accident and was on the run and driving erratically and dangerously on a busy freeway. Within minutes, this chase would be broadcast over all the local TV stations, and if more pileups occurred as a result of it, maybe even CNN.

Ridley flew down the freeway, revving his engine to the max, and when he hit some heavy traffic, he steered the bike into the emergency lane. The cop car came upon the traffic suddenly, and the driver had to hit the brakes to avoid another collision. They were at a standstill, three lanes over from the emergency lane, and it looked like they were going to lose him. Dani took over the chase for them, weaving over to the emergency lane, and soaring along the freeway toward the downtown skyline. She was coming up fast on Ridley, who thought he had lost the cops, never expecting Dani to still be in pursuit.

As the two bikes raced ahead of the clogged up freeway and frustrated commuters towards the smattering of skyscrapers that made up downtown Los Angeles, a couple of helicopters hovered overhead. One was Channel 7 Eyewitness News and the other was obviously an LAPD chopper. Word was getting out fast that a major highway chase was underway, and Dani prayed that she would be able to explain why she was in the middle of it.

In her rearview mirror, she saw more police cruisers pouring onto the freeway and coming up behind her in the emergency lane. She debated moving over and allowing them to pass, but was afraid she'd be the one arrested and Ridley would get away.

Up ahead Ridley steered his Vulcan out of the emergency lane and back into traffic, weaving in and out of cars, trying desperately to get off the freeway. He was obviously hoping to get back onto surface streets where hopefully he could shake Dani and the army of cops.

Dani followed him, repeating his moves, and soon both were speeding down the off-ramp into a dicey section of town. The helicopters were passing over the freeways, the TV crew with their cameras still trained on the two bikes as they veered to the right and headed south. Ridley was panicked now, and just sped up, in a desperate attempt to escape. More cop cars crested over a hill and were bearing down on him. Dani and a few other cop cars were chasing him from behind. And the helicopters overhead were following his every move, the news choppers pointing their cameras. He was trapped.

In a last-ditch attempt, he spun around and raced down a side street, flying out into an intersection just as a truck passed through. The driver hit the brakes but it was too late. The grill of the truck mowed Ridley down, his bike nearly split in two, and he was hurled across the road and hit the ground with a sickening thud.

Dani slowed down, allowing the cop cars to race by her. She knew she would have to explain to the cops why she was chasing their suspect. A few calls to San Francisco might help. She wasn't sure. All she knew was at this point she was not going to divulge to the cops what she believed Ridley had done, what triggered his wild driving to begin with, because she had no concrete proof and there were still too many unanswered questions. She needed to step back and just let the cops do their job. And she was going to pray Lucas Ridley wasn't lying dead on that road now, because otherwise Maria Consuelos and her father Benito Coronel just might get away with it all.

CHAPTER 36

Dani called Claire from the hospital to give her an update. Lucas Ridley was in intensive care and the doctors were not sure at this point if he would pull through. She had luckily been able to downplay her role in the chase with the cops, who just chalked up her involvement as an overeager assistant chief from another city deciding to stick her nose into their police business that had nothing to do with her. Dani was happy they only ticketed her for speeding and driving in the emergency lane. It could have been much worse. They could have tossed her in jail, but that would have raised the ire of the San Francisco Police Department, the mayor, and quite possibly the governor, and that was one headache the LAPD just didn't need. So she was basically off the hook.

She was waiting for a further prognosis from the doctors, but it was clear that she wouldn't be getting any more information out of Lucas Ridley. At least for a while. She was laying low because police officers and reporters were swarming the area, and her main objective at this point was to just keep a low profile. She didn't want to be noticed.

"What are you doing here?" a woman's voice said.

So much for the low profile. Dani slowly turned around to face Maria Consuelos, in one of her signature short skirts and a glowering look on her face.

"I suppose I could ask you that same question," Dani said.

"I'm here to check on my client."

"Lucas Ridley is a client? Isn't that a conflict of interest?"

"What do you mean?"

"You shouldn't represent people you share a bed with, Maria. That's Law School 101."

"I don't know what you're talking about," Maria said. "But I wish you ladies would stop popping up everywhere I go. There's a law against stalking, you know."

"There's also a law against tainting evidence to clear your client, and daddy, Benito Coronel."

"You're talking crazy," Maria said, brushing past Dani and clicking down the hall in her high heels.

"What's really crazy is you're doing all this to save your father, and he might not even be your biological father."

This stopped Maria cold. She spun around and glared at Dani. She looked so angry, so vengeful; Dani believed if Maria had a gun in her hand at that moment, she would be a dead woman.

"You're making that up," Maria said.

"Check his medical records. He's had a low sperm count since he was a young man, making it virtually impossible for him to father children. Someone's been lying to you, Maria. Does your brother know he's not really a Coronel? Maybe someone should tell him. I don't suppose you have any idea where we can find him?"

She stepped forward, close enough to spit in Dani's face, which Dani half expected her to do. "If you three geriatric Charlie's Angels don't stop harassing me, I'm going to file charges with the police. I mean it. Stay the hell away from me."

And with that, she stormed down the hall towards the Intensive Care Unit, her heels madly clicking all the way.

CHAPTER 37

Claire lugged the box containing files on the Benito Coronel case up from the basement. Zak was lounging in the living room in a T-shirt and shorts watching a football game on ESPN. He was recovering nicely, but still complained about soreness, mostly because Claire suspected he wasn't anxious to give up being waited on hand and foot.

Claire had made her eldest son a plate of his favorite blueberry pancakes and he hungrily devoured them from his stretched-out position on the couch. She never allowed anyone to eat in her immaculately kept living room. She didn't go so far as to cover all the furniture pieces in plastic like her mother did, but she was very protective nonetheless.

Claire dropped the box in the middle of the living room floor. Zak watched her, stuffing a forkful of his pancake stack in his mouth.

"Oh, I get it. You waited for Dad to take off before you got back to work on this case," Zak said.

"Something like that. And I don't need you to tell him when he gets home either," Claire said, lifting off the box top and rummaging through the files.

"Hey, I think it's great you're doing something you love. I could tell teaching that self-defense class down at the community center wasn't doing it for you."

"You just don't get it. I'm not doing this for excitement. I don't miss that at all. I love my quiet, boring life. I'm doing this for you. I want to make sure nothing happens to you again like what happened at that hotel."

"Why don't you just tell Dad that?"

"I already tried. He doesn't believe me."

"He's probably just afraid he's going to lose you."

"To what?"

"I don't know. Maybe he's afraid you're going to go under-cover as a secretary for some rich, hot, older guy with his own company while investigating a case, fall in love, and be whisked off to a better life."

"That's the most ridiculous thing I've ever heard. Besides, my days of posing as a sexy secretary are long gone."

"Or maybe he's afraid of losing you to a stray bullet. You can't blame him for that."

"When I was younger, yes, I threw myself into situations that were fraught with danger, sometimes naively, and luckily they just happened to work out. But now, I'm much older, much wiser, and would never do anything so stupid. Once we figure out what's going on, we're calling in the police. We're not going to do anything risky. And your father should already know that."

Zak sat up, satisfied. He lowered the volume on the ESPN game with the remote and looked over the file folders his mother was spreading out on the living room floor. "Can I help?"

"Sure," Claire said. "These are all the files related to the Benito Coronel case. I've been over them once, but I want to read them all again to see if I possibly missed anything."

"Cool," Zak said, reaching down to pick one up and flip through it. "What should I be looking for?"

"Anything unusual, anything that might hint at why Coronel

is coming after us now, or if there is someone else we're not thinking about who might be tied into what's happening."

Zak nodded, scanning the file, shrugging and then tossing it back and picking up another.

Claire went through a detailed surveillance log that she kept during the original case when they were gathering evidence against Coronel to expose his drug empire. She spent a week tailing him to his meetings, his squash games, his cocktail parties, and trips to his furniture warehouses.

Zak read a similar file with interest. "Who's Abigail?"

"Coronel's wife. We've already talked to her. She's a real estate agent now."

"Man, according to your notes, she was escorted by a bodyguard at all times. This Coronel guy never let her out of his sight."

"He's very possessive in that way. But he was also thinking of her safety. He had a lot of enemies who wouldn't think twice of trying to get to him by harming his wife and children."

Zak perused a photo that was clipped to the folder. It was a picture of a younger-looking Abigail Foster and a handsome, strapping man, about a foot taller than she. "Who's this guy with her?"

Claire glanced at the photo. "Ronaldo Soares, one of Coronel's men. He was assigned to look after her."

"You can tell they spent a lot of time together, especially the way she's looking at him."

"What do you mean?" Claire took the photo from Zak and studied it. He was right. How had the Dolls missed this before? On the surface it appeared just to be a woman being escorted by a bodyguard. But the look on Abigail's face, as she glanced up at Ronaldo, it was the same look she had when Claire met her just a couple of days ago and she was talking about her husband. There was such longing and love in them despite the harsh words spewing out of her mouth about how she never wanted anything to do with him anymore. That same look. Was Abigail having a fling with Soares behind her husband's back all those years ago? But even more importantly, since Coronel couldn't have impregnated Abigail, was the father of her two children Ronaldo Soares?

Claire jumped up and hurried over to her handbag where she fished out the digital photo of Maria that Tess had taken with her cell phone at the spa and e-mailed to her and Dani. She held the photo of Abigail and Soares up next to the one of Maria. Yes. It was so obvious. They had the same eyes. The same complexion. The same nose. Ronaldo Soares had to be Maria's father.

Claire dug down into her handbag again and found the real estate card Abigail had given her. She quickly called the office, and was told that Abigail was out showing a house but would return by noon. Claire hung up, ran up the stairs to her bedroom to quickly change, and then headed out the door, telling Zak to get some rest and not to worry about going through the files anymore. But Zak barely heard her. He was engrossed and wasn't about to stop reading about his mother's daring exploits from the past.

Claire called Dani on her cell but got her voice mail. She left a message detailing what she suspected and told her to call her back just as soon as she could. She found a two-hour parking spot across the street from the realty office and waited for Abigail to show up. Noon came and went, but by twelve-fifteen, Abigail arrived, parked her car behind the building, and disappeared inside. Claire got out of her car, ran across the street and entered through the front.

The office was bustling, and Claire searched the bullpen until she saw Abigail in a back office, chatting on the phone.

The droopy-eyed receptionist who was just doing this until some casting agent discovered her, tried her best to be civil, but was probably hungry and really just wanted to go to lunch. "Can I help you?"

"I'm here to see Abigail Foster," Claire said.

"I'll see if she's available," the receptionist said, lazily picking up the phone and punching in an extension.

Claire could see Abigail in her office, on the phone, switching over to talk to the receptionist.

"Tell her it's Claire Corley, and I want to put in a bid for the house she showed me."

That was all it took. Within seconds, Abigail was racing to the front of the office to warmly greet Claire and escort her to the back where they could talk in private. After offers of coffee and sparkling water and a myriad of pastries, Claire found herself seated in front of Abigail's desk as the woman excitedly pulled the file on the house she supposedly wanted to buy.

"I knew that was the house for you," Abigail said. "I could feel it in my bones."

"Yes, I think we could be very happy there . . ."

"Now, how much would you like to offer?"

"But we just can't afford it."

Abigail looked up from her papers, a bit perplexed.

"I know I said I wanted to put in a bid, but that was just a ruse so you'd sit down and talk with me."

"I see," Abigail said, bristling. She had no idea where this was going. "What do you want to talk to me about?"

"Ronaldo Soares."

Abigail looked as if she might be sick. But she fought valiantly to keep her cool, and wasn't about to panic in front of this strange woman. "Who are you?"

"Claire Corley."

"I don't understand. I've never heard of . . ."

"My maiden name is Claire Walker."

It suddenly hit Abigail and she gasped. She gathered up her papers and stood up. "I think it's best if you leave now."

"I'm not going anywhere until I get the truth. Your ex-husband hired some thugs to go after my sons, Abigail. I'm sure you can understand why I'm doing everything I can to put a stop to it, especially since you're the mother of two. What would you do if someone from your past tried to get revenge on you by going after them?"

"If Benito wanted to hurt you, he would hurt you, not your children."

"Apparently that's not the case."

"I don't believe it."

"What do you think he would do if he found out your children in fact weren't his?"

Abigail's eyes were brimming with tears. She had fought so long to keep this secret and now a woman she barely knew, whom she vaguely remembered from those difficult years when her husband's business was raided and he was sent to prison, was now sitting in her office tearing apart all her carefully constructed lies.

"You were having an affair with Ronaldo, who was assigned to protect you."

Abigail sighed. There was no point in lying anymore. She was caught.

"Yes," she sighed, almost relieved to be getting it off her chest. "You're right. Benito treated me like a possession, not a person. He only trotted me out at parties or work functions where it was appropriate to have his wife there. But Ronaldo, he was so sweet, so giving, and with all the time we spent together, it was natural that we became involved. It felt so right, so pure."

"That was a pretty dangerous proposition to begin with, but then he got you pregnant. Twice. And you knew Benito would go ballistic if he found out he wasn't the father of either kid, and would probably have you both killed."

"Yes, it became obvious that I could never leave Benito for Ronaldo because it would mean instant death for both of us. So we continued for several years, secretly, whenever we could. Until you girls showed up. By then, I was tending to my children, practically living in isolation, and Ronaldo was doing his own thing, even seeing other women, like your friend."

"Tess."

"Yes. And soon after that, both Benito and Ronaldo were arrested and sent to prison."

"If your feelings for Ronaldo were so strong, why didn't you two get back together when he was released from prison?"

"Because Benito still had a long reach even behind bars, and I knew that our affair had to be kept a secret forever, because Benito would never rest until he got even with both of us. I was scared. Besides, Ronaldo had changed after his time in prison. He wasn't the same sweet man I had known before. He was hardened and bitter and he frightened me. I don't know why, but I wanted nothing more to do with him."

Abigail shifted in her seat, placing her hands on the desk and pulling herself forward to get close to Claire. "Please, I don't know how you came upon this information, but you cannot tell anyone, I beg you!"

"I'll try, but answer me this. Benito knew he had a low sperm count; he knew it was impossible to get you pregnant. How did you explain your pregnancies?"

"Benito is a proud man. When I told him I was pregnant with Maria, he assumed it was some kind of miracle despite what the doctors told him. I suppose his ego wouldn't allow him to even consider the possibility I was sleeping with another man. I never came clean with him, and it just got more complicated when I got pregnant again by Ronaldo. So I decided to pretend they both belonged to Benito, because it was imperative that my children live a life of privilege, and not be cast out onto the streets, which they would have been along with me if Benito found out they weren't his."

"Where is your son now?"

"I don't know. He knew I got in touch with Ronaldo once he was released from prison and came to suspect there was more to the story that I wasn't telling him. He pressed me until I admitted that Ronaldo was his father. It was as if in his heart he already knew he wasn't Benito's son. It was like a validation that he was right after all these years. Pedro and Benito were never close, not like he was with Maria. I begged him not to tell his sister. It would kill her."

"Did Pedro contact Ronaldo?"

"Yes. He flew down to Puerto Vallarta where Ronaldo runs his bar, and from what Pedro told me it went very well."

Claire began to wonder if Pedro was even connected to the attacks. If he didn't get along with his father, what would motivate him to avenge his imprisonment? And why would he wait so long? None of it made any sense.

"Where is your son now? I'd like to talk to him," Claire said.

"I don't know. We lost touch months ago. I called Ronaldo and he said Pedro left Mexico just a few weeks after he arrived and he had no idea where he was going. He stopped his cell phone service. Maria tried e-mailing him but heard nothing. Pedro did call Maria's husband once. He and Matt are very close friends. Matt said he talked about flying to Brazil for a while, but wasn't sure if he ended up going."

Claire froze. "Brazil?"

CHAPTER 38

Tess stood in the master suite below deck of her opulent, sprawling yacht, staring at herself in the wall-length mirror. She pressed back the skin around her left eye, trying to smooth out the wrinkles. Her expensive creams weren't working as well anymore, and it was worrying her. And she didn't want to worry because that just meant more lines on her face. She had read up on the Botox craze, but was hesitant to join the millions of women who were getting shot in the face with all sorts of toxins that would freeze up her nerve endings and smooth out her features. It just sounded so barbaric, but still, as she studied her complexion, she thought maybe it was time for some drastic measure. Up until now she had avoided the dreaded *F* word . . . *facelift*. Dani didn't seem to think twice about her looks, and Claire was so goddamned naturally beautiful, stunning from every angle. But Tess, the one all the men flocked to, in a bitter twist of fate, had to work the hardest of the three of them to stay young looking. It just wasn't fair.

Her thoughts wandered to Claire. She was still upset over their sudden and unexpected fight at her house. Tess felt Claire was being grossly unfair to Bianca and it was obvious she was taking some long-buried resentments toward her out on her daughter. She had never seen Claire so put out. And she certainly had never been on the receiving end of such a verbal thrashing. Tess was distressed by the ugly scene, and all the way back to her boat slip in Marina Del Ray she went over their years together in her mind, trying to pinpoint and examine all the grievances against her that Claire seemed to have collected. Yes, there had been that ugly business with Dan Hunter, a situation Tess deeply regretted and forever felt guilty about. She hadn't known the depth of Claire's feelings. Claire was always so relaxed and quiet and unassuming. She had no idea how much she had hurt her by becoming involved with him. But were there others? Tess admittedly was rather self-obsessed in those days, and might not have been the most sensitive to her partner's feelings. But Claire could have confronted her then, and not let the wounds fester over the years. What did it matter now anyway? She had Jeb, a good man, a solid husband and a wonderful father. Claire had it all now. And the love of Tess's life was long gone. Dead and buried. She was alone. Who should feel resentful now?

A pair of large hands slipped around Tess' waist, clasping her tightly and pulling her back into the rock-hard chest of Paulo. He squeezed her tightly and began to softly kiss her neck.

Well, she wasn't completely alone.

Paulo spun her around and covered her mouth with his own. He began to quickly unbutton her blouse. She gently pulled away.

"Paulo, sweetheart, not now."

She felt bad. She rarely turned down the opportunity to make love. And she knew Paulo would take it personally, and would be afraid he did something wrong.

"What is it, my love? What's the matter?" he asked with those adorable brown puppy dog eyes.

"I'm just not in the mood. I'm sorry."

He looked at her and frowned.

"It's not you. I promise. I just have a lot on my mind right now."

He nodded and pretended to understand.

Tess turned back around and stared in the mirror again. She could see Paulo standing behind her with a hangdog look, shuffling his feet like a little boy who didn't get a gold star on his paper from the teacher. God, he was so young. What was she thinking? But that body. And his sweet disposition. And his protective nature. So many good qualities. It wasn't hard getting past his age. He slowly turned to go.

"Paulo?"

He whirled back around with an expectant look on his face.

Tess couldn't help but laugh. Sometimes he could be so linear in his thoughts. He wanted sex and it was all he could focus on. And why not? He was young and virile and wildly horny.

"Come here," she said with one of her patented come hither looks.

He pounced on her like a leopard and they fell back on the bed. He straddled her, stripped off his shirt, and fell upon her, pinning her wrists with his hands and leaning down to kiss her breasts which were now spilling out of her half-open blouse.

Tess decided at that moment, as she was consumed by her Brazilian lover, to let all thoughts of Claire and their unresolved tension go, at least for now.

Paulo stopped briefly to unzip his pants. Sweat was forming on his brow. It was hot outside and the inside of the boat was humid. It would just make their lovemaking all the more exotic and animalistic.

Tess's cell phone rang. She had left it on the table next to the bed. Paulo still grasped her wrists so she was unable to reach for it. But she managed to turn her head far enough to the right to see the caller ID. It was Claire.

She had to answer it. Maybe Claire was calling to apologize

or at least talk it out. There was a chance to get past this, and she had to seize it.

"Paulo, I need to take that."

But he was insistent. And he kept her pinned to the bed. "No. Let it go to voicemail. You can talk to whoever it is later."

"Paulo, please . . ." Tess managed to get her knee up to her chest and shove him off her. Paulo, surprised, landed at the edge of the bed. He angrily got up and stormed out of the room.

Tess reached over and answered the call. "Claire?"

"Tess, I need to talk to you. Are you alone?"

Tess turned around but Paulo was gone. She assumed he must have gone to the upper deck or maybe the galley for a beer.

"Yes. What is it?"

Claire prattled on excitedly about Benito Coronel's low sperm count and how his two children, his daughter Maria and his son Pedro, were in fact the offspring of Ronaldo Soares, the man Tess used to gain access to Coronel's Topanga Canyon estate in the eighties. But more importantly, after locating his real father in Mexico, Pedro had reportedly traveled to Brazil. She thought maybe Pedro might have been one of Bianca's attackers, so she had asked Abigail for a recent photo of her son, and, when she produced it, she was shocked to discover that Pedro Coronel was really . . .

"Paulo?" Tess said. "There has to be some mistake. Are you saying Paulo has been lying to me about everything?"

"No, he's a soccer coach all right, according to his mother, but he's not Brazilian, and it's too much of a coincidence that the two of you just happened to meet. I think he planned this whirlwind romance. I think he's part of this whole plot and I want you to get out of there right now."

Tess climbed off the bed and began to hurriedly button her blouse. Claire was right. Something was seriously wrong. And it was probably best if she just got in her car and drove back to the Beverly Wilshire Hotel. She would move out of her suite to another room and give strict instructions to the staff not to tell Paulo where she was. At least until she could sort this mess out.

Tess gasped at the sight of Paulo, standing in the doorway, a revolver in his hand. He was pointing it right at her. He must have been hovering outside and heard everything.

"Tess, what is it?" Claire said with a worried lilt in her voice.

"Tell her you're fine and hang up. Now." Paulo cocked the gun and Tess suddenly had no doubt he would use it if he had to. She didn't know him anymore. How could she have been so stupid?

"Did he come back?" Claire said. "Tess, are you still there?"

"I'm here, Claire," Tess said. "Everything's fine. Paulo has gone out."

"Good. I want you to come over to my house right now where you'll be safe."

"Okay," Tess said and then turned off the cell phone. Paulo snatched it out of her hand and hurled it across the room where it smashed against the wall and shattered.

"I don't believe it," Tess said, shaking her head. "This was your plan all along. To romance me and get close to me so you could help your father get revenge on us."

Paulo didn't answer her. He just wiped the sweat off his brow. He was fidgety and nervous and Tess was concerned he might accidentally shoot her.

"Why did you wait so long to reveal yourself? We've been together for months. You could have killed me anytime. You had plenty of opportunities."

Paulo didn't want to answer her, but Tess was insistent. "Why, Paulo?"

"Because I didn't count on . . ."

"What? You didn't count on what?"

"I didn't count on my feelings," he said in almost a whisper.

Tess stared at him. He was tortured by this new development. He had delayed revealing himself and carrying out whatever

243

plans he had for her because he had fallen in love with her, and now he was torn. But now with everything out in the open, Tess worried he might panic and choose now to kill her.

"You're an incredible woman, Tess. And it's just made everything more difficult and complicated."

"You can just walk out of here, and it won't be so complicated anymore."

"No. I'm sorry, Tess. I can't do that."

Paulo charged over to Tess and grabbed her by the arm. Tess saw the wild look in his eyes and her heart skipped a beat. This man, who only moments ago tried to make love to her, was now in a state where he just might murder her.

CHAPTER 39

When Lucas Ridley was moved out of intensive care to a private room, Dani waited for her chance to slip in for a talk with him. The only problem was Maria Consuelos. She kept a vigil over her young lover, and wasn't going anywhere. And for the sake of the other patients, Dani thought it would be best to keep her distance. Otherwise the hot young lawyer might pick a catfight and get them both kicked out of the hospital. No, Dani decided it was best to wait it out. Maria would have to leave sometime. Dani sat in the waiting area, thumbing through a news magazine, keeping one eye on the door to Ridley's room.

After a couple of hours, she heard the familiar clicking of Maria's high heels as she marched down the hall to the elevators. She was finally leaving. Or maybe she was just heading down to get something to eat in the cafeteria. It didn't matter. This was Dani's one chance. There was no police guard outside Ridley's door, because in his current condition there was little chance of him trying to escape.

Dani tossed the magazine back on the pile, hurried down the hall, and casually entered the room. Ridley was stretched out on a bed, one arm in a cast, tubes coming out of his arm, his face bruised and battered. His eyes were closed and he was resting. The television set which was mounted on the wall was on, but the volume was low. Dani cautiously approached. She toyed with the idea of continuing her tough-cop personality, getting up in his face, making threats, scaring the hell out of him so he would talk. But with her officers back in San Francisco calling her "Mom," she figured her days of intimidating suspects were long over. Maybe it was time to change her tactics. Instead of being brazen and loud and menacing, perhaps a more motherly approach was required.

She gently reached out and touched Ridley's arm. He slowly opened his eyes, smiling, expecting to see his beloved Maria. He jumped at the sight of Dani.

"Relax, Lucas, relax, I'm not here to hurt you."

"Get out of here," he said in a strained voice.

"Look, I'm sorry I was so abrupt before. I know you're in a lot of pain and the last thing I want to do is cause you any further stress. Are you cold? Can I get you another blanket?"

Lucas gave her a quizzical look. Was this the same woman who confronted him on the street and made him run and get into an accident?

Dani hated acting all sweet. What she really wanted to do was punch this idiot in the face and force him to talk. But she knew that would probably be a mistake.

"I know we got off on the wrong foot, and I deeply regret upsetting you and I feel terrible about your accident and in a small way I feel responsible."

"In a small way? Lady, you were on my ass like nobody's business! It was all your fault I got slammed by that truck!"

He was the one who was driving the bike not her. Dani wanted to wrap her hands around his throat and squeeze until his tongue turned blue. But she resisted. She had to keep working on this sweeter approach.

"I'm sorry for the way things turned out, Lucas. But I had my reasons for chasing you. I had to know if you tainted Benito Coronel's blood samples. And I got my answer."

"Yeah, what's that?"

"Of course you did it, dear. Otherwise why on earth would you have run away from me?"

"You're whacked, lady. I didn't do anything illegal!"

"I am a police officer, just like I told you, Lucas, but I'm from San Francisco. I have nothing to do with the LAPD and the charges they're going to bring against you, and I promise you I will not relay to them anything you want to tell me about those blood samples."

"Why should I tell you anything?"

"Because Benito Coronel is a very bad man and he wants to hurt my son, and I'm just being a protective mother. And I was hoping you might understand that. I bet you have a mother who worries about you and wants to make sure you're safe."

Lucas looked into her eyes, studying her, and for an instant Dani thought she had him. He was thinking about his mother and his face softened. It was almost too easy. This "being nice" business may not be overrated after all.

"Fuck you," Lucas said, turning his head away.

That did it. Screw the nice act. She'd leave that to Claire or Tess. Dani grabbed his arm in the cast and twisted it up. Lucas yelped in pain, his face full of agony.

"All right, you little shit, I've run out of patience. Do you know how many years you could get for tampering with state's evidence?"

"Let go! You're killing me!"

"Maria's given you her last blow job, that's for sure! When I'm through with you, the only sex you'll be getting is from some three-hundred-pound homie who's got more STDs than tattoos."

Lucas gasped from the excruciating pain and Dani kept one eye on the door to make sure no one walked in to find her abusing a patient.

Lucas desperately tried to catch his breath, and through his gritted teeth, he hissed, "Yes, I did it. Just let go."

Dani instantly released Ridley's arm and it collapsed on the bed with one final jolt of pain that made him grimace.

"I'm listening," Dani said.

Ridley took a few seconds to regain his composure, and then eyed Dani warily, worried she might inflict more pain on him if he didn't tell her what she wanted to hear.

"I was working in the lab. Hell, I was in charge of the tamper-proof packaging, so I was able to taint the sample before wrapping it up and sending it out for the results. You wouldn't believe how easy it was."

"Did Maria ask you to do it?"

"No. Not in so many words. But she was really worried about how long her father could last in prison and I hated seeing her so upset, and she was pinning her hopes on a new trial that was never going to happen, so when the subject of DNA testing came up, I knew that was one way I could help her."

"How did you and Maria meet?"

"In a bar. Near the lab. I couldn't believe such a beautiful girl was flirting with me. I never thought in a million years someone like that would be interested. But she was. And we've been dating for a few months now. And it's been going great."

Poor Lucas. It still hadn't dawned on him that although Maria may not have outright asked him to help her clear her father, she put the idea in his head, and manipulated him through his feelings for her and probably a whole lot of fantastic sex to get what she wanted out of him.

Why would Maria go to a dive bar near a testing lab unless she had good reason? She spent most of her time in Beverly

Hills hair salons or exclusive day spas with herbal wraps and mud baths.

Dani didn't have the heart to tell Lucas he had been duped. The fact that Maria was sticking around was just to make sure he didn't talk. Then, after a little while, with her father home and with no threat of him ratting her out, she would grow distant, perhaps emphasize their differences in values and goals, or her desire to make it work with Matt, and then quietly end the relationship with just the right amount of tears and regret. And without him ever realizing she had used him, she would disappear out of his life, changing her contact information so he would never be able to get in touch with her again. And, in the unlikely event he was unstable, and couldn't accept her leaving, if he became some kind of stalker, well, then Daddy could arrange to have him disappear in order to protect his precious girl from any harm from an overemotional ex-boyfriend. As well as keep him out of prison. It was all conjecture and theory, but Dani knew with certainty that this was Lucas's fate.

"If you tell Maria I told you any of this, I'll deny it, I swear," Lucas said, suddenly worried as he contemplated what he just admitted.

"Maria's not the one you should worry about, Lucas. You're already facing a laundry list of charges for that little high-speed chase you led me and the cops on. This little trick you did in the name of love is just going to add to your troubles."

Dani knew the state's case against Benito Coronel would be rock solid once new blood samples were tested against the sweat and blood found on the murder weapon. Because there was no doubt in Dani's mind that Benito Coronel did in fact personally carry out the murder of poor Lenny Fowler—by bashing in his head with that wooden chair leg. And if it was the last thing Dani did, she would make sure to be there in person to see Coronel tossed back in prison.

Dani turned to leave.

"Hey, where are you going?" Ridley said, straining to sit up in his bed.

Dani pulled out a tiny tape recorder from her handbag and held it up to show Lucas. "I'm done here, Lucas. You're on your own."

The blood drained from Lucas' face. How could he have been so stupid?

Dani marched out and saw Maria walking down the hall with a tray of food. Dani did an about-face and scurried off in the opposite direction. She didn't feel like dealing with her right now. That time would come once she realized that Dani had forced the truth out of Lucas, once and for all sealing her father's fate.

By the time Dani emerged from the hospital, she was on the phone with the Los Angeles Chief of Police who took her call out of professional courtesy. Within an hour, the police arrested Benito Coronel.

He was walking out of his favorite lunch spot, Delmonico's, on Pico Boulevard in West Los Angeles. He was surprised when the cops surrounded him. He was downright furious when he spotted Dani Mendez waving to him from across the street as he was hustled into the squad car. The LA Dolls had screwed him again.

Word spread fast about Coronel's arrest, and by the time he was delivered to the downtown jail, the place was swarming with reporters and TV cameras.

After dropping the tape off to the detective in charge of the case, Dani arrived back at Claire's house in Sherman Oaks, and although Claire was still out, Zak let her in and the two of them watched the highly publicized arrest on an afternoon special news report. Coronel's rage was building by the minute. There was no doubt his daughter Maria had been keeping him abreast of what the LA Dolls were doing behind the scenes, following and harassing her, working hard to blow his newfound freedom. And he was boiling mad. It showed on the television when he lost his temper and began spewing in front of the cameras. The stress had gotten to him.

"Those bitches, those Dolls, who were so instrumental in railroading me to prison in the first place, are out there working very hard to destroy my family. And I want them to know, I want you all to know, my family will not allow them to continue this vicious, ruthless campaign to defame my character and keep me imprisoned. It is up to my children now to save us."

Dani had half a mind to call those same reporters and tell them that the children Benito Coronel was counting on weren't even his. But she decided to take the high road.

Dani was already aware that Tess's young lover Paulo was Pedro Coronel. Claire had already called her with the news. She really had no reason to worry, because Claire assured her that Tess had left Paulo on the yacht and was heading back to the Beverly Wilshire Hotel. Tess was safe.

Thank God. She couldn't imagine what Paulo would do to Tess now that everything was out in the open.

CHAPTER 40

Dani pulled into Claire's driveway and hopped out of the car. Claire came rushing out of the house to greet her.

"Have you talked to Tess?" Dani asked.

"Not since I first called you about an hour ago," Claire said, her face now full of worry. "Why?"

"I've been calling her suite at the Beverly Wilshire and there is no answer."

"She should have arrived there by now. When I talked to her she was leaving Marina Del Ray. Did you try her cell?"

"Repeatedly. I keep getting her voice mail."

"Did you try Bianca?"

"Not yet. I didn't want to worry her. How did she sound when you talked to her?"

Claire shrugged. "Fine. I mean sure she was a little stressed, but I had just dropped the bomb that Paulo wasn't who he said he was."

"And you're sure Paulo wasn't there with her?"

"She said she was alone."

Dani scooped up her phone and dialed the Beverly Wilshire again, asking for Tess's suite. The phone rang and rang and Dani

253

grew more and more anxious. Something wasn't right. She could feel it.

Claire grabbed her own phone out of her bag and punched in a number. "I'm calling Bianca."

Dani hung up and sat down at the kitchen table trying to think about where Tess might have gone.

"Bianca, hello, it's Claire."

Dani perked up, praying Bianca would tell them that she was with Tess at that very moment.

"No, that's okay. I don't need to speak to Evan. Do you know where I can find your mother?"

Claire listened and nodded. "I see. Well, if you hear from her, would you have her call me here at the house?"

Dani cursed to herself. This was getting serious. Tess was in some kind of trouble. She could feel it in her bones.

"No, dear, nothing's wrong. I just need to speak with her. All right, enjoy yourselves. Bye." Claire hung up and turned to Dani. "She and Evan drove up to Santa Barbara for the day. She hasn't spoken to Tess since this morning."

"Okay, let's not panic. She's not on the yacht. She's not at the hotel. Where could she be?"

"And where's Paulo?"

Dani didn't want to think about that. Her cell phone chirped, startling both of them. She saw on the caller ID that it was Bowie. She quickly answered it.

"Hi, sweetheart," Dani said.

"Hey, Mom, I'm at the Puerto Vallarta Airport about to board a flight back to Miami, but I wanted to fill you in on what I found."

"What are you doing in Mexico?"

"I flew down this morning. I was following up on a lead and I think I turned up something you might find interesting."

"What is it?"

"I have a buddy in the Miami Police Department, a detective. Actually we dated a few times, but that's another story."

And one Dani wanted to hear, but another time.

"Anyway, he slipped me the late Doobie Slater's address, an apartment building in the Art Deco district. So I went over there and broke in before his family arrived to clean out his stuff."

"What did you find?"

"Just a big mess. Doobie apparently wasn't a big believer in keeping his space clean. It was like a hurricane hit the place. But I did manage to find a few bank statements and his checkbook in a pile of bills and supermarket flyers. I went through the cancelled checks and one really stood out. It was made out in the amount of ten thousand dollars."

"You think that's some kind of payment for taking a potshot at you in Mexico City?"

"At first I thought so, but the check wasn't from anyone connected to the Coronel organization. It was drawn from a bank in Puerto Vallarta. The signature on the check was illegible, just chicken scratch, so I decided to hop a plane south and pay a visit to the bank. I made it there with about twenty minutes to spare before closing, and I didn't think the teller was going to cooperate with me, so I threw out your friend's name."

"Tess?"

"Yeah, she sure does open a lot of doors."

"Tess has some properties in Mexico that were probably financed through that very bank."

"Next thing I know I was ushered into the bank president's office and he couldn't have been more helpful."

"Was he able to identify the signature?"

"No. But he was able to tell me whose account it was drawn from. The Blue Parrot. It's a bar downtown near the beach. I went down there and it was all boarded up and nobody was there. I checked with a few locals but nobody would tell me the name of the owner."

Dani looked up at Claire, who was wringing her hands nervously. "You ever hear of a bar called the Blue Parrot?"

"Yes. Tess mentioned it. That's the name of the place owned by Ronaldo Soares. She went there and talked to him and then crossed him off our list of suspects."

Dani's stomach did a flip-flop. It was all coming together now. "Bowie, honey, that's a big help. Thank you. Call me when you land safely back in Miami."

"Will do, Mom. Love you."

"I love you too, sweetheart."

Dani hung up.

Claire sat down with her at the kitchen table. "What is it? Is it Ronaldo Soares?"

"He paid Doobie ten grand to try and kill Bowie down in Mexico City. He missed, but killed an innocent man in cold blood."

"But why? He was just a bodyguard. I can't believe he'd go to all this trouble to get back at us for putting his boss behind bars."

"But he's the one. He has to be. Benito Coronel wasn't the one who hired a bunch of lowlifes to go after our kids. It was Ronaldo Soares."

Dani instinctively reached for her cell to call Tess again, but deep down she knew she wouldn't answer. And it sent shivers through her entire body. Was Tess even still alive?

CHAPTER 41

Dani and Claire didn't expect to find Tess on her yacht, but it was the only place they knew to look. They were desperate. The ride over the 405 freeway from the valley to Marina Del Ray was interminable. They drove in silence, both worried about what might have happened to her and trying not to think about the worst-case scenario. When they parked the car and ran past the line of expensive boats towards Tess's slip, Dani's heart began to race. She feared they might find their friend's body and had horrible visions of what Paulo might have done to her as they climbed aboard the yacht and did a quick search. Fortunately, they found nothing. No trace of Tess or Paulo or anyone.

"She's got to be with Paulo. But where?" Dani said more to herself than to Claire.

Claire looked around, knowing that if Tess had any idea where Paulo, aka Pedro, would be taking her, she would undoubtedly do her best to leave behind some kind of clue or message that would point them in the right direction. She checked Tess's closets and drawers in the main stateroom. Meanwhile, Dani was calling the Beverly Wilshire Hotel on the off chance they were

257

wrong about the whole thing and Tess might be just returning from an afternoon shopping spree.

"Dani!" Claire called out from the stateroom.

Dani stuffed her phone in her pocket and hurried down the steps below deck to join her.

Claire was pointing at a glass-top coffee table where Tess's bag was tipped over, the contents spilled out.

"Okay, so she was obviously here and taken away by force. She never would leave this boat without her bag."

Dani sifted through the makeup, the compact, some hand-written notes to herself and found a thick wad of cash. Obviously her kidnapper wasn't after her money. This just worried Dani more. Paulo was out for revenge in the name of his father. His real father. Ronaldo Soares. But why?

"Look at this," Claire said, kneeling down and studying some markings on the glass table top. There were several letters scrawled out in what appeared to be a pink shade of lipstick. "She tried to write out a word or something. T-O-P-A . . ."

"What does it mean?"

"I have no idea. I've never even heard of that word," Claire said studying the hurried markings. "If it's a word."

"She probably didn't have a lot of time. Maybe just a few seconds before he dragged her off."

"Do you think that's just part of the whole message?"

"I would bet on it. Those letters could be an acronym for something."

They stood there looking at the hasty lipstick message but nothing came to them. Dani was about to give up trying to think what Tess's message meant when she gasped with the sudden realization.

"What is it?" Claire said, turning to her.

"It's not an acronym. Tess just didn't have a chance to spell out the whole word. Topanga. Paulo must have told her he was taking her to Topanga Canyon."

"Benito Coronel's ranch."

"It's got to be at least a half hour from here," Claire said, pounding up the steps toward her car.

Dani was right behind her. She was praying they wouldn't be too late.

CHAPTER 42

Even after he was sent to prison, Benito Coronel refused to sell his beloved Topanga Canyon hideaway. Abigail didn't want it when they divorced. In fact, she tried to convince Benito to sell it, but he refused. The house had sentimental value to him, it was the centerpiece of his criminal empire, and although his lawyers managed to scrape together what little was left of Coronel's fortune to pay off the back taxes, it had fallen into disrepair from years of neglect. Coronel hoped to make a triumphant return someday when he was released from prison and restore the sprawling ranch-style house into the glorious showpiece it once was. But now it was dusty and rickety, the house itself in desperate need of a paint job, with a few broken windows from trespassers and homeless squatters.

Paulo told Tess where he was planning to take her even before he hustled her into a rental car and drove her up the Pacific Coast Highway towards Topanga Canyon, which is why she tried to go back for her purse that was sitting on the coffee table. She pretended to knock it over buying her a few precious seconds, quickly grabbing her lipstick and writing out as much as she could before Paulo stormed back and grabbed her by the arm and hauled her out of the stateroom. She didn't even know how much she had managed to write with the lipstick, or even if it was legible enough, but she had to hold out hope that Dani and Claire would be able to figure everything out because Paulo was on edge. He was jumpy and nervous and about to do something stupid. Tess held her breath waiting for the inevitable.

When they arrived, he dragged a wobbly old chair to the center of the living room, pushed Tess down and tied her up with some rope. She was lucky he didn't gag her. She couldn't believe this young man, for whom she cared so deeply and so passionately, had completely tricked her, made her feel like a fool. How could she have been so wrong about him? How was it possible after all the intimate moments they shared?

She wanted to kick herself. Her radar was usually so good at discerning a man's motive and intentions. Her hardened shell had been a result of inheriting her late husband's vast wealth. So many men wanted a piece of it, and Tess was the most direct path to the keys to the vault.

But Paulo had been so gentle, so unencumbered by greed and ambition. He was such a breath of fresh air. She had been right about him though in one sense. He wasn't interested in her money.

"Why now, Paulo? You must have known Maria was working hard to come up with new evidence to free your father. Why did you feel the need to come after me at a time when she was so close to getting him released?" Tess asked as Paulo watched her, his eyes narrow, so full of anger.

"Do you think this was about avenging *him*? He treated me like dirt my whole life. I have no allegiance to that murdering drug dealer."

"Then why?"

"For my father," Paulo said his voice low and troubled.

"But Benito Coronel isn't your father."

"I know that. I'm talking about my real father."

Ronaldo Soares.

Paulo just stared at Tess. "I never dreamed it would be so easy to get close to you. Not in a million years. I knew you were based in Brazil. Who doesn't? The papers write about you all the time. I had a friend in the school system there, a teacher, who e-mailed me and told me they were looking for a soccer coach, so I applied. Then I heard you would be hosting a benefit to help save the athletic program. I had only been there a couple of weeks before you showed up for the event and I was able to introduce myself."

Tess felt so stupid. She had played right into his hand, always the sucker for a hot Brazilian athlete, who now it was clear wasn't even Brazilian but was able to pass as one. But she was done analyzing this scam love affair and her predictable behavior.

"Paulo, I understand why you didn't kill me, but why target Bianca? Why put me through that if you really did feel something for me?"

"What are you talking about?"

"The thugs who tried to snatch her in Rio, the ones who shot at Dani's son in Mexico, and the others who beat up Claire's son the night before his wedding."

Paulo gave her a puzzled look. "I don't know anything about that. I had nothing to do with it."

"If that's true, then the only thing you've really done is break my heart," Tess said her eyes welling up with tears. "Untie me now and we can just go our separate ways."

Paulo raised his shirt and pulled out his handgun. "No. They'll send me away for kidnapping. I can't just walk away from this. I have to take care of this now."

"Paulo, please . . ."

He pointed the gun at Tess. "You're so beautiful. What a waste. I'm sorry, Tess."

Tess struggled against the ropes, but he had done a good job of securing them in a double knot. She was helpless.

Paulo's hands were shaking and his aim with the gun was unsteady. Tess took a deep breath. She thought he was desperate enough to actually pull the trigger.

But he didn't. He kept the weapon trained on Tess but he was still hesitating, wrestling with himself.

Tess knew if she was going to save herself, she had to take advantage of the conflict raging inside of her young lover. But how? There was nothing left for her to do, nothing left for her to say.

"Paulo, I love you," she said, dropping her head and fighting back tears. She wasn't lying. She did. She had broken her own rule. She vowed never to fall in love again after the death of her husband. And she had remained steadfast in her conviction. But Paulo had gotten to her over the last few months with his sweet, dancing eyes and joyous devotion. He hung on her every word and constantly proclaimed his passion for her. There was no way he could have faked that. He may have conned his way into her life, but as she sat there tied to the chair, she knew she had seen the real Paulo, or the real Pedro Coronel. It wasn't all an act. And he wasn't the only one who gave over his heart. She had let her guard down. She had developed real feelings for him.

Paulo's eyes were now brimming with tears. He believed her. He knew this wasn't some kind of desperate trick she was attempting to save her life. He lowered the gun but kept it aimed in her direction. He was consumed with emotion. Grief over his actions. Confusion over how they got to this point. Despair over his current circumstances. He was trapped. And he had to do something to save himself. And a big voice inside of him was yelling at him to take care of business. Do away with Tess and run far away from this seriously botched revenge plot.

Tess read all of this in Paulo's face. He was either going to shoot her or let her go. And she knew in her heart he was leaning toward letting her go. Unfortunately, however, the decision was made for him.

"Do it, Pedro. Do it now," a male voice said from behind Tess.

Paulo looked up, surprised. Tess was bound too tight to turn around. But she didn't have to because she recognized the voice. She knew who it was.

Ronaldo Soares entered the filthy, weathered room. His towering presence startled Paulo, who absentmindedly lowered his gun and gaped at the man who had so suddenly interrupted the scene.

"What are you doing here?" he asked in a shaky, cracked voice.

"Look at you, Pedro, finally ready to be a man and carry out the plan we talked about," Ronaldo said with a smile as he walked around in front of Tess and leered at her. "And look at you, Tess. All tied up and unable to get away. This is a fantasy I've been dreaming about for years."

"How did you get here, Ronaldo?"

"Abigail called and tipped me off that you and your two friends were closing in on the truth. She was panicked. She didn't want Benito to find out. I staked out your yacht in the marina and I followed the two of you here. I was hoping Pedro would save me the trouble and do away with you himself, but I've learned not to count on him for the dirty work."

Tess knew it was easy for anyone to track her. She had forfeited her eligibility for undercover assignments the day she married her super-rich shipping magnate husband. Now she was a fixture on the society pages worldwide and there was absolutely no way she could keep a low profile and hide from anybody. Just how much was this inconvenience going to cost her?

"So I guess it's up to me to take care of business," Ronaldo said, edging closer to Paulo and his gun.

"You two planned this together?"

"Yes," Ronaldo said leering at Tess. "We wanted to get revenge on all three of you. Pedro was going to start with you.

What better way than to make you fall in love with him and then betray that trust and kill you with his bare hands? Just like you once betrayed my trust. But Pedro got soft. He kept postponing it, kept feeding me a line about waiting until the time was right. The fact was, he had fallen so hard for you he couldn't do the deed. And then he stopped taking my calls. He cut me out completely. So I had to move on with a new plan."

"Going after our kids," Tess said, sickened.

Paulo stared blankly at Ronaldo Soares. He didn't want to believe it. "That was you? We never discussed that. Why would you do that?"

Ronaldo flashed him a smile and then made a quick grab for Paulo's gun, snatching it out of the shocked man's grasp.

Tess let out a desperate sigh. This wasn't good. Paulo was her only shred of hope of making it out of here alive and now he was unarmed.

Ronaldo toyed with the gun as he stood menacingly near Tess. He looked Paulo up and down with disgust. "I had to. You proved to be an embarrassing disappointment. I only wish my other boy, my real son, was still alive to make me proud. But you three Dolls made sure that was never going to happen."

Tess looked at him as she replayed the events over in her mind. And then she remembered. "That boy, the one in the guard shack, the one you were training to work for Coronel one day, that boy was . . ."

"My son. Yes. Marco. And you killed him."

"No!"

"You distracted me while your two friends raided the compound and started shooting up the place. My boy got shot. You murdered him in cold blood."

"How can you say that? Coronel had twenty men firing guns and that boy was caught in the crossfire. Nobody could possibly know who was responsible for shooting him."

"You three raided the place. You set everything off. You're responsible! All three of you! You have no idea the pain I've been living with all these years. He was a good boy. He was my whole world."

"Where was his mother?"

"Dead. Car accident in Mexico. She was the love of my life. I was raising him myself. Teaching him the business."

"What about Pedro and Maria, the two children you had with Abigail?"

"They were never mine. Not really. They were always going to be Benito's. I had to accept that and move on with my life. Benito would have cut my throat if he knew the truth, so I focused on the one son I did have until you took him away . . ."

"How did you get Pedro to help you?" Tess said as she shot a look at her young lover, who just stood there with a lost look on his face.

"When Pedro found out I was his real father he came down to Mexico to see me. It didn't take him long to fully appreciate the pain you three Dolls caused me. The pain you caused his mother and sister, and yes, even the father who mistreated him. And Marco, my son, Pedro's half brother, shot dead because of you. We had a few drinks at my bar one night and decided it was time to make the LA Dolls pay. Pedro was only too happy to do whatever he needed to do to help his real father finally find peace."

Tess craned her neck to look at Paulo. "The man you thought was your father rejected you all your life, so when you finally came face to face with your real father, you were willing to do anything to win his approval and love, is that it, Paulo? Is that how you got mixed up in all this?"

Paulo didn't move. He just kept his eyes fixed on the floor, unable to look at Tess.

"Except he was weak," Ronaldo spit out. "And foolish. I warned him about you. How you can get a man right where you want him. And yet he still let you manipulate his feelings like you did mine all those years ago. He got all wistful and whiny and said he didn't want to hurt you. He backed out of our plan."

"So you went with Plan B," Tess said with disgust. "You used that recent financial windfall you told me about at your bar to finance your revenge. I knew there had to be a reason you didn't fix up the place. We're probably not talking about a lot of money, because you couldn't afford to hire anyone halfway competent to carry out the job you had in mind. You got yourself a bunch of idiots who came cheap, like Doobie Slater in Florida. And they screwed up big time."

Tess's eyes flickered over to Paulo who had slid down the wall and was now sitting on the floor, his knees pulled up to his chest, his face streaked with tears. He was watching the scene, trying to process all that was going on, and at a complete loss as to what to do next.

Ronaldo still fingered the gun and kept his eyes glued on Tess.

"When your buddies didn't get the job done, you figured that was it. You could bide your time and try again when you could finally get your act together and pay for some real hit men. But you never expected the three of us, Dani, Claire, and me, to band together after all these years to find out who was behind it all. So you and your mercenary buddies began keeping tabs on us to make sure we didn't uncover any connection to you. I'm betting one of your Miami thugs shot Doobie Slater in Florida before he had the chance to give Dani your name. Because the one certainty in your life is that you'll never survive another ten years in prison. You wouldn't be able to take that. You were so sure we were going to blame Coronel because we were so hot on his trail, and you thought we'd go to any lengths to pin it all on him and then you would be in the clear. But it just didn't work out the way you wanted it to. So what now, Ronaldo? What are you going to do now?"

"Well, for starters I can shoot you," Ronaldo said, suddenly raising the gun and pointing it at her face.

Tess squeezed her eyes shut and braced herself for the inevitable. But it didn't come. Suddenly she heard a struggle and opened her eyes to see Paulo fighting Ronaldo for possession of the gun.

Paulo had made a last-minute decision to spring forward and attempt to save her life. Ronaldo punched Paulo in the face in an effort to push him away so he would let go of the gun. But Paulo was younger and stronger and fought back delivering a forceful blow to Ronaldo's solar plexus. The air whooshed out of him and his grip on the gun loosened just enough for Paulo to make a grab for it. But Ronaldo was expecting this, and slipped his finger around the trigger and squeezed back. There was a loud pop and Paulo, clutching his stomach, blood seeping through his shirt, collapsed to the floor.

Tess screamed with anguish and struggled mightily against her bonds to get to him but it was impossible. She couldn't move. Her body went limp and she just kept shaking her head and saying, "No . . . no . . . no . . ."

Ronaldo straightened up and stared at Paulo, who was still alive but just barely. As their eyes met, the enormity of what he had just done seemed to finally seep into his consciousness. He had shot his own son. The life drained out of Paulo and his head tilted downward. He was gone.

Still gripping the gun, Ronaldo slowly twisted around and turned his weapon on Tess. She gazed at him defiantly, refusing to allow him any satisfaction by showing even the slightest hint of fear. She sat back in the chair to accept her fate.

Ronaldo pulled the trigger. There was a click. The gun was out of bullets. He hurled the weapon across the room and lunged at Tess, wrapping his big hands around her throat, choking the life out of her.

The chair tipped over and the two went crashing to the floor.

The right leg on the chair snapped off, freeing Tess's left foot. She began kicking out at Ronaldo hard, hoping the pain might get him to back off, which would buy her maybe a few more seconds of life. He shifted his weight, trapping her free leg, pinning her to the floor. Her hands were still tied behind the back of the chair. There was nothing left to do but wait until she lost consciousness.

The front door was suddenly kicked open. Tess couldn't tell what was happening at first, but she knew someone was dragging Ronaldo off of her. She was light-headed and barely conscious, but she felt someone untying her hands. Everything was blurry but she was able to open her eyes and see Dani pummeling Ronaldo with the butt of her own gun, while holding Ronaldo by a fistful of his hair. And then, when she was freed from the chair, she saw Claire helping her up, and she finally felt safe. Her friends had rescued her. Just like old times.

Dani snapped a pair of handcuffs on Ronaldo. Dani never left the house without her handcuffs. And Claire gave Tess a bottle of water she had brought in from the car. Tess took a sip, feeling replenished and relieved, but then she saw Paulo's body sprawled on the floor. She began weeping all over again as she staggered over and threw herself on top of him. It was all so pointless, so senseless.

It also wasn't over. None of them had heard the other car pull up. Dani had set her gun down on a table in order to join Claire in comforting Tess. After all, there was nobody up here except for maybe a pack of wild coyotes foraging for food.

This was why the three former LA Dolls were surprised by the sudden appearance of Maria Consuelos in the doorway. She had a pistol in her hand and a seriously deranged look on her face. Maria was here for one reason. She was hell-bent on avenging the only father she had ever known—Benito Coronel.

CHAPTER 43

Maria's eyes gazed at her brother's twisted, dead body on the floor. She choked back tears as she whispered softly, "Pedro . . . Oh God, Pedro!"

"They did it!" Ronaldo screamed, his hands cuffed behind his back. "Those three killed him, just like they murdered my boy, my Marco!"

Dani and Claire helped Tess maintain her balance. She was still dizzy, but she was otherwise all right. Claire kept a hand firmly on her elbow to steady her.

Dani shook her head. "No, Maria, it was Ronaldo who shot him."

"Pedro called me and said to meet him here. He sounded panicked and desperate . . ."

"He was in trouble. Ronaldo had gotten him mixed up in some bad business," Tess said, still weeping and holding the limp hand of her dead lover. "He wanted you to help him get out of it . . ."

"He didn't sound right and it made me suspicious so I brought this just in case," Maria said as she raised the gun at the women. "My father always taught me to protect myself."

"Put the gun down, Maria," Dani said evenly. "It's over."

"No, it's not," Maria hissed, cocking the gun. "Wherever you three go, death and destruction are sure to follow. Somebody needs to stop you."

"Listen to me, Maria, don't make things worse for Benito. He's already being sent back to prison. That's going to be tough enough on him," Dani said. "The last thing he needs is to know the daughter he loves is going on trial for a triple murder."

"You said he wasn't my father," Maria spat out. "Now you're saying he is just to save yourself?"

"He's the father who raised you, provided for you, but it's true, your biological father is Ronaldo. Look at him. You're the spitting image of him," Dani said.

Maria didn't want to look, in fact she fought the urge. But her mounting curiosity got the best of her and she glanced over at Ronaldo Soares, and as hard as she tried to deny it at first, it was so obvious, so apparent. He had the same eyes, the same nose, the same complexion. Her hands began to shake. She nearly dropped the gun.

Dani seized the moment and leapt across the room. She pounced on the pretty lawyer who went down kicking and screaming. Maria became a wildcat, trying to scratch Dani's eyes out and rip her hair right off. Dani's only concern was the gun. She could handle a few cuts and bruises. She made a grab for it.

Claire kept her eye on Ronaldo. Tess was still weak from nearly being strangled to death and was sobbing over the body of Pedro, or Paulo as she would always know him.

Ronaldo thrashed about, trying to free himself from the handcuffs and join the fray, to help his daughter, but it was useless. Claire shoved him back against the wall.

Dani finally managed to yank the pistol out of Maria's grasp and then gave her a hard powerful shove. Maria slid across the floor, knocking into the broken chair where Tess had been tied up. She was curled up on the floor and sobbing quietly. Dani was pretty sure Maria wouldn't have shot them all dead, but she couldn't take the chance. She handed the gun to Claire, who kept it trained on Ronaldo and Maria, and put her arm gingerly around Tess's shoulder.

"You okay, honey?"

Tess nodded. She was still overcome with emotion and couldn't take her eyes off Paulo's crumpled, still body.

Dani went to Claire's car to retrieve her cell phone and called the police. Within an hour, cops were swarming all over the property, arresting both Soares and Maria and questioning the three women about the details of what happened and how they all ended up on Benito Coronel's abandoned property. The police were just getting started with their investigation, but as far as Dani was concerned, the case was finally closed. And their kids were safe.

CHAPTER 44

A few days later, Pedro Coronel's funeral was held at Forest Lawn Cemetery in Los Angeles. Abigail Foster, who had been interviewed by the *LA Times*, specifically asked that Tess not attend her son's services. She was not at all sympathetic to her grieving since she held Tess, as well as Dani and Claire, completely responsible for her only son's tragic death.

Tess decided to abide by her wishes and did not show up. She waited until after the burial to visit his grave to get a little closure. It was heart-wrenching for her. Despite his initial motive in entering her life, Tess knew that her young paramour had grown to care for her deeply, perhaps even love her, which was why in the end he just couldn't hurt her.

Tess's only focus now was getting out of town. She had been in Los Angeles long enough throughout this ordeal and was anxious to return to her home in Brazil, where she could disappear into seclusion for a few months, grieve properly, and then re-emerge from her cocoon and get on with her life.

But Dani wanted one more meeting with her two former partners. Tess was reluctant. She was afraid Dani might try to talk her into staying permanently, kick-start the business, and she had no intention of doing that. It was totally out of the question.

It was bad enough that her daughter Bianca dropped the bombshell at breakfast the day before that she was moving to LA to pursue a career as a model. That was horseshit as far as Tess was concerned. She knew exactly why Bianca wanted to stay and it had nothing to do with being the next Kate Moss. She wanted to be closer to Claire's son Evan.

They had been spending an inordinate amount of time together, and Claire's worst fears were becoming a reality. They were pursuing a relationship. Another reason for Tess to blow town. She didn't need to be a punching bag for Claire's anger over the relationship. Tess knew Bianca's heart. She knew the girl was sensitive and caring and would never hurt Claire's younger son. But there was no way to convince Claire of that, so it was best to let her discover it on her own.

Dani had asked Tess and Claire to meet her at the Burke Williams Spa where they could wind down with a massage and clock some time in the Jacuzzi. She chose the Sherman Oaks location in the Pacific Galleria Mall. Tess scowled to herself as the limo moved at a snail's pace up the 405 freeway to the San Fernando Valley. No, Dani couldn't have picked the Santa Monica location, which was much more convenient to Tess's boat slip in Marina Del Ray. No. She had to go with Sherman Oaks, a stone's throw away from Claire's house. She was always making things easy on Claire, completely ignoring Tess's interests. Oh well. This would be the last time they would be seeing each other for a while, so she decided to just grin and bear it.

Upon her arrival, Tess discovered that Dani and Claire were already being worked on by their respective massage therapists. Tess checked in, took a quick shower, and then slipped on a robe. She was then ushered into a treatment room by a short Japanese girl with a bright smile and remarkably big hands for her otherwise petite size.

After a luxurious ninety-minute Shiatsu treatment, the therapist led a drowsy Tess back into the ladies spa, where she found Dani and Tess waiting for her in the Jacuzzi. Tess dropped her robe and stepped into the hot bubbling water.

"How was it?" Dani said, her head resting on a towel rolled up at the tub's edge.

"Heavenly," Tess said, picking up a cup of ice water with a wedge of lime and taking a sip. "Thanks for the treat."

"My pleasure," Dani said.

"So have you spoken with Bianca? Has she told you?" Claire said.

So much for massaging out all the tension. Claire was wasting no time bringing up the recent developments in their kids' lives.

"Yes," she said, sighing. "Yes, she has."

"So what do you think?" Claire asked.

Tess could lie and tell Claire she was concerned about the budding relationship, but the fact was, she was not. She thought it was sweet. She decided to be honest. "I think it's great. They seem to really care for each other."

"I think so too," Claire said quietly.

Tess's eyes popped open. She couldn't believe it. Claire saw her reaction and couldn't help but laugh.

"Really, I do," Claire said. "I just want them both to be happy."

Tess was relieved to know there wasn't going to be an argument. Everything was cool between them. They didn't need to talk it out or analyze the situation, or even offer mutual apologies. They had never done that in all the years they had known each other after they had a fight. It was over. Done. Finito. And it was time to pick up where they left off.

"I've got enough worries right now than to spend time obsessing over Evan," Claire said. "He's a big boy now. He can take care of himself."

"Worries? You mean Jeb?" Dani said.

"He's calmed down quite a bit. And now that our little adventure is over, I promised him that was it. It was just a one-time thing. And there is virtually no chance anything like this will ever happen again. So I'm pretty sure that emphatic assurance was what in the end saved my marriage."

Tess held up her glass of ice water. "I'll drink to that."

"That's what I wanted to talk to you two about," Dani said right on cue. Both Tess and Claire were waiting for this.

"Forget it, Dani," Tess said.

"Now wait. Hear me out," Dani said. "I was offered the job of Police Commissioner for San Francisco this morning."

"Honey, that's great," Claire said. "You've wanted that job for a long time."

"I turned it down."

"Why, Dani? You've been waiting years for this opportunity. Why on earth would you say no?" Tess asked.

"Because I'm older and wiser, and I don't have the stomach for all the politics involved anymore. I admit it would be fun going back the boss and making life difficult for all the little assholes who didn't take me seriously because I'm a woman and old enough to be their mother, but after talking it over with Bowie, really thinking about it, I decided I already accomplished what I set out to do there, and I want a fresh challenge."

Claire turned to Tess and smiled. "I knew this was coming."

"Believe me," Tess said. "I did too."

"I'm not talking about anything official, or even permanent. But I have been seriously considering re-opening the business, taking on a few cases. It would strictly be a one-woman operation and I could enlist Bowie to do a lot of the legwork. But I was thinking . . ."

"Here's where we come in," Claire said, nudging Tess.

"Maybe I could call you, only on occasion and only if you're interested, and maybe once in a while you could help me out. I don't mean go undercover or anything; I'm aware more than either of you that our days of dressing up in a stewardess costume are over."

"Speak for yourself," Tess said haughtily.

"So you're open to undercover work?" Dani said, smiling.

"No, I'm just saying I could still pass as a hot flight attendant."

"She's right, Dani," Claire said grinning. "Most of them work right up to their sixties."

Tess splashed water from the Jacuzzi in Claire's face.

"All I'm saying is . . . we've always worked well together. And I know you both have busy lives now and don't have a lot of time, but I'm just asking you to consider, on the rarest of occasions, joining me if a really challenging case comes up."

There was a long pause as Tess and Dani considered. Tess couldn't believe she was actually thinking about it. She just wanted to wing her way back to Brazil, hide out for a while, and then grace the party circuit of the rich and famous again. But how hard would it be to do a little investigating on the side? Especially if Dani was chasing after someone with money, who perhaps inhabited Tess's social world? After all, she did know a lot of dirt. And why not share some of it every so often?

"Let's face it," Dani said. "If this case showed us anything, it's that we're just as effective, if not more so, than when we started this thing all those years ago when we were in our twenties."

Tess couldn't argue with that. "Okay," she said tentatively. "As long as it doesn't become a habit."

"Of course not," Dani said.

"I can't believe you agreed," Claire said, astonished. "I was waiting for you to be the bad guy and say absolutely, unequivocally no. And then I was just planning on shrugging and backing you up. Now if I say no, I look like the intractable bitch!"

"It's your choice," Dani said.

Claire folded her arms, in a state of shock. "Jeb didn't believe me when I said it was over for good. I can't believe he's turning out to be right."

Dani nearly leapt with joy. Tess could see in her eyes how happy this was making her. And her excitement was infectious. Still, the last thing she wanted to do was show her enthusiasm. Dani would probably press her into returning full time and she refused to do that, not with her social calendar.

"So what should we call ourselves?" Dani said.

"What are you talking about? We are and always will be the LA Dolls," Tess said, amazed that Dani would even consider the notion of changing the name of their long-dormant detective agency.

"Well, I just thought we might be a little old to be referred to as Dolls, don't you?"

Tess puffed her chest out. "No, I do not think that."

Claire giggled. The bickering was already starting.

"Okay, what do you suggest?" Dani said, tossing Claire a conspiratorial wink.

"You know, just off the top of my head, what about the Menopausal Murder Club?" Claire said, laughing.

Dani howled with delight.

"I don't see the humor in the word menopause. None whatsoever," Tess said, her face reddening from the thought of that awful word.

Whether it would be the LA Dolls resurrected or another moniker sans the word menopause, all three women knew, whether they wanted to admit it or not, that a new and exciting chapter in their lives was about to begin.